BENEATH THE LOTUS
A REVENGE THRILLER
DACOTA ROGERS

Copyright © 2025 by Dacota Rogers

All rights reserved.

No part of this publication may be reproduced, distributed, or transmitted in any form or by any means, including photocopying, recording, or other electronic or mechanical methods, without the prior written permission of the author, except in the case of brief quotations embodied in critical reviews and certain other noncommercial uses permitted by copyright law.

This is a work of fiction. Names, characters, places, and incidents are either the product of the author's imagination or used fictitiously. Any resemblance to actual persons, living or dead, events, or locales is entirely coincidental.

First Edition: January 2025

This book is for all the

Garretts
Rogers
Atkins
Brennans
Morgans
and
Hancocks

You were not inspiration for this book

I

Its origins were a mystery. Stark white pedals and sharp lines, it was as seamless as anything I'd seen, and I'd spent countless hours studying its every feature. The glass globe magnified the pink lines in my palm, the contrast like blood against snow. It was so perfect. Each delicate curve offered calm amid chaos, pulling me away from the storm of my thoughts. At night, I'd stare at its yellow heart and, gradually, silence would fill me until sleep came. How that flower had become what it was to me I don't know, but two truths are no mystery: I loved that lotus.

And it killed my mother.

We'd moved to a new house in a new town. We were on the run from the Mexicans mom had robbed in Vegas, and it was the first day of school. I was trying to escape the house without interacting with the rest of the Torqueres.

"I've done it, Jimmyboy," mom said as I edged past the basement stairs into the kitchen, careful to avoid the creaking floorboards. Dirty dishes, a half-eaten apple, crumpled and torn magazines, and an assortment of hand tools were piled on the table in front of mom, all except for a square space directly in front of her. Parallel white lines filled the space. "I've found the perfect combo."

I shook my head. Most mothers would be making breakfast for their families at this hour, but here she was.

The point of a syringe cut into her arm at the top of a traveling scar. She swirled the needle in tight circles. "Come on you bastard." The needle came out, a fat drop of blood following it, and she cut a new hole above the last. "Got you!" Her thumb pressed, and her eyes rolled back. "Coke and heroin in the arm." She plugged a nostril and pressed her face to the table. "Meth in the nose."

Funny the things you get used to. Watching someone shoot heroin was a disgusting thing to witness, but when it's your morning routine it becomes just that: routine. I went blank, as I ever did.

Mom's head lifted from the table. "Fuck-ing per-fect."

She bit her bottom lip with little studs, the remnants of her teeth implants. Black and silver, she'd lost her teeth one by one over the years.

Song stood over the sink but watched mom over his shoulder, slanted eyes gazing from beneath hair that mom cut with a knife whenever it got too long. He was short, had dark hair, and his eyes were creased. I caught his attention and, eyebrows high, exaggerated an eye roll. The chain around his neck rattled as he twisted away from me.

"I need lunch money," I told mom.

She leaned back, closed her eyes, and took a long, slow breath through her nose. Her head rolled back and resembled a boiled skull. One of her hands reached for her pants pocket while the other traced a line from her stomach, up her chest, around her neck, and into stringy blonde hair.

"You're stupid, Jimmy," she said through a gust of breath, "not to try this."

I had very little to say to my mother in general and less when the drugs mixed inside of her. Since she'd robbed those Mexicans, the drugs were always mixing. She always said shit like that. Things most parents warned their kids off, she wanted me to try. I hated it. I ignored it.

I ate an entire apple as she dug in a pocket with one hand and rubbed her nose with the other. I crossed my arms and waited. Eventually, "Mom!"

She fought an eye open. Inside, the pupil vibrated. "Wha?"

"I-need-lunch-mon-ey."

"Food'n fridge." Her chin rolled and settled onto her chest. "Make some'tin."

I slammed the refrigerator door. Condiments clattered. "I have school today'n don't have time to make some'tin," I mocked.

"School?" She slumped forward, hair sweeping through meth lines on the table, and pulled her hand from her pocket. A wad of cash filled her fist. "Fuck school," she said and dropped the money onto the floor.

It was all hundreds.

She was a despicable person. The type to rob you, leave you for dead, and spend your money on dope. If anyone deserved to have their money stolen by their son, it was her. I knew it. Hell, anyone she'd ever met knew it. But she stole. I didn't.

I picked up the wad and spread it open. Buried within I found a ten, a five, and three ones. I took the five, threw the rest in her lap, and turned to leave.

"Check your brother," mom mumbled.

I sighed.

Tiptoeing, I approached the top of the basement stairs and peeked down. Stupro's door was shut. I crept on, careful of my footfalls. The doorknob turned.

I stomped through the living room and bolted up the stairs two at a time. At the top, I stopped and tried to hear if he was following.

Tap, tap, tap, tap...

The sound came from upstairs, not down, and I shoved a finger into each ear. *They decide to start early on the first day of school?* I thought as I ran by the twins' door to Pecu's room. I removed my fingers from my ears, opened Pecu's door, and slammed it behind me.

Little jean overalls were buckled on one side, and he wore no shirt beneath. Chin-length blonde hair was tucked behind both ears and a stray bang hung to the middle of his face. Shining baby blues topped chubby cheeks, and his grin was shy. Staring down at his countenance, the thought struck me as it had so many times before: *He must be the cutest, most innocent baby alive.*

Cutest maybe.

I said, "You good in here?"

He nodded, eyes wide. Nodded a little too long, eyes a little too wide. He kept his hands behind his back.

"What you got, Pecu?"

He tucked his head into his chest and shook it.

"What is it?" I asked. My stomach turned.

He shook his head hard.

"Give it here, Pecu,"

"No!"

"Pecu, now!"

Eyes wet enough to drown in, Pecu brought his hands from behind his back and presented what was in them. His guinea pig. It was sliced open down the center of its back, and fur flapped like butterfly wings. I tasted apple and caught the bile before it was added to the gore.

The guinea pig writhed in Pecu's hand, its body convulsing. A moan pressed from my lips, and I let the tears fall. My shoulders slumped, and I clenched my eyes closed.

"Damn it, Pecu." I turned away. "Kill the poor thing."

"No," he said in his same pout.

"Now!"

A thump then silence.

My eyes eased open. Sunlight beamed from the window and through the space between me and Pecu like a wall. Bloody fingers folded in front of him, Pecu rocked back and forth on his heels. He wiped a tear from his cheek, but left a streak of blood.

"I've told you about this, Pecu," I said and lifted the limp guinea pig from the floor. "You know better."

A flow started from his eyes. "I'm sorry, Jimjim." He sniffled and wiped more blood onto his face. "Are you mad?"

"Clean this mess up then go tell mom you need a bath."

He nodded. Already his tears were gone. *I got to get out of here.* Dead guinea pig in two fingers, I swung open Pecu's door.

TAP! TAP! TAP! TAP!...

"God damn it!" I ran past the twins' door and down the stairs straight into a smell that only comes from one creature in the world: a six-hundred-pound man who'd shit. Dad snored like a chainsaw on his bowed couch. I thought about getting Song, signing to him in our way that dad needed cleaned, but I had to get out of here. Now.

Escaping out the front door, I ran headlong into solid flesh. My head cranked back until I could see his face. Soot-black hair hung to shoulders encased in leather. Oil, stale smoke, and something like copper wafted from him. Words he'd said a hundred times echoed through me, "Six-six, three-fifty, and every bit of it dangerous." He smiled behind a blazing cigarette.

"Hey Stupro," I whispered, heart audible between the words. "Good morning."

My eyes went to his feet.

His cigarette butt hit me in the chest, spraying embers, then he pushed me aside and the door thudded closed. Stupro's heavy steps creaked past the living room and descended the basement stairs. I swallowed, shook my head, and picked up the guinea pig off the porch. I sighed.

Guess I better dig a grave.

Moving from town to town had its benefits. There was always a time where kids left me alone. Whether it be jocks, geeks, music kids, or skater kids, it was only a matter of time before I was recruited, but when we moved towns it was like starting fresh. It let me focus on my schoolwork without the expectations that came with having friends, and thus keep up my perfect grades.

My desire for straight A's, if I'm honest, was slightly narcissistic. It tickled my ego that someone from my background could be more successful than the normal kids. Nope, nothing important like a dream of going to a decent college or getting a decent job, just good old superiority complex, the mainstay of all great feats.

I deserved to be proud of my grades though. I once watched mom bury a man in our backyard, then aced a geometry test the next day. "He overdosed," was all mom would say about the sudden patch of missing grass out back. The dead man had been the most traumatic experience I'd lived through at the time, but the geometry test had been simple. We moved before I got the results, but I know I aced it.

Of course, my family had a lot to do with my grades too. None of them had done well in school, so I would.

Third period social studies had posters of presidents, maps, and timelines on the walls; the teacher droned on about the syllabus, ranging from Columbus to Clinton; and the kids hardly hid their whispers, recounting their summer to anyone who'd listen.

I read the textbook with half an ear on the teacher, enjoying the separation I felt from the other kids. No one dared include me. I sat mid-center and hunched low to blend in so the teacher wouldn't call on me. Given a few weeks like this, I'd finish the textbook.

A finger tapped my shoulder.

My hand tightened around the edge of the desk, and I leaned over my book.

"Hey, new boy," someone whispered.

I put my head down, sighed, then turned.

Thick, black mascara surrounded her eyes. Powder clumped in the wrinkles of her face. A blush in an awkward tan color was thick and glistening on her cheeks. Her hair was brown like bark, straightened, and adorned with a pink bow the same color as her sundress. Her nose was upturned, her eyes were too big, and her lips were thin. She set her pen against her lip and smiled.

I cleared my throat.

"Where you from, new boy?" she asked and leaned toward me in her desk. A black lace bra peeked from beneath her sundress, and I felt guilty for noticing.

"Around."

"Oh," she said.

I tried to keep my eyes on hers, but they veered. *Am I no better than the twins?*

"Are you going to lunch with anyone?" she asked.

"I don't know anyone, so no."

"You are now."

Her name was Amanda Raymond, and she had an old Subaru hatchback. She was a senior in high school, hated her father, and wanted to be a veterinarian. She would dance on a pole to pay for college. I learned all this on the walk from the school to her car.

"Where do you want to go?" she asked, throwing the gearshift into reverse. Fast-food wrappers, soda cans, and crumpled paper covered the floorboard.

"I only have five dollars," I said, thinking about the wad of cash I had in my hand this morning.

She giggled. It was small and sweet. "Well," she drawled. "We could just drive."

"Cool."

She drove us through Casper. September this far north was steamy breath in the morning and staying indoors at night. Amanda was insane to only wear a sundress. Of course, she had an agenda to dress in such a way.

"So really," she said. "Where do you come from?"

"I don't really come from anywhere. I've lived everywhere."

"Why?"

"My family —" I scratched my head. "Likes to move." This line of questions led one direction, and I knew how to stop it. "What about you?"

"I've lived here my whole life. It stinks. I wish I had your family." Then she explained about growing up in Casper, which involved underage drinking, sports, and waiting for a short summer. She said it all like the worst curse imaginable, but it sounded nice to me. She talked and I let her until she seemed to forget that I had had an upbringing at all.

I stared out the window, watching trees pass, their burnt-colored leaves still clinging. *Casper is nice*, I decided. Maybe it was the absence of city life. Casper was a city, but it felt like less. A place where neighbors help neighbors and everyone's your neighbor.

Amanda cleared her throat. Eyes on the road, both hands on the wheel, she made a point not to give attention to me looking, but she knew I was. The way her upturned nose pointed toward the roof, the way she shook her hair out of her face, the way her eyebrows set high on her head. It was all calculated. One eyebrow drew in as she considered something.

"Do you skip school?"

I once read that a kid will turn out one of two ways, exactly like their parents or exactly the opposite. I figured it had to do with how the child felt toward their parents, whether consciously or unconsciously. Well, I'd be the opposite. That meant following rules. All of them.

But she's staring at me expectantly.

I tried to sound confident, but it came out a croak, "Sure I do."

Paved streets turned to dirt. Fields of long, yellow grass spread in every direction. Eventually there was no sign of Casper, and she turned us into a cove of pine trees. Cool, grass-laced air rolled in through the open window, but my nerves had me sweating.

"Get in the back," she said.

Suddenly, I was in the back.

It wasn't ten minutes of frantic sex and we were back on the road. She stared into the mirror as she adjusted the bow on top of her head, and I could have laughed at the futility. Makeup ran down her face, lip gloss spread an inch around her mouth, and her hair was wet and stuck to her face, but she worried about her little pink bow? If I wasn't a coward, I'd tell her how she looked.

"You look great," I said.

"Shut up." She didn't smile, didn't giggle. I felt like a piece of meat. "Where do you need to go?"

"Uh —" We had just had sex. Weren't we supposed to cuddle or something? Her sudden dismissal felt similar to the time mom had forgotten me at a gas station, and I'd sat on a bench alone for hours until she remembered I existed. The rejection felt no better now. "Back to school I guess," I said, voice barely above a whisper.

She nodded and stared at the road ahead. Had I messed up? Maybe I'd done a bad job? I'd had sex before, but to say I knew what I was doing would be a lie. Maybe it was just me. I wanted to say something, anything to fill the silence, but any words I had to say would've just been noise. I let my insecurities hang.

She stopped to turn into the school parking lot. My breath caught.

Hair flowing behind him, motorcycle roaring, a huge man drove toward us from the opposite direction. Amanda waited for him to pass. I held my breath and stared.

It was uncle Stupro.

Jaw square, tight, and strong, he looked ogre-like as he roared by. The motor faded behind us as we turned into the parking lot, but I frenzied. *Had he seen us? Did he know I was skipping school? What about Amanda? Should I tell her we can never see each other again? Will she care? Why'd I agree to skip school? Had he seen us? What do I do?*

"You good?" Amanda said.

"Oh." She had stopped at the end of the front entrance to school. I'd been staring at the dashboard. I opened the door and stepped out. "I'll see you —"

She sped off before I could close the door all the way, and I stared at her taillights until she turned. *I really am just a piece of meat.* I inhaled deep the clean Wyoming air.

It's no different from any air, I realized.

2

I made it to my final class — thankfully — and walked home after. Our new house was better than most we'd lived in. There was plenty of space, inside and out. Our closest neighbors were far enough away that we could scream bloody murder on the front porch without them hearing. Inside, there was space enough that everyone had their own room, which prevented us from having to scream bloody murder.

I took a final breath of fresh air, strode into the living room, and closed the door behind me. Dim light spilled from the old box television dad had on a milk crate in front of him, and it made him glow. His face, neck, and half his chest, coated in barbeque sauce, reflected the action on TV.

A plate perched on his belly; a pile of chicken bones perched on the plate. Mom used to shave the sides of his head for him, but now he had a pate like a bowling ball with wisps on the sides.

"What you watching, dad?" I asked.

He grunted through wet chewing and hard breathing then pointed at the screen with a chicken leg. The question had been rhetorical. Dad watched Jerry Springer or reruns of Jerry Springer. A girl pulled another girl's hair while a man watched with a proud smile. Dad traded a chicken bone for a cigar in his glistening fingers then caught his breath before taking a puff.

"Anything left to eat, dad?"

As I moved around his couch, dad heaved. I stopped and stared. His fat jiggled with every cough, and the plate fell from his stomach and clattered on the floor. His hands pressed into his throat, and he leaned over, almost crashing onto his TV. I was frozen.

I should do something.

I smacked my palm against his back three times as hard as I could, and a glob of chicken soared and splattered on the TV screen. His breathing sounded like he'd just been pulled blue from the ocean and given CPR. I shook my head and left him there.

The twins were in the kitchen.

Coitus's teeth were sharp. Her black, rat eyes were too close together. She was overweight and, at nineteen, she'd already started to sag at the chin, arms, and stomach. Her hair was thin, brown, and oily. Coitus was the second ugliest person I'd ever seen. The first sat across the table from her, hands clasped to hers, finger through finger: Coitum, who shared every feature but with a masculine tint.

"Well, hello, Jimmy," Coitus said, her voice nasally.

"Coitus." I acknowledged her, and kept it short with her brother too, "Coitum."

Two long strides and I reached the pantry doorknob. "We're not going by that right now," Coitum said and giggled. Coitus did too. I turned the knob. "She goes by Tussy now."

"And he's Tummy," Coitus said.

I opened the door and moved to step in.

"Jimmy, wait!"

"What?"

"Don't you want to know why?"

"No," I said and hurried to close the door.

"Cause she's the finest damn Tussy in town," I heard Coitum say anyway. And Coitus, "And he's always in my tummy."

God damn it.

Song was squeezed into a ball the furthest he could get from the door. There was enough room for a man to lie if he tucked his knees. Boxes and cans of food filled the shelves above him. The chain that mom kept bolted to the floor clinked as Song relaxed. He tensed for everyone in the house but Pecu and me.

"Hey." I sat on his blanket, scooted some chains to the side, and grabbed the antibiotic ointment I kept next to the oatmeal. "You all right?"

He replied in a flurry of Cantonese.

"I know, I know," I said. "Come here."

I massaged a generous amount of ointment into his neck, under the steel collar. The weight of the chain caused the collar to chafe, and the wounds never truly healed. Mom said it was a part of his punishment and it served him right. Song kept his eyes closed and turned his head when I needed to reach a different spot on his neck.

Finished, I stood. "You want out?"

He stared at my mouth, and his lips moved without making a sound.

I opened the door and pointed. "Out?" He pushed himself as far as he could into the corner. "I understand. Trust me, I understand." I grabbed a cheese stick and a Pepsi from the fridge, avoiding eye contact with the twins.

"Don't see why you're so nice to the stupid jap," Coitus said as I hurried out the kitchen.

I started for my room. "He's Chinese –"

Stupro stepped in front of me. Suddenly, I was in Amanda's car and watching him pass on his motorcycle.

"Sorry, Stupro." I laughed and heard the shakiness in it. "Didn't see you there."

He glared down at me.

"What did you do today?" I asked. It was a stupid question, one I would never ask. Stupro's eyebrow tilted. "I mean, do you like Casper?"

Shut up, idiot!

"What's to like?"

"I —" I swallowed. "The people seem nice."

"Really? Make a friend, did you?"

The buzzing of the refrigerator suddenly sounded far away. *Make a friend?* He knew. He had to know. *He'd seen us.*

"You're funny, Stupro." I tried to move, but he was a big man to move around, and he moved for no one. "A friend? Yeah, right."

He grunted and turned so I could pass.

I tripped up the stairs on my way to my room.

❦

The next day I went to school searching for Amanda. I would tell her it was all a mistake and that was that. I'd be the asshole, she'd tell her friends about me, and I'd be the talk around school for a while. I ran a hundred scenarios through my head of how the conversation would go as I waited for her to show up for social studies, but she never came.

The day after she rushed in and sat on the opposite side of the room from me a minute before class was to start. I tried to force her attention to me all class, waving, whispering, everything but standing and screaming her damn name, but she ignored me and at the end of class rushed out faster than she'd rushed in.

The third day I waited in a bathroom stall, tapping a frantic beat with my feet. When all movement quit in the hall, I hurried into class. The seat behind Amanda was empty, and I sat.

"What's up?" I whispered.

She stared forward.

I tapped her shoulder.

"Hey, Amanda," I said louder. "Why're you ignoring me?"

She whipped around. Her face was red and her eyes were two thin creases. "I don't need someone like you in my life. Leave me alone."

Someone like me? Her bottom lip trembled, the slightest movement that I would've missed had I not been remembering how that lip felt against mine. "What do you mean someone like me?"

She leaned closer to me. "I don't want you in my life if all you want is to jump my bones," she whispered. Her head swung with every word.

"What!" I said a little too loud. "You jumped my bones."

She huffed and whipped back around.

"Listen," I whispered in her ear. "Let's go to lunch and talk. Just talk."

"No," she tossed over her shoulder.

I should've left it there. It'd been my intention to quit this, whatever it was, anyway. But puberty is nature's brainwashing mechanism and all I could think about was her thin and delicate neck and her cute little ponytail. "Come on, Amanda," I said. "Let me make it up to you."

We went to McDonald's, ate in her car, and I apologized for seeming like all I wanted from her was sex. The next day we spent the entire school day having sex. Then weeks went by. Most days we skipped a few classes, others we skipped all day. If we were ever called to the principal's office, we'd ditch and meet at her car.

Skipping school was nothing like doing drugs. I wasn't sleeping with my sister or eating myself to death. Skipping school wasn't nearly as severe as keeping a slave for Christ's sake. I wasn't like my family. I just wanted to be around Amanda, someone who gave me attention like I'd never had before. Was that a crime?

She was my first real relationship. A nice girl. Had her problems, but she was mostly sweet.

My family were strict Christians was the explanation I gave Amanda as to why I never went out after school. She bought it without question and only a couple times did she try to convince me to sneak away to a concert I just had to go to or a movie I just had to see.

"What happens when your mom finds out you've been skipping school?" she asked one day when we were both supposed to be in third period but we were walking into McDonald's for an early lunch.

"I don't even want to think about that," I said.

I paid for the food with money I'd taken from mom that morning, and we waited by the jungle gym. "You're such a gentleman."

"Why do you say that?"

She wiggled closer to me and kissed my cheek. "You always pay even though you know I got money."

I could've laughed. It wasn't funny, but the absurdity was hard not to laugh at. *I'm a gentleman?* I'd stolen money from my mother. She'd stolen it from a house full of Mexicans, along with a whole lot of drugs. After she and my uncle killed them all, of course.

"Why you smiling all weird?" Amanda asked when I got back with our food.

I shook my head and ate. I kept pace with Amanda, and we were done in moments. I wasn't sure if we were hurrying to get back to school or go for a "drive." I left those decisions to Amanda. I led her through the front door.

And stopped dead.

Uncle Stupro puffed a cigarette from atop his motorcycle, leaned back and comfortable. His hair whipped around his face in the wind like those little flags people leave with flowers in a graveyard. Slow, he removed his sunglasses and made eye contact with me. My eyes were captive. He shook his head, then he leaned forward and kicked his bike to life. He was gone before I could breathe.

"Who was that?"

I remembered who was next to me. I remembered how she made a little squeak when I tickled her and how her hair stuck to her face when she sweated and how her lips felt when she said Jimmy into my neck. I swallowed.

"I don't know," I whispered.

"Out!" mom yelled two days later as I came into the kitchen. The twins dashed out the room, hand in hand. Song flipped the two-pound steak sizzling in a pan: dad's dinner. "Where you been?"

Her face was tallow-white. Her eyes were black pits. Her jaw muscles wormed. The usual. Her wiggles were tight, though, not the usual flails. Her eyes could hold mine and didn't dart indiscriminately. She had the sense of mind to appear angry. From her, sense of any kind meant one thing: she'd skipped a shot.

"School," I mumbled and went looking for food, playing casual.

"EIGHHH! Wrong answer. Where you been?"

She knows. "What're you talking about?"

"Don't play stupid. You've been skipping school. I want to know where you been."

I shrugged. "I went to lunch."

"You fucking went to fucking lunch?" she said in one word. "Went to lunch every other fucking day?" I tried to make sense of that. Had Stupro been following me longer than I knew? "Your principal says you're on thin ice," she said. "Screw your principal. I want to know who you're with."

"No one," I said, maybe too quick.

Mom glared and sucked her lip. Her teeth implants peeked through the crease. The moment held.

Then she shrugged. "Hand me a rig, you little fuck."

I handed her a syringe from the butter drawer. Song's chain rattled behind me, kept rattling. He always shook, but he only quivered like that for one person.

Stupro stood outside the kitchen.

"Skipping every day, huh?"

He smiled.

That smile kept me up all night. He knew I'd lied to mom. He knew I skipped all the time. He knew who I was with. Those facts cycled on repeat as I tossed and turned.

What have I done?

When she missed third period the next day, I knew. I stood in the middle of the teacher explaining the scope of death during the Civil War and headed for the door. She yelled something at me, but the words were a blur. I sprinted home.

Stupro kneeled next to his bike in the driveway, cranking a wrench. Breathing hard, I tiptoed by him. His attention stayed on the bike, but I couldn't be sure if he noticed me.

The twins were on one couch, sucking each other's faces. Dad slept, or pretended to sleep, on the other couch. No one noticed me.

"The fuck are you doing?" mom spat from the kitchen.

I took the basement stairs two at a time, twisted the knob — locked — pressed with my shoulder. The door wouldn't budge. I backed up four steps and charged. It snapped and crashed open.

The basement was silent and black. It smelled like blood.

"Jimmy, what the fuck?" Mom screamed. "You know better than to..." her voice faded as she disappeared from the top of the stairs.

A beam of light fell from the single, small window in the top corner of the room. Dust swirled within. I stood and stared, attempting to make sense of what that light illuminated.

A sawhorse. A naked girl. Blood shining on her ass.

A familiar ass.

I ran. Her wrists and ankles had been bound together; her body bent over the sawhorse. A rag was tied over her mouth.

"Amanda," I said and brushed a wet clump of hair from her face. "Oh god." It was a purply, mushy mash, unrecognizable, like a bag of grapes beaten against cement.

She moaned.

"You're alive." A table was next to her. "You're alive." Metal instruments fit for surgery crashed from the table in my panic. I found scissors. "Stay with me, Amanda."

My hands were moist. They shook. The rope was thick, and the scissors were dull. Back and forth, I cranked. My hands hurt. I glanced back at the door, at the bottom stair glowing from the forty-watt bulb in the stairwell. I had to go faster — *Faster!*

The rope finally burst. I eased Amanda off the sawhorse. She moaned but was limp. Her crotch and ass were coated in blood, and her face was destroyed, but her body was unmarred.

He'd left it to admire.

I put my face close to Amanda's. "You've got to get up. Come on." I shoved my arms beneath her shoulders and lifted. She was unresponsive. "Shit, shit, shit," I mumbled. I had to carry her. She was too heavy.

My shoulder pressed to hers, I pivoted. I got her up and onto my shoulder and pushed her up with my legs; they shook but I stood. Her hair and arms draped down my back, and I forced myself to concentrate on taking steps, not on the blood on her ass and what it meant. One difficult, small step, and I was shaking with her weight.

The stairs creaked.

I should've been scared, terrified. This man was a monster, one deserving of fear. But that's not what I felt.

As tender as I could, I set Amanda down. Stupro crept onto the bottom stair, blocking what little light came from upstairs. I picked up the scissors and slinked further into the basement's darkness. Stupro glided his fingers over the busted door frame.

He froze.

Then flicked the light on.

Slaughter was everywhere. A pile of organs, intestines, hearts, livers, brains, lay next to an old meat grinder. Feet from it, bones took up the bulk of the basement floor. Skin was in a third pile: three bodies, heads still attached.

I vomited onto the pile of bones.

Stupro laughed, full and hearty.

Bastard. *The bastard!*

I ran with the scissors up. He stepped aside, and I slipped by him, arcing my swing as I passed. The scissors went into his thigh and out. He dropped to a knee, and suddenly I was behind my uncle, the worst part of my life, with an industrial pair of scissors and a direct shot at his neck. I swung down but stopped. For some reason, I stopped.

Stupro lurched to his feet and glared at me with eyes that had seen the skin peeled from his victims. The glare changed as he realized what had happened, as he saw me stuck with my arm posed to strike. He smiled.

He ripped the scissors from my hand and swung.

I landed. Everything spun. I pushed myself back with my feet. My hand pressed into something wet and squishy, flesh or organs or whatever else lay on the floor. I found my feet and tried to regain my senses.

He held Amanda up by her hair. Her feet dangled. She squirmed, finally conscious. She met my eye.

As our eyes touched, Stupro slid the scissors into her stomach slow and deliberate. She screamed, but only once. He let go of the scissors, and they protruded from Amanda's stomach. She quit fighting. He licked his lips, smacked her ass, then she landed at my feet.

I stared at her, but I could see nothing through the tears in my eyes. Stupro's laugh brought me back. I charged him. Weaponless, shameless, hopeless, I charged him.

The world flashed white, then everything went black.

3

The globe was warm in my hand, but the rest of me was cold in this new house. I'd held the lotus, staring at its soft curves and delicate tones, for days. It was all I could do. If I took my mind off of that flower, it'd quickly turn to carnage.

The carnage I caused.

Stupro had knocked me out. After, mom drugged me long enough to pack up the house and the Torqueres and get us out of there without a fight from me. I'd regained consciousness in my spot in the van, just like any other time we'd moved.

Pecu had sat next to me, petting a puppy I'd never seen before. Mom had one hand on the steering wheel, the other fingering the jewelry box she always kept next to her when we moved towns. The twins were in the back, sneaking kisses. Past them, out the rear window, dad's trailer trailed.

Through the window, staring at me through long, whipping black hair, Stupro passed on his bike. He smiled a crooked, demeaning, victorious smile, one just for me before he roared ahead.

There'd been a weight in my pocket. I didn't know how it got there — someone must have placed it — but I had pulled out the lotus flower and studied its calm features. I'd been staring at it since.

We'd followed the setting sun until buildings began to block my view of the sky. A red and white sign flashed by *Welcome to Sacramento*. Mom made some calls, then we stopped outside a run-down house squeezed between other identical houses.

My room was in the basement. A yellow stain ran down the drywall. The carpets smelled like cat piss. It didn't matter though. Nothing did.

Days went by in that house, maybe weeks. Now and again I had to climb the stairs for food or the bathroom, but otherwise I stayed in bed, never really sleeping, never really awake, focused on my lotus.

How that flower was able to do what it did to me, I never really understood. I considered myself pretty grounded – I believed in what I saw, and I wasn't drawn to pseudosciences like astrology or homeopathy. Yet, the lotus had an effect on me that defied logic. I'd gaze into the solid glass globe and the darkness around me would fade. Its yellow core and delicate petals seemed to illuminate a path, the only way out.

"You going to pout your life away?" mom asked one day as I dug in the fridge. "It's time to pull your head out your ass."

I ignored her.

"Either go to school or get a job. I don't need two of your father."

"My uncle..." I couldn't say it. "I think I'm allowed to be sad."

"I'm out of dope, and it's your fucking fault. Either get to school so you can get a good job, or go get a job so you can bring me some money."

"My fault?"

Her face twisted, eyebrows drew down, eye twitched. She sucked her gums and two silver points squeezed through her lips. "Your fucking fault," she said. "If it wasn't for you, we'd still be in Wyoming."

Her eyes were flat lines. No amusement. No laughter. She meant what she said. She truly believed it was my fault. I squeezed my hands into fists. "I'm not doing anything for you."

"Remember your grades? What happened?"

"What happened?" My voice tore. "What happened? Quit acting like nothing's wrong!"

Song fumbled at the sink. A plate slipped from his hands and shattered on the floor. He dropped to his knees, letting out a stream of words that sounded apologetic. He scooped porcelain with his bare hands.

"Gah!" Mom crunched her foot into Song's ribcage.

"Stop!" I put myself between them.

She took two deep, loud breaths. Song's chain scattered porcelain as he fled to the farthest from mom he could get. "You'll provide for me Jimmy, one way or another."

Tears glistened on Song's cheeks. He poked at the porcelain in his palm. His breathing was shallow, and he flinched every intake. I met mom's eye. "I'm not doing anything for you."

"Fine." She shrugged. "Get out."

I looked up from Song.

Leave? A man so obese he needed assistance in all he did, eat, sleep, and shit. Twins that took out their teenage frustration and fancies on each other. A metal-mouthed, evil woman that only had eyes for her next fix. *I could leave?*

Squishy flesh pressed into my lax hand. Pecu's smile was shy. His eyes were round and questioning. He swung my hand back and forth, smile turning inward. "Jimjim?" his little voice came.

I squatted so that I was eye-to-eye. "Sup, buddy?"

"Love you." His arms squeezed around my neck, and his hair pressed against my cheek.

Tears filled my eyes as I rubbed his back. I stood and faced the monster that'd somehow created him. She knew as well as I knew. "I can't leave."

She laughed.

Pecu's Velcro sneakers crunched over porcelain as he went to Song. He patted Song on the head, and even he smiled. Pecu had that effect on everyone. He turned toward mom and put his arms up. She picked him up, bounced him on her hip, and tickled his nose with her own then set him down.

How could this awful person, someone who could help Stupro escape after the murder of a teenage girl, show so much affection to anyone? Had she shown me the same affection? For some reason, the thought made something lurch in my chest and I had to get out of that room.

"Let's go, Pecu." He took my hand. He had a bulge on his back, under his shirt. "What's that?" I slid out the scissors he had tucked in his waistband. Shaking my head, I put the scissors on the table and led Pecu to his room.

There was a pile of weed on dad's tray, and I took a handful on my way out.

I never smoked. Weed is a gateway drug, so said every teacher I'd had since the second grade, and that meant I'd smoke it today and tomorrow I'd turn into my mother. I don't know why I did it. I wanted to rebel. I wanted to find relief in something besides the heart of my lotus flower. I wanted everything to just go away.

The joint I rolled from bible paper was a cone. Stems pierced the paper in three spots. It lit though. I inhaled and laid back, waiting for escape to take me.

It was no escape.

Mom shooting cocaine and heroin into her neck while Pecu sits in his high-chair, crying, shit in his diaper, food on his face, slamming his arms down to get her attention; me coming in after school, finding a rash on Pecu's bottom from sitting in the mess so long and shivering cold as I hurry him to a hot bath, the tears not stopping, the heaviness in my chest, the scrubbing until the water is murky.

It's just weed though. I wasn't like her. I got straight A's.

A live rat in a shoe box being buried in the ground. A cat screaming from a tree, twelve staples holding it up by its tail. A guinea pig with its back flayed wide. The neighbors knocking, asking if we'd seen Goldie, Saber, Gato, Jerry. Pecu smiling up at me with that innocent smile.

Scissors *protruding from Amanda's naked stomach. A smiling Pecu stealing scissors from the kitchen.*

I jerked up off my bed, and my lotus flower fell from my lap. Everything was clear. I ran to Pecu's room.

My mind was hazy, my eyes were heavy, and my mouth was made of polyester, but it didn't matter. I had to save Pecu. I had to get him away from these people.

We have to run.

Thoughts whirling, I barged into Pecu's room without knocking.

Rusco, Pecu's puppy, was tied belly down to the seat of a wooden chair, his legs spread and connected to each leg. He squirmed but yarn secured his body to the seat too. Pecu stood next to the chair with a pair of scissors in his hand. Both their eyes landed on me, wide and shining, Pecu's guilty, Rusco's pleading.

I ran and pulled the scissors away from Rusco's tail. Rusco cried, sounding eerily human. I cut the yarn. When the last of it fell to the floor, Rusco bolted out the room. I dropped to my butt, back against Pecu's bed. I looked up at Pecu.

He grinned.

My family. My dead girlfriend. My uncle running free. My little brother becoming my uncle. The weed crushing it all together in my brain. I cried. I laid my head back on Pecu's bed and cried.

The clarity I'd had a moment ago was bludgeoned to death by reality. It'd taken too long to recognize what I needed to do. It was too late.

How long I cried, I don't know. The tears just came, like a ceiling that'd taken rain for months had finally caved. The damage was done. It was too late.

Pecu rubbed my back and petted my head. When I became conscious of it, I glanced up into his baby blues. They glistened and two wet lines shined down his cheeks.

I cried harder.

"Don't cry, Jimjim." Pecu hugged me. "Please, no crying."

"It's all I can do."

"Why cry?"

He stared into my face, searching. "You can't hurt animals, Pecu." I'd told him that dozens of times already.

"I can though."

I shook my head. "You should protect them, care for them. How would you like it if someone tried to hurt you like that?"

Pecu's eyebrows tilted. Eventually he straightened his back and put his fists on his hips. "I'm strong," he said. "No one hurts me. I'm strong enough to bend to my will."

Bend to my will? "Pecu, who told you —" I stopped. I lifted Pecu and set him in front of me, our faces inches apart. "Stupro is bad, Pecu. You can't listen to him! He's bad. You get it? Bad."

"Pecu?" I softened my voice. "Pecu, who would you rather be like, me or uncle Stupro?"

His eyes were defiant. Stupro had always treated Pecu differently, letting him hold tools as he worked on his bike, taking him for rides, speaking to him in a tone less threatening than he spoke to the rest of the world, even bringing him to parks a time or two. Pecu loved his uncle.

He looked at me then looked away.

He never answered.

I went to my room and lifted the lotus flower off the floor, analyzing the conversation with Pecu. As the weed faded and thoughts began to move in their familiar sequence, something became clear. Pecu had asked me why I was crying over him hurting animals. He didn't understand. He was a damn toddler for Christ's sake. His thoughts weren't his own. Not yet. Maybe it wasn't too late.

Whisking Pecu away was a great idea, but it wasn't so easy. We'd need money, a get-away vehicle, a destination.

So I got a job.

There's a special kind of anger felt when working under a lesser man, and not only for the working man. Deep down, the lesser man knows he's lesser too, which only furthers the resentment. The better man knows that every decision his boss makes is obviously wrong. The lesser man knows he's hated and makes decisions out of spite. It's an uncomfortable arrangement, but it seems to be common. For whatever reason, people are not awarded the coveted positions in any workplace based on merit. It's all about the ass and how well you kiss it.

I never did learn the art.

At my first job, the ass to kiss was Greggory's. Not Greg. Greggory. He was twenty-seven and the manager of the McDonalds that had hired me in Sacramento. White-and-red topped pimples covered his oily face. Red, greasy hair peaked from beneath his visor.

I put up with him though. It was what normal people did, and normal I was determined to be. I'd thought a lot about it since getting serious about fleeing with Pecu, and in order for it to be worth it I had to give Pecu a normal life once we got away. That meant I needed to be normal.

I wasn't normal though.

Normal people stress over paying their bills. I stressed over if our house was going to be raided by police. Normal people were happy when they got off work and got to watch a movie. I was happy when the twins quit their pumping before midnight so I could sleep. Normal people were sad when their favorite TV show ends. I was sad my little brother lusted over causing pain.

"What're you thinking?"

Rachel's pudgy cheeks creased with the smile that she always wore. Little strands of dark hair clung to her forehead under her visor, and she held my stare for longer than was typical. I slid her the half-made burger in front of me and started the next one. "I'm thinking I need to be more like you."

Her smooth, tan cheeks turned an adorable crimson, and she studied her hands. "I'm nothing special," she mumbled.

"You do exactly what you should be doing. Working and saving money. Going to school and getting good grades. I bet you have a plan for college. You probably even know how many kids you're going to have. I wish I had it together like you do. You're —"

"What the hell is this, lovey-dovey hour?" The piercing, cracking voice made me wince. "You two need to be working, not telling your undying love for each other."

The jealousy that twisted Greggory's tone and pressed his eyebrows together was so obvious that even naïve Rachel noticed. "Oh no, Greggory," I said, all innocence. "I would never love a woman you so obviously desire. Even if it would save you a prison sentence."

It was my ongoing dig. The guy might as well have ravished the underage girl, the way he undressed her with his eyes. The minor advances Greggory made toward Rachel and the way he leered at her cut right through my filter and drew out whatever words were at the forefront of my mind.

"Clean up your station, Jimmy." Greggory fixed me with his best scowl. "Rachel, will you start the inventory?" he asked, turning to her and sounding sweet. "Merdle's coming to do her deposit, and I'd like to be done when she gets here."

Rachel had a quality that everyone seemed to like, a sweet innocence that she still clung to even though she'd had to have gone through some things, seen some things, living in the part of Sac Town that she did, West Sacramento. It drew me to her like a fly abandoning its pile of shit for a lonely bulb in the darkness.

"I've had enough," an angry whisper came from Greggory. I'd forgotten he was there. "Don't mock me again."

I straightened my back, and squared my shoulders. I was thin, but I'd been working out the past few months and had made the big gains that come with starting. After Stupro handling me like an unruly toddler, I was ready to work myself into a bigger body. I towered over Greggory.

His jaw tightened. A thick vein crawled from beneath his visor, crossed his head, and connected with an eyebrow, traversing grease and whiteheads on its way. His hands made fists. His face turned shades. I only stared. He opened his mouth to speak.

"Greggory!" a raspy voice called from the back of the store. "Now, why'n the hell aren't these boxes outside in the trash? And why does this beautiful girl have your inventory sheet in her hand? I've told you once; I'll tell you again. That's your damn job."

Greggory sped away from the cooking area for the back of the store, yelling sorrys and you're rights. Merdle, the owner of the store, was about ninety and wore every year of it. The stoop in her back put her at four-ten. Her hair hung white from her head in scattered strands. I'd never seen her smile, even if I'd only seen her a few times. She hated everything. Especially Greggory.

I liked her for that.

That shift came and went as they all did. I cooked burgers, prepared burgers, and cleaned. I wondered if that was what it was like to be normal, to waste away at something you hate. After, I reported to Greggory as I'd been instructed to. "I'm finished."

He glanced up from his chair in the closet-sized office. Merdle sat next to him. Stacks of green money sat in front of her. "And?" Greggory's eyebrow went sideways.

I bit my cheek. "And you told me to let you know before I leave. I'm leaving."

"Here," he said. "Take your paycheck."

He lifted an envelope between us and I snatched it. *My first whole paycheck.* I'd been paid once, but I'd started during the pay period. This was going to be what I received check to check. I tore into the envelope and took out the piece of paper.

$743.47

I stared at that number. I'd worked two weeks and made under seven hundred and fifty dollars. Two whole and dreadful weeks slaving under Greggory for under seven hundred and fifty dollars. I wanted to crinkle that paycheck into a tight ball and throw it into Greggory's face. Hell, I wanted to clench my hand into a ball and throw it into Greggory's face.

It would take me forever to save enough to get away with Pecu at this rate. I figured I'd need five grand to get away. I'd have to spend some of my paycheck on gas to get to work every day. I'd be lucky to save five hundred a paycheck.

"You need something else?" Greggory demanded. His and Merdle's eyes studied me. I turned toward the back door.

"Hold up, son." Merdle stopped me. "Walk me out." She stuffed the cash in front of her into a black bank bag, zipped it, and flicked Greggory on the ear. "I'll see you in a month."

Her nails felt like claws on my upper arm. I gave her my best smile, and she gave me the happiest scowl I'd ever seen on her. "The back door?" I asked.

Outside, we stopped behind a multicolored minivan. The vehicle made me smile. I knew how successful her McDonald's was but she chose to drive a rickety old minivan.

"I've seen that look before," Merdle said at my smile.

"I figured as successful as you are you'd drive something a bit more modern."

She cackled. "I meant that look you gave your paycheck. It's the look of someone who needs money. More than they have."

More than they'll ever make working at McDonalds. I only nodded though.

"My nephew doesn't like you. You know what that tells me?"

I scratched my chin "Your nephew?"

"Well, my niece's husband's son from another marriage. I don't know what the hell to call him. Greggory. The little prick running my store. He doesn't like you."

I thought of the way he talked down to me, squeaking while trying to sound intimidating. I thought of the way he glared at me, eyes crossing while trying to appear menacing. I tried not to giggle.

"Him not liking you is funny?" Merdle snapped.

My mirth vanished. "No, ma'am."

Her eyes narrowed. "It's hilarious, you ask me. A kid ten years younger than him." She shook her head. "You know what his dislike for you tells me?"

I shook my head.

"It tells me that he's afraid of you. Be it your stature, your quality, or whatever else, our little Greggory is threatened by you. Now, what does that tell me?"

I shrugged.

"That you're probably smarter than Greggory. Probably a better worker than him. Better people person too, I'd bet. Son, he's threatened by you for good reason."

"Thank you," I mumbled.

"Oh, don't let it go to your head. It don't take much to be better than that twerp. I'm telling you because I saw the desperation in your face when you seen your paycheck. I've been there, poor as a baker's fourth daughter. Just stick it out. You never know, you might get a promotion quicker than you think." She winked at me once, tucked her bank bag under her arm, and waddled to the front door of her van.

She turned back. "Oh, and whatever it is you do to piss off little Greggory." Her lips had a sinister slant to them. "Keep it up."

I walked over to the clunker of a car I'd bought with my first check, smiling myself.

Sacramento was a fine enough place. The City of Trees. Capital of the great California, where cultures collide and breed. Where white people wear durags and black people wear top hats. Where Asian people speak Spanish and Mexican people speak Ebonics. If America is a cultural melting pot, California is the burned crust on the bottom of that pot.

Being the capital, California's prize pig, the city was in good repair. Streets, sidewalks, that sort of thing, all nice. You got the Sierra mountains on one side. Not too polluted, nothing like LA, people loved to tell me.

I'd have liked it there, if I wasn't who I was, living with whom I lived with.

I walked into the kitchen and greeted Song in broken Cantonese. He smiled and responded, speaking more than I knew to understand. He knew that it was too much, but went on anyway. I let him.

I'd always been intrigued by the way the man acted. Our house basically sat on top of our two neighbors, so close that I sometimes mistook the neighbors' humping for my siblings', but Song made no attempt to alert anyone to his situation. In his situation, I'd wait until Spinny was gone then I'd scream bloody murder until the police came knocking. Song was silent as death.

"Sit." I forced him onto our kitchen stool. This daily ritual went back as far as I could remember. No matter how much ointment or other treatment I provided, Song's collar burns stayed red and leaked pus.

"You're wasting your time."

Mom's voice made my skin crawl.

"Let it scab," she said and drug herself to the fridge. Huge black circles surrounded her eyes, and her skin was a nasty pale. "You let it scab. Then it will callous. What you're doing doesn't do shit but prolong it. Your helping is making it worse."

I ignored her.

"You'll learn the truth one day." She carried the gallon to a kitchen chair and collapsed into it. "Generosity is what's wrong with the world. Everyone thinking they know what's best for everyone else. If everyone worried about their damn self, the world would be better off."

I couldn't let it go. "With all the people like you in the world, someone's got to try to make it a better place."

"Oh, so noble. Well, answer me this, you little fuck. Are you helping him? Say you never cleaned his wounds, they got infected, and he died. Wouldn't that be better?"

"No," I answered instantly.

"Oh, yeah?" She scoffed. "Look at him."

He lifted a glass from the drying rack and wiped it with a towel. At the sudden silence, his eyes peeked over his shoulder. Noticing our stares, he fumbled the glass, scrunched his shoulders, and released a peep of a moan. His chain rattled with his shakes.

He lived his entire life this way. The man's life had to be miserable, living with this family.

Worse yet, he had to know better. As far back as I could remember, mom shot dope and never ran out of money. Same with the rest of the family, they'd always been the worst type of people. It was my normal. Mine, but not Song's. He must have had a life before being the household slave to the Torqueres.

Would never waking up again be better than waking up in terror every single day? *It might.*

But with death, life is not even possible.

"No," I decided. "At least alive there's a chance."

I dashed to the fridge, pulled out an apple, and tried to escape before hearing her response.

"You're naive, Jimmy. Some people don't have a chance worth living for."

In the living room, dad's snores were interrupted by the front door banging open. I stopped behind the couch. It was Stupro. The bastard made eye contact with me, let his lips tilt into a sneer, then went up the stairs. I was stuck there, heaving, trying to catch my breath. It was like that every time I had to gaze upon the sick parody of a man.

Our new house was two stories and had a full basement. Mom and Stupro had the upstairs, dad had the main floor couch, and the kids got the basement. Mom had decided that we'd be here for a while, so Stupro's hobbies were forbidden, thus him living upstairs rather than down. I stepped off the bottom stair and thought I smelled blood. The faint smell scratched at my memory every time I came into the cool, damp basement.

Pecu loved it though. "What's up, buddy," I said, closing his door behind me.

He jumped into my arms. "Jimmy! Guess what! Guess what!"

I felt the smile on my face. "What?"

"I kidnapped with a stripper."

"You what?"

He pointed to the TV that I'd put in his room. I spent most every moment I was home with Pecu, so I'd moved my video games in with him for something to do. "The game. I picked up a stripper, now I'm kidnapping with her."

"Do you know what a stripper is?"

His little head wiggled side to side.

"Do you know what kidnapping is?"

He shrugged. "Sleeping like a kid?"

I laughed. "I think we should play a different game."

We sat and did the same thing we'd been doing since moving to Sacramento: hung out. The video games seemed to be a healthy outlet for Pecu's affinity toward causing pain. As far as I knew, Pecu hadn't hurt anything, anything in reality, since his last dog almost lost its tail. It was proof to me that I could save him. He only needed attention. And distance from the evil side of his family.

"Jimmy, when do we get to go on our trip, just me and you?"

My mind had been on mom and the conversation we'd just had. "It'll be the three of us, buddy. Me, you, and Song. We'll leave soon."

4

"Nice haircut," I told Rachel as I bumped her out of the way so I could clock in at the monitor at which she was stationed. "What you doing out here?"

"You're the first to notice." She curled a stray lock around a finger and smiled with both cheeks. "Greggory wants me out here now. He didn't say why."

I snickered. "He probably thinks I'm stealing you away."

"I'm not to be stole from anyone!"

"I'm just telling you his thought process."

"That's so creepy. He —"

"He's standing right here!" Greggory's face was a bright red shined with grease, and his eyes were narrow slits as he came around the corner from the drive-through window. "That is not why I put her out here, so shut up."

I straightened my back and saluted like a good little soldier. "Yes, sir. Sorry, sir."

"I put her here so she could learn the register, and I could teach her."

"Whatever you say," I said and winked at him, tilting my whole head with it. I whispered, "Good luck."

"I don't need —" He stomped a foot down and balled his fists. "Get to work!"

I nodded at Jerry as I took my place next to him at the sandwich station. Jerry was pleasant enough, though he was still more convict than McDonald's employee. After thirty years in the pen, he spooked easily and was prone to jumping into a fighter's guard. Greggory never spoke to old Jerry the way he spoke to me.

"He talked to me like that I'd get him," Jerry had said after Greggory and I got into one of our verbal fencing matches. "Nobody, not ever, going to talk to me that way."

"What do you mean get him, Jerry?" I'd asked.

He pulled up his pant leg and showed me a little knife, very prison-shank looking, sheathed at his ankle. "I'd fucking get him."

We worked through the dinner rush, and I was cleaning the grill for the next shift when Jerry started squirming. At two hundred and sixty hard pounds, he squeezed in next to me. I stopped scrubbing with the grill brick.

"You seem all right for a square," he said.

Instantly defensive, I responded, "What makes you think I'm a square?"

"Look at you." He laughed. "Clean cut. Always flirting with that little Christian girl. Man, you fit right in with her. Shit, when I was your age, I wasn't trying to do no working. I was robbing. Stealing and robbing."

I told the ex-con for some reason, "I've grown up doing crime. Runs in my family."

"Oh, is that right?" His tone was curious, not condescending.

"Sure. I dress like a square on purpose." I smiled. "No one ever suspects the square."

"Shit, you ain't lying." He rumbled a hard laugh. "I knew you was all right. Felt it in my gut."

The back door crashed open. "Greggory!" Our leader rushed between me and Jerry, pushing by me and ricocheting off Jerry. "This place looks like shit! I knew I shouldn't have hired such a little weasel, no matter how much my sister insists you're family. Ain't no blood of mine so damn stupid."

"Sorry. I've been so busy. We had —" Greggory's voice faded as Merdle led him into the office like a dog who'd pissed on the carpet.

"I like that old lady," Jerry said, and we laughed. I went back to cleaning up and ten minutes later Merdle's cracking voice called me into the office. "Hey." Jerry put his arm out, barring my way. His eyes were conspiratorial. He lowered his voice. "Pay attention."

That was all he said, and his arm moved.

Merdle sat in front of her safe with stacks of cash in front of her. Greggory stared at me with more anger in his demeanor than normal. "Give him his paycheck, Greg," she said, adding a new stack of money to the table. She leaned back in her chair and faced me. "Despite Greg's complaints, I gave you a raise. Keep up the good work —" She nodded her head at Greggory and winked behind his back. "And there will be more where that came from."

"Thank you," I said and really meant it.

She leaned forward and started stuffing stacks into her bank bag. I stuck my tongue out at Greggory and closed the door on his whiney face. My hands tore through the envelope and pulled out my latest paycheck.

$802.87

Not too shabby, I thought. Not good, but fifty more dollars than I'd been getting. Fifty dollars closer to making our escape. Fifty dollars for annoying Greggory.

"Did you see it?" Jerry asked me. Our area was clean, and it was time to go.

"See what?"

Jerry's eyes roamed over the store and landed on Rachel. She stared at us with her cute little smile. "Meet me at your car after work," Jerry said out of Rachel's view.

I clocked out and waited in my car. The parking lot emptied, all the evening shift workers left, and the overnight shift settled into their jobs. I was ready to leave when the passenger side opened and Jerry squeezed into the seat. "Sup?" he said.

I waited for him to speak more. "Sup, dude?"

He shook his head, and his wide eyes caught the reflection of the McDonald's sign above us. "Did you see it?"

"See what, Jerry?"

"The bank bag? All that cash?"

"Yes…"

"That lady comes in here once a month for her deposit. Once a month, then she just walks out with it."

"And?"

"And? Do the math, kid. This place pulls in at least a grand a day, easy. That little old witch walks to her car all alone with thirty Gs in her mitts."

I knew exactly what he was thinking. "Listen, Jerry. I know what I said earlier —"

"I know you was lying, kid," he interrupted. "But you got it in you. I can tell." *Is that supposed to be a compliment?* "I need someone with a car. That's it. All you do is drive, and we'll go fifty-fifty. Think about it, kid. Don't say no yet, just think about it." He opened the door and stepped out. With his head in through the window, he continued, "And so we clear, I'm not going back to prison. So if you got thoughts about telling, you best think them against your life. See you tomorrow, kid."

I focused on keeping my car between the lines, trying to keep my mind blank, but all I could think about was Jerry's words. I wasn't paying attention as I got home, and I walked straight into mom.

"What the fuck is this about a trip?"

I choked. "What trip?"

Her face contorted, revealing the pointy screws in her mouth. "Pecu says you're saving money for a trip."

"Oh, that." I swallowed. "I told him I'd take him to Disneyland."

She glared. "With Song?"

I probably should have made it clear that leaving was a secret. "Pecu asked if he could come. I only agreed to shut him up."

She strode forward and stood an inch from my face. "No matter what you think of me, Jimmy, I love my baby. If you ever even think about taking him, it will be bad for you. I'll find you. No matter where you go. I will find you."

The door crashed behind me, and I ran down the stairs to my room. I tried to control my breathing. Two full paychecks were all I'd gotten so far and only had a little over a grand saved up. It wasn't enough. I wanted to flee right then, but it wasn't enough.

"No one gets hurt."

Jerry's eyes took me in from the passenger seat of my car. It was the third time I'd said the words since we'd gotten off work and drove around the corner to change into black jumpsuits. Each time I said it he gave me that same blank stare.

"Say it, Jerry. I'll do this, but you got to promise me no one gets hurt."

He stared.

"Say it!"

The door slapped behind him, and he disappeared into the walled enclosure behind the store. My car was a hundred yards from the back door of the McDonalds. I had a clear view of Merdle's minivan as well as the door leading into the store, but my car was camouflaged behind a wall of shrubbery.

Jerry would take Merdle's bag, then run the other way. I'd watch and casually drive my car around the corner, picking him up out of sight.

An easy crime. Little risk. Massive reward.

My choice was easy. Pecu over Merdle. I was sure she'd understand if I was able to explain it to her. She definitely wouldn't agree with It — no normal person would — but she'd understand.

Everything I'd saved had been spent on things I thought would be immediately necessary. Clothes for each of us so no one at the house would see me packing. A week's worth of food so I wouldn't have to stop driving for anything other than gas. A phone for the app I'd learned about: a translator to speak to Song. It was all in the trunk of my car. I'd get my half of the cash, go home, and pretend like nothing happened.

I wanted to run that day, flee as soon as the money was in hand, but I had to make sure that I wasn't suspected of this robbery. Not showing up for work the next day would be suspicious. Mom was going to be on my trail, I knew. I didn't need the police chasing me too. A week from that day, that was the plan.

The back door to the McDonalds opened and Merdle waddled out. Old, helpless Merdle.

What am I doing?

Jerry stalked out of his hiding place and pulled something from his black jumpsuit. He came around the corner of Merdle's van pointing a black pistol at her.

I yanked the door handle and barreled around my car, past the bushes, but it happened too fast.

Jerry said something and Merdle shook her head. The gun went up as the McDonalds door cracked open. Jerry's arm crashed down. Merdle collapsed. He crouched and reached for the bag.

"Jerry?"

The voice came from the doorway. Rachel stood there.

"No!" I shouted.

Her eyes locked with mine.

The gun fired.

In the closing darkness, her blood sprayed black against the building like water shot from a cannon. A nickel-sized hole dotted the center of her forehead.

I collapsed.

5

"Get up, kid!"

My eyes focused. I was on my knees. It was dark, and I was in the back parking lot of my job. Jerry tried to get me to my feet. I stood then followed him. I dropped into the driver's seat, closed the door, and settled my hands onto the steering wheel.

"Drive!"

I nodded and pulled the gearshift. My car pulled out from behind a wall of shrubbery, and I headed home from work. I knew the way well, and the car practically drove itself. Jerry counted bills next to me. His lips moved in silent numbers and tears dripped off his chin into his lap. *Why is he crying?* He was so large and intimidating. It seemed ridiculous.

Somewhere between McDonalds and the I-5 my senses returned in a flash.

Oh, god, what have I done?

Jerry stacked money into two piles in his lap. A gun lay on the center console between us. *The gun that just killed Rachel.* I threw the steering wheel right, slammed on the brake, grabbed the gun, and crushed the barrel into the bridge of Jerry's nose.

"What the fuck —"

I drove the butt into his temple and released a guttural roar. "You stupid son of a bitch! You? Why did you –" I choked on snot. "Put the money back in the bag." His red and wet eyes met mine. I shook the gun in his face. "All of it." His jaw clenched, but he filled the bag. "Now get out."

"We're on the interstate! The cops —"

I ripped the money from his hand. "Jerry, if you don't get out of my car in two seconds, I'll pull this fucking trigger."

The door opened, and I floored it. Jerry rolled behind me.

I drove, wiping at my swimming eyes, remembering a sweet Christian girl, like how she'd say such cute things or how her cheeks went round when she smiled or how her brains looked splattered on a back alley wall.

I slowed my car to a stop in front of our house and laid my head on the steering wheel. How could I be so stupid? Trusting a man who had spent most of his life in prison to commit a crime with such a high reward and not resort to violence. By the way he'd attacked Merdle, it seemed he'd been planning to go about it that way from the get-go. I was a fucking idiot.

Rachel's death was on me. Just like Amanda's.

Devoid of any other options, I opened the door and started for the house. Each step was a challenge. I focused on acting normal, but my knees wouldn't bend, my feet were too heavy, and the sidewalk seemed to have more cracks than I remembered.

Dad was on the couch. Awake. And not eating. I swallowed, then said, "Hey, dad."

I tried not to look his way as I strode toward the kitchen. "Jimmy," he gurgled. "Jimmy. Sit down."

I froze. Slowly, I sat across from him.

"You can tell me anything, Jimmy," dad said. "I'd help you. Somehow."

"Sure dad, I know." The last thing I knew was that.

"Is there anything I can help you with now, son?"

He took massive breaths in through his nose like the speech had been exhausting. I stared, trying to decipher his thoughts, trying to convince myself his decision to start talking now was a coincidence. "No, dad. Why?"

His arm lifted from his side. He clicked a button on the remote.

"—blue sedan heading north on the I-5. Police have one man in custody, but believe there was an accomplice. The driver of this vehicle —" A picture of the car I'd parked out front filled the screen, "is believed to have shot and killed a sixteen year old girl during a robbery at this McDonalds. On the scene, we have Julia Rom —"

Dad clicked the button again. "Is that your —"

I surged to my feet, bolted for the kitchen. *No. No. No. No. No.* I slid on the linoleum, and Song crashed against the far wall. I made eye contact with him. *Why am I here? What am I doing? Why am I in the kitchen? What do I do?*

I had to escape. Now. *But how?* I'd thought about it for months, but now I was frozen. I stood and stared at Song, at the slave I was supposed to save.

Song shuffled forward and pressed two knuckles to my chin, lifting my head. His eyes were usually wide as he assessed every threat around him. Usually his lips creased a deep frown.

That face was gone. His head was tilted back, and his chin was high. His frown was a straight, hard line. This face was not the face I knew. It radiated strength. Without words, he showed me strength.

Be strong.

The floor creaked behind me and I swung around, bringing Jerry's gun up out of my waist. Coitus's eyes made saucers. "What the hell, Jim —"

"Shut up. You're going to do exactly what I say. Exactly! Understand?"

She glanced back at Coitum, her constant tail.

"Exactly!"

"I understand. Calm down. We can talk —"

"Sit in that chair. Coitum, go in the coat closet and get the duct tape. If you're not back in five seconds, you won't have a twin anymore."

No one moved.

"Now!"

Coitus plopped into the chair, and Coitum was back before I could get the barrel to the side of my sister's head. "Start wrapping that tape around her and the chair, Coitum. If you don't do it tight enough —" I poked her with a gun.

I stepped back as Coitum wrapped the tape around her. My breathing slowed, and my heartbeat quit hitting so hard. Live or die, I was getting Pecu out. We were going to escape. My little brother was going to be normal. I couldn't think about McDonalds. Or Merdle.

Or Rachel.

The crinkling of tape stopped. Coitus's legs were silver from ankle to knee. Her arms were pinned to her sides.

"Hold your hands together, Coitum." He obliged. Song moaned next to me. His mask of strength had disappeared. I gestured with the gun toward the duct tape then to Coitum's clasped hands. Song shook his head. "Tape him, Song!" He closed his eyes and pressed his palms over them.

"Coitum, if you try anything, anything at all, I'll kill you. I don't want to, but no one's stopping me. Keep your hands just as they are and sit."

The chair creaked with his weight, and he lifted praying hands to his face. I set Jerry's gun on the counter, unrolled a strip of tape, and advanced toward Coitum.

His shoulder pounded into my midsection, and I lifted off the ground, crashing into the cabinets over the sink. He tried to pull away, but I locked legs around his torso and pulled him close. With my free hand, I searched the counter beneath me for the gun. Soon as I found it, I hammered the gun onto his head.

CLACK!

It kicked as it fired. I slammed the barrel into his face. He opened his mouth to scream, and I shoved the gun in. Hard. Coitum gagged.

Everything stopped.

Blood poured out of his nose and over my hand. "Please, don't," I whispered. "Coitum. Please."

He nodded carefully. Tears fell from his eyes and blended with dark blood. I lowered myself off the counter, while I kept the gun steady. "Back in the chair now and —"

"Who shot a fucking gun in my —" Mom stopped and stared at the gun in my hand. "What the fuck, Jimmy?"

I ignored her. "Tie this freak to the chair, just like Coitus."

"Jimmy, what do you think —"

I ripped the gun from Coitum's mouth, aimed at her feet, and fired. "Sit down, Coitum," she whispered. "Just do what he says. He's obviously going through something —"

CLACK!

"No talking!" I screamed.

There was a small part of me, maybe a large part of me, that wanted her to make a wrong move, forcing me to pull the trigger. I was here, gun in hand, because of her. If she was anyone besides who she was, none of this would be happening. If she moved...

Could I if she did?

"Now what, Jimmy?" she asked when Coitum was secured. "Tie myself up?"

"Give me Song's key."

She looked confused. "What?"

"The key, mom!"

Slow, she lifted a gold chain from her neck. The little key landed at my feet, and I pushed it toward Song with my toe. He stared at it. No expression on his face, no movement in his body. He didn't even seem to breathe.

"Song!" His eyes came up. They were full and wet. "Song, unlock yourself." I put my hand to my neck and twisted it like a key. "Free, Song. Unlock it."

His eyes never left mine. He shook his head and spewed Cantonese. He kicked the key back toward me, his tone rising.

Mom laughed. "He can't leave, idiot."

I didn't understand, but I didn't have time to. "Get in the chair, mom." She lowered herself and folded her hands in her lap. "Do I need to knock you out?"

"Get on with it, Jimmy. We get it. You're serious." I put the gun down, took up what was left of the duct tape, and tied her like my siblings.

"I hope you're not thinking of doing what I think you're doing," mom said. "I'll find you. I'll kill you."

I cut the tape with my teeth. "My life is worth saving his." She opened her mouth, but I crushed a length of tape over it.

Two strides and I ripped the key up off the floor. One stride and I shoved it into the mechanism on Song's collar. The chain clattered to the floor. Eyes wide, he rubbed at the raw flesh of his neck.

I pushed him in front of me, but he stopped after a step. I pushed him again. He stopped. "Go Song!" His head shook. He moaned then spewed words. "We have to get out of —"

"He can't, Jimmy," Coitus said.

I pushed and kept pushing. He fought every step, but I got him into the living room.

"What —" A gasp of air, "— is going on?"

Dad stood above the couch.

He was too big. The bones, the muscles, the joints, they couldn't support him. It was impossible. But there he was.

"I'm leaving." I turned to Song, forced eye contact. "Go to the van." I made a motion with my hands like I drove a car. He shook his head, but I pushed him hard toward the door. I turned back toward dad. "I'm getting Pecu away."

"I —" Tears fell down his face as he sucked for air. "I —" He blew out air in a gust. "I. Understand."

I took the stairs to my room two at a time, ripped open the top drawer of my dresser, and pulled out the lotus. It still felt warm to the touch, though I hadn't held it since this morning. In its place, I left the gun that had killed Rachel. I couldn't stand to touch it any longer.

Pecu was in his room, sitting on his bed, wide-eyed and shook from the commotion. "Am I in trouble, Jimjim?"

"No, buddy." I lifted him and placed him on my hip. "It's just time for our trip, that's all."

I hurried up the stairs. At the top, the front door burst open.

A streetlight shined behind and hid his features. I could see his silhouette though. Only met one man that made a shadow that large.

"The fuck you doing off your ass —" The floorboards bent with Stupro's weight. Stupro scanned me from my feet to my eyes. "And what are you doing?"

His smile was genuine. I swallowed. "I'm leaving," I whispered.

He shrugged, then nodded. "How's Spinny take that?"

"Doesn't matter."

He kept nodding. "Don't think she'd be very happy with me, I let you just walk out. Especially, with Pecu."

"You don't have a choice."

"Come on, Jimmy. We've been here before —"

He stepped forward. I stepped back. "You ain't killing nobody. It ain't in you." He took another step.

"Stop!" I cried. I felt like a toddler throwing a tantrum next to this monster. "Don't take another step!"

He stepped forward; I stepped back. "Give it up. I'm not letting you leave without your mom's permission. I owe her too much."

He stepped forward, and the floor shifted again.

"Stop!" He stepped forward. "Please! Stop."

He reached for my neck, I dodged, and my free hand snapped out. The globe of the lotus flower slammed into Stupro's temple. I felt the crunch vibrate through my entire body. Stupro crumpled. Pecu screamed.

I looked down at my uncle, the man who had caused so much in my life, so much in the lives of so many. He was disgusting. He preyed on the weak and fed off their misery. He deserved this. He deserved so much more. He deserved to die.

I looked at my hand. In my palm, the lotus flower had a smudge of blood like a fingerprint left by my violence. I wiped it, but a hair would not move. *Not a hair,* I realized. A crack ran the length of the globe.

I shoved it into my pocket and ran out the door as fast as I could. Neighbors stood in doorways all down the block, their eyes on the bloody man leaving a house where multiple gunshots had fired. I sprinted to my car, popped the trunk, and took out the two duffel bags.

Song stood next to the van. "Get in!" I screamed as I put Pecu and the duffel bags in the back. "We don't have time."

He shook his head, so I went to where he stood, opened the door, and manhandled him into the van. His cries were manic, but he finally complied.

In the driver's seat, I took a deep breath and tried to still my thrashing heart. *I did it.* Pecu was away from those people. He'd never see the things I've seen. That was all that mattered. Not Merdle. Not Rachel.

I couldn't think of them. I looked back at Pecu. "Are you ready for our trip, buddy?"

He nodded through small sniffles. Tears were wet on his cheeks, but they'd stopped running. Song's head was in his lap, and he shook from the sobs. I shoved my arm back into one of the duffel bags and found the cell phone.

I tapped until the translator appeared on the screen. "What is wrong with you?" I said into the phone.

Song's back straightened as the translator rattled unrecognizable words. I tapped at the phone to show him how the translator worked and handed it to him. His eyes squinted and his jaw clenched and unclenched. The phone jerked out of my hand, and Song tossed it out the window.

"You've killed my family!" he shouted.

6

My entire life, every day, I'd seen Song. Seventeen damn years I'd been around him. I stared at the mystery beside me. A honk came from beside the van. Long blonde hair whirled in the wind, and the woman within the whirl showed me two middle fingers. I turned my eyes to the road.

"You speak English?" Seemed like a good place to start.

"You have to bring me back."

"I can't, Song. I —"

"You don't understand. My family is in danger. You have to —" He put his face in his hands and shook with sobs. "You have to take me back."

I couldn't accept the flawless English coming from the man's mouth.

"Song, I'm not bringing you back."

"You have to!"

"I can't."

"My family —"

"My family is in the backseat!" I shouted. Pecu whimpered, so I reached back and rubbed his knee. "I have to get away, Song. Pecu is my family, and he's been in danger all his life."

"Drop me off. I'll walk."

"I'm not stopping."

"But why?" he whined.

I thought about my car's picture on the news. I thought about the same car parked outside of a house with my tied-up family. I thought about the cops having Jerry. I thought about the bank bag I had next to my seat. I thought about the unconscious, possibly dead old woman I'd stolen the bag from.

I thought about a beautiful young girl whose life I'd cut short.

I tried to think of something that would justify my actions without revealing what I'd done, but his eyes demanded the truth and he deserved to know why my priorities were more important than his. So I told him. Everything.

After I stopped talking, the rattle of the van was the only sound. I'd run out of words and let the silence hold. Eventually, I relaxed my grip on the steering wheel. West on the I-80, with a life of pain behind me. That was the most important thing. No matter what we went through, the worst had already been lived. I quit shaking and the adrenaline drained from my body, leaving me exhausted.

He pointed at a huge green sign. It read: Vallejo. "Get off here."

"Why?"

"Because I don't want to show up in San Francisco in the van your mom will have to report stolen by the man that tied-up her whole family and stole her child." He glared my way. "That's why."

Pecu was asleep when we rolled into the cheap, one-floor hotel parking lot. I got us a room, laid Pecu on the bed, and found the TV remote. It took some browsing before I found what I was looking for.

"It was so scary, so terrifying," mom said on the tiny box television. "He ran in, pointing a gun, and made all of us tie each other up." The tears on her face almost looked so genuine they almost fooled me. "He kidnapped my two children! My sons, please, someone find them."

A sketch of a man appeared on the screen, and the anchorman explained the situation. The man was black, had a massive afro with a pick-comb poking out the side, and, most importantly, was not me.

I'd been kidnapped by Jerry and his accomplice after work, forced to show the way to my home after they'd argued, then my brother and I were taken by the predator. As much as the police knew, it was obvious dad had helped craft the story, and I silently thanked him. As long as Jerry kept his mouth shut, I wouldn't be blamed for Rachel's murder. If he was smart, he'd blame everything on mom's fabricated black man at the first opportunity.

Either way, the cops would be searching for us. Two young people kidnapped by a murderer? An amber alert already proclaimed? Before long, all of California would be flipping rocks for us. We had to get further away.

We'd stolen a car in Vallejo to get away from the van. *What was one more crime?* Song spoke enough to direct me to San Francisco, but no more. I was relieved to let him lead, even if San Francisco was entirely too close to Sacramento. Now that I could breathe without hyperventilating, it was time to figure out how we were going to escape.

"Song." He sat the bed next to me while Pecu snoozed behind us. "Why are we in a motel in San Francisco?"

"My family is here," he whispered.

"Where? Let's go get them. We can all —"

"They're probably already dead."

I swallowed and looked at my hands. "We have to be able to do something. That's why you brought us here, right?"

He shrugged. "The man that traded me to your mother has my family. If I was ever to try and escape, he promised he would kill them."

Pecu's snores were fast and small. I watched his little chest move. Though the stress of the day still had my nerves fraught, a weight had been lifted that I'd been carrying for too long, possibly my entire life. There was one less Torquere in the world because of the crimes that I'd committed. It didn't justify anything, but the fact still brought relief.

I couldn't make it for nothing. Every moment I spent doing anything but driving was a moment longer for my mom to find us. We needed to be on the road, no matter what Song needed.

But he'd suffered beneath the Torqueres longer than Pecu had, longer than I had. It wasn't my fault that he'd somehow become a slave to my mother, but I still felt responsible.

The smart thing to do was leave him, I knew.

"We have to find them," I said. "We will steal your family away, and they can come with us."

He scoffed. "Mr. Long is first born to *the Mr. Long*, the man's heir. You don't steal anything from Mr. Long."

"You can steal from anyone."

"No! I won't hear of it." He sounded as though he was angry that I'd even considered stealing from the man.

"Song, he has your family hostage."

His hands wrung in his lap. "He's been too good to me."

Too good to him? "You don't make any sense. How are we going to get your family back if we can't steal them from the man who has them?"

His eyes met mine and actually seemed to see me for the first time since I'd abducted him from slavery. "There's only one way." He started popping the knuckles on each finger. "We ask."

I went that night. Would have left the same hour, but it had taken some time to convince Song that I had to go alone. He felt like he was disrespecting the man, Mr. Long, by not going himself, which was ludicrous. If someone had Pecu, I'd have no problem stealing from them. No matter who their daddy was.

Song had relented when I pointed out how angry Mr. Long would be that he'd run. It would be better for him to hear the explanation from me. That had been what convinced him. Not that someone needed to stay with Pecu. Not that the man might tie him up and send him back to mom. No, Mr. Long's anger was the convincing argument.

That gave me pause.

Good idea or not, going alone was the only option. Song was unaware of it, but he was our leverage, the little we had. I was useless to this Mr. Long. For whatever reason, Song wasn't. He refused to tell me the story, but mom had made a deal for Song specifically and the death of his family was the seal that kept Song from running. Mom wanted Song. Mr. Long wanted mom to have Song. Giving up Song for nothing would've been stupid.

Plus, if Song's family was already dead, I didn't want him to be there to hear it.

I sat in the back of a cab and watched San Franciscan lights streak by. It was obvious when we entered Chinatown. Four-story buildings built with one car width of space between them, clotheslines hanging from window to window, clothes draping from each line and every piece of line. The predominant color was red.

The taxi stopped. "This is it," the driver told me.

"It," was a building like all the rest, tall, square, and red. A stairwell led to an indistinct door. "You sure?"

The man's smile showed all his teeth. "Been here more than once, sure as sure. I tell you, this is it."

I handed him a twenty, got out of the car, and watched him speed off.

Bells jingled as I walked into a closet-sized reception room. One chair, one chest-high desk, and one chest-high Chinese woman were all that was in the room. "Welcome! You come for massage, manicure, or pedicure? You want sauna first? You tell me."

Three steps, and I had my hands folded on her desk. "Mr. Long."

"What you say?"

"I want to speak with Mr. Long."

Her head turned left then right like there might be someone else I was talking to. "No. You get massage. No Mr. Long here."

"Listen. Go back and tell your boss that Jimmy Torquere, Spinny Torquere's son, is here and he's not leaving until he gets to speak with

Mr. Long." She turned toward the door behind her. "Tell them no one else is leaving either."

I lowered myself into the chair as the door banged shut behind the woman's desk. This was insane. I wasn't a tough guy, and I felt like anyone who looked at me would know as well as I did. I reached into my pocket and rubbed a thumb against the little hair-sized crack on the lotus flower's globe.

A peaceful talk with a powerful man, that was my mission. Everything would be fine. I'd get Song's family, and we'd be on our way.

Bells jingled, and I surged to my feet. A Chinese man stood in the doorway.

"We're closed," I told him.

His head tilted, and he stuttered some gibberish. He tried to push past me, but I stood my ground. "I said we're closed," I growled, trying to sound confident. The door slammed as the man ran off.

At the same moment, the door behind the desk swung open.

The room filled with young Chinese women. They wore white robes, and the only difference between one and another was the length of their glossy black hair. Ten, fifteen of them surrounded me.

A woman cut through the center of them, identical in dress and look except her hair was road-snow grey. "Mr. Torquere, I have been instructed to entertain you." Her English was as pristine as Song's. "Master Long is on his way."

"Um. Thank you."

She nodded. "Which girl would you like?"

Which what was that? "Which girl?"

"Multiple, sir?"

"Oh, uh —" I stuttered. "No girl. Girls. I won't be here —"

The woman snapped her fingers and shouted a word in Cantonese. The women funneled back through the door until it was only me and the old lady. She fixed me with a stare that was almost expressionless. She wore it like a death stare. "Anything else, sir?"

I shook my head.

She left, and I ran my hand through my hair. I came with threats, demanding that I see the owner, and they give me my choice of their wares? You don't treat someone like that for no reason.

My name is enough to make a slave trader treat me like royalty?

I tried not to think about what my mom could have possibly done to instill that type of respect in these types of people, but I knew it wasn't by treating them well. Most likely, I was giving myself over to someone who would love to kill my mother.

I should have left Song and ran.

"Mr. Long is ready for you, sir." I jerked from my thoughts. The grey-haired lady stood in the doorway behind the desk. "He's out front."

Outside, a black limousine beckoned me. The farthest door to the rear opened and a man climbed out. He was sumo wrestler big in an expensive, two-sizes-too-small suit. "Mr. Torquere?"

I nodded.

"Mr. Long is waiting." I moved to enter the door, but he stopped me with a palm. "Very sorry for the inconvenience, but I must frisk you."

At his direction, I put my hands on the top of the limo and let him pat me down. The only thing I had on me was the lotus flower. He took it out, gave me a funny look, then slid it back into my pocket. He tapped my shoulder and waved toward the door.

A seat in the back, a seat running on the one side, a mini bar opposite it, and a seat under the window to the cab. Mr. Long sat the leather couch across from the bar and twirled a dark liquid in a wine glass.

He was tiny. My knees nearly touched my chest with my feet on the floor, yet his feet hardly touched the floor. The leather seat bounced and rocked as the sumo wrestler sat next to me.

"Howie, sit up front tonight, please." The words came from Mr. Long.

The large man's hand froze on the door handle, and he met the eye of Mr. Long. Eventually, he nodded and uttered, "Sir," as he left me alone with Mr. Long.

Mr. Long leaned forward and tinkered with his bar. Deep creases surrounded his eyes, accompanied by black circles. Gouges bordered his mouth and connected to both sides of his nose. Grey peppered his hair at the temples and flowed into the rest of his slicked-back do.

"Nice limo," I said as calmly as I could. I gripped the lotus in my pocket for dear life.

He smiled. "I find it to be an extravagant waste of money that I could find a much better use for, but father insists that a certain image be portrayed. Uphold the image or lose the name, he says. So, I wear this suit and I ride this limo."

"Your father sounds... demanding."

Mr. Long poured from a bottle into a wine glass. "Demanding is not near strong enough a term." He held the glass between us, gesturing with his eyes to take it. I hesitated. "Come now. I hardly think your mother will mind."

I swallowed. "My mother —"

"Your mother," he said, voice overpowering my own, "*she* is demanding. I just got off the phone with your mother as a matter of fact."

I sipped at the wine. It was disgusting. "What did you talk about?"

"First, let's speak of you. You must know something about me, the type of man I am, because you correctly sought out one of my establishments. Knowing whom you deal with, why would you put yourself in such danger?" He paused. "You do recognize the danger, yes?"

"I needed your attention fast."

"That I understand, but tell me why."

"In a nutshell? I need Song's family. Tonight."

He swirled his wine. "You willingly put yourself in my hands for another man's family?" His tone turned solemn, "That is very courageous, honorable even. Why?"

I told him what I'd told myself. "Song is family. His family is my family."

He studied the wine in his glass. "Well, then," he whispered. "I must welcome you to the family."

What?

"I was hoping to never speak to your mother again, Mr. Torquere. When she rang, I was not happy. Twenty-some years it has been."

"What did she want?"

"In a nutshell? Song's family murdered, and her two sons held until she arrived."

Until she arrived. Of course she knew this was where we'd go. She knew once I found out about Song, I'd have to try and help him. She'd been using my conscience against me since I'd developed one.

"Mr. Torquere." Mr. Long sounded different. "I'm going to be frank. Your mother has power over me. Not only me, but my family. If I could, I would defy her. If it was but me, I would defy her. But it is not. My father will not allow it. I'm forced to do whatever your mother demands."

Tears dripped off his chin and left little dark circles where they absorbed into his suit. I expected this man, this slave trader, to be ruthless. I expected to be the one crying as I begged him to let Song's family go. His tears were hard to understand. His words were harder.

"Did you —" I swallowed a lump. "Did you already..."

"Kill Song's family?" He scowled. "The family I took in as my own?" Then he shouted, "The family I have taken care of all these years?" His face was red, and his fists were balls. "Did I kill that family!"

I stared.

He deflated, and his eyes turned down. "I love them."

I was afraid to speak, like my words could unsettle whatever balance this conversation teetered on.

He took a shaky breath. "But it must happen."

"No," I whispered. "There has to —"

"Where are Song and your brother?"

I pulled the door handle to jump out. It was locked. I turned, made eye contact with Mr. Long. I moved to grab him, but a little snubbed nose revolver pressed into my chest.

"Mr. Torquere." He breathed. "Don't make this difficult."

7

I was about ready to stop making it difficult. I needed sleep, but they wouldn't let me. I needed food, but they wouldn't feed me. I'd been chained in the moist cellar for ten hours at most, but the excitement of the previous day made it feel like weeks. I was drained.

The single door opened, and Mr. Long's pointy-toed shoes clinked on the floor. He was the only person I'd seen since Howie had secured me to the chair. He had been surprisingly gentle, that giant.

"I just got off the phone with your mother."

"Good for you," I snarled.

His eyes were barely higher than mine though he was standing. They glared. "She is still dealing with the police in Sacramento over some kind of wild kidnapping —" He eyed me, an eyebrow drooping. "But she wanted you to know that she will see you shortly. I need the boy before she gets here."

I clenched my teeth.

"I've been thinking of some unordinary methods to use against you, Mr. Torquere. What is the best torture for one who would risk losing everything to save a slave and his family? And I know how much you're risking."

He turned and tapped the door twice with his knuckles. In came four women of varying ages.

A mother and three daughters, I realized.

Mr. Long's voice was confident, but his eyes were wet and his face was tight. "Ladies, introduce yourself to Mr. Torquere. Tell him a little about yourself and your relation to Song."

The oldest spoke first. "Song and I escaped China with the help of the Long family. He is my husband." Tears spilled from her eyes. "We had three beautiful girls together. I miss him so —" She collapsed into Mr. Long's arms and cried.

I'd seen Song every day of my life. I'd known he was an older man, known that he must have had a life, but I'd never given thought to what that life might've been. Seeing it in front of me, seeing what my mother took from him... Mr. Long chose the perfect torture.

"My name is Vanessa," the oldest daughter said. "I am a dentist and have two young sons. I was seven when dad left. I remember him doing sock puppet shows for me before bed, and how he used to make me breakfast even when he was late for work." She glanced at Mr. Long at that, and they shared a sad smile.

Another woman strode forward. "Mom says I was three when dad was taken, and I don't remember too much about him. One memory I see clearly is Christmas. There was a huge present that took up most all the front room. All it was was a big box with a series of smaller boxes inside. I guess the year before I cared about the boxes more than the presents. The box idea was dad's."

The last daughter must've been my age. Her beauty was debilitating, the kind that was hard to focus around. Right then, I hardly noticed. "I never got to meet my real dad, and he has —"

"Stop!" I shouted. "All right. I get it. Just stop."

"Thank you, ladies," Mr. Long said. "You may go."

The room emptied but for the two of us. We both cried. Unrestrained, we cried for long minutes. "Do they know?" I finally asked.

"Do they know their father has been a slave all these years? No. Ling suspects, but —"

"Do they know you'll murder them?"

His face drooped, and he aged decades.

I breathed deep, in through my nose, out through my mouth. "Get me a phone."

He pulled a cell phone from his pocket and pressed a button. He held the mouthpiece close to my face as it began to ring. The first was cut off. "You have them?"

"Hi, mom. Miss me?"

Silence. "Did you give him Pecu?"

"That's why I'm calling. There's only one way I'll give you Pecu."

"Listen here, you little fuck, you'll give me my son or you're done."

"Mom, you'll never find him without me —" *Maybe a lie.* "And I'll die here if I have to —" *Not a lie.* "You're not in a position to demand anything from me."

More silence. "Fine."

"Song goes back to his family. They go free."

"No," she said instantly.

"Fine. Have fun searching for Pecu. Mr. Long, hang up the —"

"Wait!" I could hear her huffing into the phone. I counted breaths. Seven. "Fine. Give me back my baby."

Her words made my tears start afresh. Mr. Long took the phone away. "Samantha," he said, his smile making him young again. "Bring the photos. Or you get nothing."

His thumb tapped a button, and his arms were suddenly around my neck. "Thank you." He sobbed into my ear. "Thank you so much."

Seagulls protested in swirling flocks above, and I watched them dive into rocking water. The sky was grey as the sun fell. Hundreds of shipping containers towered around us, and the seagulls used them as resting places between clawing at the ocean. It all seemed so quaint, like everything was exactly where it was supposed to be. Except us.

No one told me why we were meeting at the docks, and I didn't ask. The docks, the city, or fucking Mexico, it didn't matter. I'd lost. Hardly twenty-four hours and already I was giving up my chance at saving Pecu.

My only chance.

Tiny fingers pulled at the corner of my mouth, and I took my eyes from out the window of Mr. Long's limo. Pecu's huge blues glistened up at me atop his little baby frown. He used his fingers to curl my lips up. "Smile, Jimjim. No more sad."

I gave my best attempt. "Sorry, buddy."

I held him tight, squeezed him with everything I had, like I was making up for all the moments I should've been holding him since he was born. I let the tears stream down my face.

"Jimmy?"

"What, buddy?"

"I can't bweave."

I released him, snorting snot with a laugh. I wiped my face with my sleeve and fixed my eyes away from him. "Isn't this a little suspicious?" I asked Mr. Long. "A limo sitting at the docks for an hour."

He shrugged, eyes looking moist themselves. "A man parked in his own docks isn't illegal."

"His own docks?"

"Yes." Mr. Long cleared his throat and wiped his eyes.

The massive crane, the massive ship, and the massive truck on massive tires all pointed out the obvious: massive money.

"Jimmy." Song put his hand on mine. "Jimmy this is all so much. Thank —"

"Don't," I said. "Please. Don't."

He nodded.

I went back to watching the seagulls and tried to think. At that point, I wished I was more like my mother. I wished I could have left Song in slavery back in Sacramento, or at least abandoned him once we had gotten to San Francisco. Pecu and I would've been halfway across the country, but no. I was giving him up instead.

A black sedan entered at the other end of the docks. It sped toward us, and the tires squealed as it slid to a stop, drifting sideways ten feet from the limo. The driver's side door opened, and an open-toed sandal came out followed by the vilest woman ever to breathe air. She closed the door and leaned against it, puffing a cigarette.

"All right, let me go first." Mr. Long climbed over my legs and out the door. Mom caught my eye before the door closed again. She grinned.

"Mom." Pecu rapped his knuckles on the window. I pulled him further away. His little hand waved at her. "Mama!"

Mom and Mr. Long spoke. Their words were hidden behind seagulls, waves, and machinery, but Mr. Long's hands waved in frustration. When they stopped, he crossed his arms. Mom's smile lost its vigor. She tapped two fingers on the window of her car. It inched down, and an ornate wooden box slid through the gap. It was only three inches tall, six inches long, and had a heart engraved on the top like a little girl's jewelry box.

I couldn't see it from my seat, but I was familiar with it. Whenever we moved, the box never got packed. It rode in the center console next to mom's hand. I'd wondered more than once what was in that box, but she kept a lock on it. A lock I'd never seen the key to.

Mom flipped the box end over end and caught it with a flourish. Her smile returned, and her lips moved. Then the door was open. I slid out using my legs, my arms grasping Pecu, and stood next to Mr. Long.

"You fucked up seriously this time," mom growled. "I told you what would happen."

"Mama!"

Pecu reached toward her with both arms, squeezing both hands open and closed. I clenched my teeth. Here I was risking my life to save this little boy's future from the cretin, trying to do anything to give him a chance, and he wants out of my arms at the first sight of her? He didn't know any better — I knew that — but it still put a hole in my chest.

"Give me my son," mom demanded.

"Give me the photos," Mr. Long said. He held mom's eye. The box clattered and clanked all the way to Mr. Long's feet. He lifted it. "The key?"

"Threw it out years ago."

The stare that he pointed at her was impressive for such a tiny man. At that moment, I knew this man was used to getting things done his way with little resistance. This situation clawed at an ego that had little scarring. Even mom swallowed as she took the blunt end of that stare. "They better be here." His jaw clenched. "Or this will turn for you."

Mom shrugged off the tension. "Don't threaten me, Richie. Just open the damn —"

The box shattered on the ground, and I flinched. Mr. Long lowered himself and picked up the contents that spilled out of the box. Three Polaroid photos. He cycled through them, then his eyes rose. "You may go. If you're seen in San Francisco again, you'll be killed." He faced me and patted my cheek. "Thank you. You won't regret it."

I shuffled left so he could get into his limo. As soon as the door closed, he was gone. And we were alone.

Mom yanked Pecu from my arms. "I can't fucking believe you, Jimmy." She opened the back door and passed him to Coitus, who gave her a roll of tape. "Put me through all this, and for what? to give him back a day later?" She ripped a piece of tape off the roll. "I ain't half as mad as Stupro though. He might kill you, Jimmy, after you hit him like that."

"I —"

The tape slammed over my mouth. "Not now, you little fuck. You don't get to talk. Hold out your hands." I saw no reason to resist, so I presented them. "This is all bad for me. Very bad. I've been sober for two nights now. Seen things I haven't in years. All of this hurts me, Jimmy, but you know what?"

She went silent and stared into my eyes, waiting. I shook my head.

"It's going to hurt you more. Much more." She slapped my face harder than she ever had. "Get in."

I stared at my hands and edged toward the door. "Oh no. You ride in the trunk from now on. Coitum!" *Prunk*, the lid bounced as it popped. My hands were blurry all of a sudden, but I went around the car and got in the trunk.

What choice did I have? She had Pecu.

We started moving.

I focused on the hum of tires on pavement. I couldn't start thinking, not then. I brought the lotus flower out of my pocket and put them on my lips. Just listen to the tires, listen to the pavement. Concentrate. No thoughts.

Screech!

I rammed forward. Everything was silent, still. Then screaming. All around me; I couldn't make out the words. Glass shattered.

"Get out of the car!"

The shout was clear. I kicked at the trunk lid. I yelled into the duct tape. The shouts around me continued, clearer now but all melding into one indistinguishable sound. I positioned my shoulders on the back seat and brought my knees in, ready to donkey kick the trunk lid.

It popped open. A too-large man in a too-small suit, wearing a black ski mask. "Howie?" I asked but it came out, "Mowee?"

He lifted me by a fistful of my shirt. We were on an on-ramp to the interstate. Black Audis were parked haphazardly around mom's car.

Men weaved between them. Black suits, black face masks. Black rifles. They pointed at the ground at three of my family members.

"The boy's in the car," Howie said, nodding toward one. "What you want with them?"

I mumbled into the tape. He grinned then ripped it from my face. "Ah!" I wiped my mouth. "What do you mean, what do I want with them?"

"Mr. Long said it's up to you." He pointed at mom, Coitus, and Coitum face down with hands in zip ties behind their backs. "The choice is yours."

Mom's face lifted. A vein on her forehead pulsed. She thwacked her head down and shrieked with the full force of her lungs. A trail of red dribbled down her face like a single bloody tear.

"Leave them," I told Howie. "Put them in the car and tell them to go."

"You sure you don't want them..."

"Dead?" I turned away, toward the Audi with my little brother in it, and wiped my face. "I'm responsible for enough. Let them go."

8

"When's mama coming, Jimjim?" Pecu asked again. We'd been brought to a beautiful home — a mansion, really — given a room, and left to our own. I'd watched Pecu play video games all night.

"I don't know, buddy," I answered.

Pecu kept his eyes on the TV and let his next question drift away. The flat screen was an addition newly added. It sat directly in front of a huge wall painting, one of those abstract, in the eye of the beholder types of art. The painting fit the bedroom. The TV did not. Pecu had stared at it since we got to Mr. Long's. I'd stared at my lotus flower, and the new crack in its globe.

The door opened. Mr. Long strode in with a maid in tow. "Good evening, gentlemen."

"Hi!" Pecu squealed and lifted the controller close to his face, tapping buttons frantically.

I smiled. "Hey, Mr. Long."

"Please, call me Richard."

"Wait." I did the math. "Your name is Richard. Like —"

"Mr. Torquere, do not let the next words out of your mouth be a variation of Dick and Long."

"Right," I said somberly. "Call me Jimmy."

"Jimmy, would you mind sending Pecu with Tamara here so we may speak? She can take him to the kitchen to get some ice cream."

"I scream!" The controller hit the floor, and Pecu ran at the lady. She took him up in her arms.

Mr. Long sat on the bed next to me. "Mr. Long — Richard. Thank you for what you —"

He silenced me with a hand. "It was nothing compared to what you provided me. I still feel indebted."

The room went silent, so I asked, "How do you know my mother?"

He studied my face. "How well do you know your mother?"

"I've lived with her my whole life. She only cares about one thing." *Two, counting Pecu I guess.* "She'll do anything for her fix."

He nodded. "I met your mother twenty-five years ago when my baby sister got out of juvenile detention. She was a troublemaker back then, my sister, and thought because her father was powerful she was powerful. The short of it, she slapped her teacher, was charged with assault, and went to jail.

"While there, she met your mother. My sister convinced father to let Samantha come live with us since she didn't have anywhere else to go. My sister is the only person alive that can change my father's mind on a matter, and even she had trouble in this case, with your mother's... ethnicity. As soon as she got out, your mother —"

"What was my mom in jail for?"

His demeanor changed, frowning for my sake. "Murder." He stared. "She'd murdered her father when she was fifteen."

Mr. Long stared like the news should touch some sentimental part of me. I would have been sad for the grandfather I never met had I taken some time to think about it, but the information was shrapnel next to the things I've seen of my mother.

"But my sister convinced us all she was a good girl," he continued, "just had been through some hard circumstances. We believed her. I mean, what kind of nineteen year old girl is bad? I'm still not positive if truly bad people even exist."

"They do," I said.

"Well, your mother had a drug problem already, but we helped her through it as much as we could. We treated Samantha like family." His head sagged.

"It wasn't hard for your mother to figure out what the family business was. The way everyone treated father, the strange schedule we all kept, the occasional glimpse of men with firearms. We tried to keep business out of the house, but your mother is a smart woman. Too smart."

He sighed. "She met Song and found out what he did for the family. She —"

"What did he do?"

He met my eye and seemed to consider if he should tell me or not, or how much he should. "Song is a chemist. He used to manufacture certain chemicals." Certain chemicals. Gears tumbled into place. "Your mom wanted him to —"

"I know what she wanted."

"Right. Well. Your mother decided she was to have him."

He reached into the chest of his coat and pulled out Polaroid photos. He handed them to me. "It was an elaborate plan, one none of us would have thought her capable of." The pictures were of a much younger Mr. Long. "I'm in charge of one of the more controversial branches of the family business." In the first photo, he was standing outside of a massive shipping container like the ones at the docks I'd seen. "Your mother knew this." The second photo, he was opening the container door. "That knowledge gave her leverage." The third photo, he was inside the container surrounded by dirty-faced Asian people.

"Someone called the police that day. They arrived moments after I left, too close to be a coincidence. I went to jail because I owned the shipping yard and the boat. The police couldn't prove that I had any knowledge that this was going on so they were forced to release me. They had no case. Anyone could have been responsible for those... those slaves.

"No sooner was I home, than I received a letter. Within was a copy of those three photos and a list of demands. It wasn't signed, but I knew by the demands who wrote the letter."

It was more information than I'd gotten living with my mother for the last seventeen years. I thought about the one lesson mom was so keen on implanting into her children: never call the police. She'd always been so insistent. Was it guilt over what she'd done to Mr. Long? Mom? Capable of guilt?

"That's why she was always so hard on him," I whispered. Mr. Long held a question in his eyes. "Song. She must have beaten him because he wouldn't make drugs for her."

"He wouldn't?" He laughed. "The agreement was that Song would go with her, and if he tried to escape I would kill his family. No one ever said he had to do what she told him to do." He shook his head, smiling. "Anyway, father forced me to do what she demanded. I was ready to go to trial against those damn photos."

The room fell quiet. For a long time, we sat like that.

"You see now though?" Mr. Long said eventually.

"See what?"

"The kind of enemy you have in your mother. She is smart. She is conniving. She will do anything to get what she wants."

I shrugged. He said nothing new.

"What is your plan, Jimmy?"

I shrugged. "Find a safe place to raise Pecu."

"Stay here."

"What?"

"Why not? Your mother won't be able to get to you. You won't need for anything. You can send your brother to the best private school. I owe you a debt. Let me pay it."

Stay here? Just stay here and imbed myself into this community? I couldn't. I had to raise Pecu in a normal environment. Two white people in the center of the Chinese Mafia were as abnormal as it gets. Plus, if we stayed here, mom would know right where to find us.

As would Stupro.

"Can I think about it?" I asked.

Mr. Long smiled. "Take as much time as you need."

I'm a hypocrite.

Every person in this world, at one time or another, does something that they said they would never do, no matter how intact their integrity is or how hard they try against it. It happens. A true hypocrite is something different. A true hypocrite is someone who decides to live by a definite set of principles, to make decisions according to those principles, then breaks them, obviously and utterly, not once, but over and over, each time with the understanding that what they do goes against what they believe. That's a true hypocrite.

And I am one.

The first two months of our new life, I was the most honorable man I'd ever known. Well, besides Song, but few people get the chance to give up a perfect life for one of slavery to save their family. I'd freed my brother from the Torqueres, and that alone made me feel like I'd killed Hitler single-handedly. I was the best person I could be. I'd proved it. But, as I said: complete hypocrite.

Pecu and I moved into Song's house. It was an empty-nest situation when it came to Ling, her youngest daughter recently leaving for her first year of college, and a coming-home-from-war situation when it came to Song, his war lasting next to twenty years.

All Ling wanted to do was pamper me and Pecu, the savior and the baby. All Song wanted to do was pamper his wife. They were gone every weekend, visiting their three girls, but when they were at the house they filled it with a giddiness that was uncomfortable. I counted days between their trips.

My days were filled with the mundane, which I should've been able to enjoy. Mr. Long, through Howie, had helped me obtain a new identity. I was now Jim Thompson, and Pecu was Paul Thompson. It was a specialty business of Mr. Long's, I learned. I took my GED test, aced every section, and after the test was the one time I'd seen Mr. Long since he'd asked me to stay.

"The doors are open to you," he'd told me.

"Which doors?"

"All of them, Jim." He said the words as matter of fact as he said any words, like if he said it it would become true because he said it. "Decide what it is that you want to do, and I will help you to do it."

That was largely why it was so difficult to enjoy my sudden picturesque life. I'd made my escape. Pecu was safe. Now I had to do *something* with it.

School was the obvious choice; I knew I had the brains for it. Dissuading myself was easy though. I'd ruined my chances of going to a real school, one of those fancy Ivy League places that you have to go to if you want to be something above average. Kids that get into those places work their entire lives at it. No matter how well you scored, you didn't get in with a GED.

Besides, what would I go for? If Mr. Long was going to pay for my college, I had to pick something and stick to it. Decide my entire life at seventeen years old? What sense does that make?

The next choice was work. I could get into some kind of job and work my way up. That, or try to think of a business I could start myself. Not too many people have a backing like the one I had in Mr. Long, and I knew a business loan was well within my list of askable favors. I just had to think of something feasible, something profitable. What could I do or produce that people would want to give me money for?

So I sat idle. We put Pecu in a fancy preschool — he, at least, was going to go to an Ivy League college — and I waited for him to get home each day. Ling tried to get me fat, something I enjoyed, and Song tried to get her pregnant, something I ignored. I had to do something with my life, now that I had one, but the choice I made had to be a good one.

"Are you ready for lunch?" One strand of hair hung loose from Ling's tight bun, the only evidence from the commotion she and her husband had caused. When it came to Ling, that single out-of-place hair equated to total dissemination.

"Didn't we just have brunch, Mrs. Chan?"

"I'm bored. You're eating."

"You didn't sound too bored."

Her eyes narrowed, only slightly. That look equated to outright disbelief. "I missed my husband."

We both laughed.

"What's so funny?" Song asked, pulling out a chair from the table at which I sat.

"Nothing —"

"Jim thinks our lovemaking too loud, honey."

My cheeks warmed.

"Better than Coitus and —" He stopped as he realized what was coming from his mouth.

"Much better than that." I finished for him.

He cleared his throat. "What's for lunch, my porcelain angel?"

"Grilled cheese."

"Grilled cheese! You've been in America too long, woman. Forgot your roots."

"I remember hot dogs and tater tots for lunch most days," I said.

Song glared. "Traitor."

We all giggled. Almost the exact same banter happened every day. I wondered if it felt as fake to Song and Ling as it did to me.

Three hard raps on the front door snapped the smile from my face.

Song said he'd get the door. He had a look on his face, one that must've been similar to my own. I held my breath until I heard a familiar voice. "Howie!" Ling smiled and patted his shoulder.

"How are you, Mrs. Chan?"

"Tired," she said. "My husband insists we spend every possible moment together, and sleeping doesn't count."

"I don't blame him. You're as beautiful as ever."

She beamed. "Will you eat with us?"

He sat across the table from me. "How are you doing, Mr. Thompson?"

"Fine. And you?"

He nodded. The butter sizzling in the pan was the only sound, and it filled the room with the awkwardness I'd found in every room since I'd escaped the Torqueres. As soon as pleasantries were over, everyone remembered what we'd been through, and it settled thick between us.

"I actually came to see you, Mr. Thompson. I —"

"Call me Jim."

"Jim. I thought I'd come and see if you had plans for the day."

I'd bet my life he knew I had no plans. "What'd you have in mind?"

"Maybe go to the shooting range. Maybe the gym after. Get some food."

"Sure," I answered. "I haven't been out of the house much. I want to be home when Pecu — Paul gets here though."

He nodded.

We ate our sandwiches, and I told Howie to meet me in his car while I got some workout clothes together. Song followed me to my room. "Be careful, Jimmy," he told me. "Howie, he's a..."

"A what? A bad man? A gangster? A —"

"A killer. Just don't forget who he is, what he is, and who he works for. Be careful. That's all."

"Thanks, Song." I hugged him how I thought someone would hug their father, then ran out to Howie's car, an all-black Audi. I stopped and stared at it. "Fancy," I told Howie.

"I know, huh? It's Mr. Long's ."

He threw it in drive, and my back pressed firm against the seat.

I shivered at the purr as he floored it. His car or not, I was intrigued that he got to drive around such an expensive car at such a young age. Howie might've been thirty, but I would've placed him closer to twenty-five. Too young to be driving a hundred thousand dollar car.

"So what's your story, bro?"

He wore a blue button-up T-shirt and a pair of jeans, like he tried to look normal. My previous description of sumo-wrestler big still fit, but I noticed now that he was almost all muscle, not fat. Three-hundred pounds is a hard weight to get to, but Howie made it look cut.

What does he want though? He'd shown up in a fancy car, wearing disarming clothes, for what? to hang out with me? I'd lived around Spinny Torquere my whole life. I knew the scent of an ulterior motive.

"You know most my story," I said. "What's your's?"

"All I know of you is that you demanded a meeting with Mr. Long, and he actually gave it to you. Then he tortured you with his own hands. He saved you from some tweaker lady. Then he treats you, a *gweilo*, like some long-lost family member. I'd say you know more about me, bro."

He laughed. It was infectious, and I laughed too. "Does make me sound mysterious, put that way."

"So, what's up? Who are you?"

"No one." He glanced ove rand tilted his head. "All right. I'm someone that was trying to save his family, messed it up, and ended up saving someone else's. Mr. Long's apparently. He decided to reciprocate."

He nodded. "Sounds about right."

"So who are you?" How do you know Mr. Long?"

"My dad worked for the — his family his entire life. Came to America through them. My dad was murdered when I was seven. Mr. Long helped my mom financially, then helped me decide what I wanted to do with my life."

"Sounds like a hobby of Mr. Long's."

"You could say that. Got to say, though, you're the first *gweilo* in his collection."

The way he said that word, *gweilo*, I wasn't sure if it was an insult. "Lucky me. So what did you guys decide."

"On my life? The military. I was a navy seal."

"Hence why we're headed for the shooting range?"

"What, you don't like to shoot?"

"Never done it."

He smiled at me. "If you don't like this, there's something wrong with you."

"There's something wrong with me regardless."

We both laughed. It was comfortable.

No one was at the outdoor shooting range. Mr. Long probably owned it, and I'd bet it was reserved for his employees. Howie used a key to unlock a hard, silver case in the trunk of the Audi, and he started to assemble different parts of a rifle.

"You ever seen one of these?"

"No," I whispered, watching him move efficiently.

"Barrette fifty cal with a ten-round magazine," he said. "My baby. Come on, I'll let you shoot her."

The rifle had a bipod on the end of it, and Howie set it up so it stood on its own, pointing down range toward some human-shaped dummies. "First things first. Hold your hands up like this and put my head in the hole." Palms facing me, he cupped both hands in front of his face and made a little hole to look through. "Good. Now, with both eyes open, can you see my face?" He stared through the hole in my hands. I nodded. "All right, close your left eye. Can you still see my face?"

His face disappeared behind my hands. "No."

"Open both eyes. Still see me? Kay, close your right eye. See me?"

His face was still in the hole. "I see you."

"You left-handed?"

"No."

"Weird. You can put your hands down. So you're left-eye dominant, but right-handed."

"Which means?"

"Which means you're going to learn to shoot with your left." He helped me get into position to the right of the rifle and told me to put my earmuffs on when I was ready. "Think about your breathing. Pull the trigger, don't squeeze, on the end of a breath."

The dummy wobbled and swayed, but looked like it was a foot in front of my face. I inhaled. Exhaled. Inhaled. Exhaled... And pulled. The butt pounded into my shoulder.

"Did I hit it?" I yelled.

His hand did something to the scope. "Try again."

Inhaled. Exhaled...

KAPHUNK!

The power made me shiver. A chunk of the dummy flew straight up and floated down. "Dude!"

He laughed. "I told you. Try to hit the further target."

I got lost in it. It felt funny, doing anything left-handed, but I was almost comfortable by the time Howie quit giving me pointers and let me shoot. Eventually he realized I'd continue until he made me stop. "All right, bro. We better hurry if you want to make it home for your brother."

My heart was still thumping as Howie drove us away from the shooting range. "That was awesome," I said.

"One of my favorite things, bro." The way he said bro sounded like bra.

A silence settled, one of a different kind. Not the awkward who's-this-white-guy kind I'd been feeling. It was like I was a normal person to Howie. A person in the same circle as him. I wasn't a savior that he had to respect and be nice to. I wasn't a kid that he owed a debt to.

"So who do you want to be?" Howie asked.

I shrugged. "Who do you want to be?"

"Honestly?"

"No, lie to me."

He smiled. "I want to open a little store. Sell something. Food, maybe, or furniture. I don't care. I just want to own a business. Something legit. Something to be proud of. I just want to be..."

"Normal?"

"Exactly." He popped his neck, staring at the road. "Normal."

95

"Why don't you?"

"I'm trying to. I've been saving money. Mr. Long knows of my plans though, and I feel like he pays me just enough to keep my business dreams out of reach."

"He doesn't want you to have your own business?"

"Mr. Long is very altruistic, don't get me wrong, but he has a hard time giving up an investment."

"And someone with your training is pretty valuable."

He shrugged. "So, who do you want to be?"

"Same as you, I guess."

"A businessman?"

"Normal," I said. "That way my brother can be extraordinary."

"I can respect that. Maybe not agree with it. But I can respect it."

"What's not to agree about?"

"You can't live your life for another person, even if it's a kid. You have to have something for yourself."

"I'm happy just to give my brother a real chance. I don't need more than that."

He turned into a parking lot, and the car stopped. "You know how to fight?"

Fighting with Stupro in a basement, dismembered bodies scattered. "Honestly?"

"No, lie to me."

"Then, yes. I'm a karate expert."

Ten minutes later I was in basketball shorts and a T-shirt on a squishy blue mat, facing a sumo wrestler in a skintight leotard. "Is it too late to change my mind about this?" I asked.

"Yes."

I sighed. "What's up with the onesie? I thought sumo wrestlers wore thongs."

"You think now's the time to tease me, bro?"

"Seems smarter than fighting you."

"We're not fighting. We're sparring."

"I think we better wait until I have my own onesie."

He laughed. "Come on. Try to take me down."

I knew I had a better chance of removing a tree stump from the earth barehanded, but it's better to just get these types of things over with. I let my posture bend into what I thought a fighter's pose would be. Right hand forward and open, I slapped at his hand, searching for something, unsure what. My fingers struck out, wrapped around his wrist. I yanked down on the arm and spun my body around him, trying to get to his back.

I thudded onto the mat and three hundred pounds dropped on me.

"That it?" Howie rocked back onto his heels then stood, nimble as a 300-pound Bruce Lee.

I coughed but stayed where I was. "Aren't there weight classes for sumos?"

"Get up. There are no weight classes in life. You might be pretty big for a youngster, but eventually you'll come across someone bigger than you."

Wasn't that the truth. I climbed to my feet.

"When you're fighting someone larger than you, you can't try to overpower them. You have to use your own strengths. Looking at me, what would you say your strengths are over mine?"

"I'm faster?"

"Maybe."

"More flexible?"

"Probably."

"Better looking?"

"Not on your best day, bro. You have to use what you got against me, at least what you think you got. Try speed. Throw some strikes."

"You want me to hit you?"

He nodded.

"Are you going to hit me back?"

"I won't hit you. Take a swing."

I closed my eyes, my head sagged, and I snorted a deep breath. Eyes closed, head down, I struck my fist out as fast as I could toward his center. He palmed it like a golf ball. "Come on, bro."

Bouncing on my feet, throwing one-twos, I tried to break through Howie's guard. He was not only bigger than me, stronger than me, and nimbler than me, but he was faster than me too. After an hour of bouncing off Howie, I was covered in sweat and gasping air through my mouth. His head had but one bead of sweat on it.

"When —" I heaved. "Can we — stop this?"

"Done already? Come on. I'll take you home."

The drive home, my lungs burned, my body sweated, and my back was bruised, but I felt good. My body from using it, but felt good in my head too.

"All right, bro." He stopped in front of Song's house.

I opened the door. "Thanks, Howie. I had fun."

"No problem." I went to close the door. "Hey! Hey, tomorrow I lift weights. We could stop by the range first. I'll help you learn to shoot a pistol left-handed. You in?"

I didn't have to think long. "Sure."

I walked toward the house, smiling. As I got close, I heard crying. *Pecu!* I ran, crashed through the front door, found Pecu on the couch, red-faced and tear-streaked, with Ling trying to console him. I rushed to his side.

"What's the matter, buddy?"

"Mama!" He blew a snot bubble. "Where's mama?"

I'm a coward. A coward and a hypocrite.

"She's coming, Pecu," I said. "Don't cry."

9

"What's up with the van?" I asked as I hopped in. Howie had parked it across the street from Song's. It had two seats in front but was all open space in the back except for a duffel bag. No windows but the two up front.

"Happy birthday, bro," Howie said. "Do you do anything special for your birthday?"

Birthdays had never been much in the Torquere house. Mom was usually too far gone to know what month it was, forget the day. She remembered once though. She'd even got me a gift. It was my fourteenth birthday, and I got a rainbow assorted bag of pills.

"It's ecstasy, Jimmy!" she'd told me. "For years I've kept one of every sort I came across. White devils to black angels, I got all sorts. I say we snort the dust at the bottom of the bag."

"No," I told Howie. "So what's with the van? We going to work out or what?"

"I need it for work today."

"Got something to move?"

His eyes touched mine. "Yes."

I stared out the window as we drove. Howie and I had been hanging out every day while Pecu was at school. We'd work out, go to the shooting range, or eat food. It wasn't much of a life, but I was starting to enjoy it.

Howie drove us in a direction that was not familiar then suddenly we were in Chinatown. My stomach dropped. *Howie had work to do.* My fingers fidgeted with the door handle.

He parked the van next to a large brick and seemingly inconspicuous building. "Jim, Mr. Long asked me —"

"Do you only hang out with me because he makes you?"

His eyebrows scrunched together. "He doesn't make me hang out with you. He suggested that you might be bored and could use a friend."

"But if he wouldn't have suggested..."

"Would I have hung out with you that first day?" he finished for me. "Probably not. But that's not why I still hang out with you. You're my friend, Jim. I don't have many."

"And if I don't do whatever it is you're about to ask me?"

"Damn, *gweilo*, you're paranoid. Yes. *We are friends.* I don't give a shit what your relationship is with Mr. Long."

I stared at him.

He shook his head. "There're some bad people doing some bad things to women in that building. Mr. Long wants us to save them. We'll have to break in. It's illegal. But it's a good thing."

"Us?"

"Listen, bro, I'll keep it real. I can do this myself. For whatever reason, Mr. Long asked me to ask you if you wanted to come. Notice the phrasing. He told me to ask you."

"Aren't there people who do this sort of thing for him already?"

"Plenty."

Kidnapped my little brother to get him away from criminals. Committed crimes so that I could get to a point where I could stop. Promised myself I would be normal the first chance I got. I chose a principle to live by: law-abiding. I chose the type of person to be: normal. Those thoughts were crystal clear in my mind.

"What do I have to do?" I asked.

That's a true hypocrite.

He frowned. "Mr. Long sold some... wares to a —"

"Call them what they are."

"Mr. Long sold some *slaves* to a man, and the man is breaking the contract."

"There's a contract when buying a slave?"

"Buy a slave from Mr. Long there is. They have to be treated a certain way. If they're not, he sends people like me to repossess them."

"So we go into this building and make sure the slaves are being treated fairly?"

"This time —" He held up a finger, "we go in assuming they're not because we have word that there is some dirty shit going on. But normally yes, we go in nicely."

"If we're not going in nicely, how are we going in?"

His hand disappeared beneath him and brought out the silver 9mm Ruger I'd been shooting every other day for months. "Hopefully, we don't have to shoot, but we have to get those girls out." He held out the butt toward me but yanked it away as I reached for it. "It has bullets in it."

I swallowed, nodded, then took the gun.

"There will be men in there." He dug in his pocket. "Take these zip ties. Get the man on the door. Try not to kill him. I'll incapacitate any others. The last man, Pretty Chang, we have to speak to." He grabbed his door handle, adjusting his own pistol in his waistband. He met my eye. "You ready?"

My hands were sweaty. My body shivered. My throat was too tight to make words.

He patted my shoulder. "You're ready." I followed him onto the sidewalk in a daze. "Put the gun away!" he demanded in a whisper, and I shoved it into my pants. "Jesus Christ." He rushed down a narrow stairwell. There was enough room at the bottom for us both to squeeze in front of the door.

He put his lips next to my ear. "The door swings to the left," he whispered. "A body should be to the right. He's yours. Get the ties on him before you do anything else."

"Are you sure I can do this?"

He shrugged. "You ready?"

No.

He kicked the door at the knob and it flung open. Howie pushed in, and a man sprawled onto the floor. Howie's steps were sure and solid, gun up as he followed where it pointed. As he stepped past the man on the floor, he kicked out. The man's gun clattered across the floor.

The inside of the building was brighter than outside. The man at my feet tried to get up. I fumbled in my pants pocket, grasped the zip ties, and dropped them on the ground. Two gunshots cracked.

I jumped on top of the man, fighting him while I tried to find a zip tie. He jerked against me, but felt weak. I got one wrist back, then two, but I couldn't get a tie around them. He jerked too much beneath me.

What do I do?

Howie's foot crushed the man's face, and his body went limp. I froze for a moment, staring at the limp man's crooked jaw. "Bro." Howie was shaking his head. "Get the ties on him. Let's go."

I bound the guy's wrists behind his back then stood. The room's ceiling was lined with luminescent lights, and they hung over long, broad tables. Four rows of them, each fifty feet long. Howie was on the far side of the room, screaming in Cantonese. Between us, countless naked women lowered themselves onto their stomachs.

Their nudity was not attractive. Their heads were shaved bald. On their backs, rib bones and vertebrates were countable. The meat of their butts had vanished, legs running seamlessly into their backs. Faces, the ones I could see, were so sunken that their eyes bulged like a toad's.

On the tables were paraphernalia I would've had trouble making sense of on their own. Glass jars, little camping stoves, newspaper clippings, electronic scales, boxes of baking soda. Wasn't hard to figure out though. Giant piles of cocaine filled the tables.

"Aye!"

Howie stood beside a door, glaring. I rushed over, hopping over starving bodies. There was a zip tied man at his feet, a bullet wound in each shoulder, moaning and rolling in pain. "I'll go in first," Howie said. "Go in fast and to the right. Ready?"

No.

Howie crashed through the door, and I sprinted to the right, pointing my gun in every direction, trying to find what I was supposed to point at.

I found him. A striking figure of a man sat behind a desk carved to appear as though four lions held it up with their paws. His hair was perfectly messy, somehow pulled back, scattered, and in place at the same time. His eyes were barely slanted —*probably half white*, I guessed — and they were sky blue.

He puffed a cigar like all was as it'd always been. A pile of cocaine was scattered in front of him with spirals drawn through it like he slid his nose through any time he wanted more. His suit was perfectly tailored. It was covered in powder.

"You broke your contract with Mr. Long," Howie said.

The man puffed his cigar, bellow hiding his features. "Did I?" His head dropped into the pile and snorted. He came up with coke on his forehead.

"Do you remember the terms?"

The man tossed his cigar to the ground, opened a hinged box in front of him, and chose a new one. Using a pair of little scissors, he cut through the end. "I remember." A silver Zippo lit the cigar.

"You violated those terms."

The professional way Howie spoke contrasted with the room, the man, and the situation. All I could do was watch Pretty Chang. He dropped his head, still blowing smoke, and snorted more.

"What does this violation mean to me?" He sounded hardly interested.

"You leave town. Never return."

"And if I don't."

Howie shrugged. "You don't leave this room." His gun came up.

"All right, all right, all right, I'll go. Let me pack some —"

"No. A car waits outside. It will bring you to a place to heal."

"A place to —"

Howie rushed the man before he could finish. "Hold his head back, bro." I reacted, ran over to the man's back and held his head by his hair. Howie took both the man's hands in one fist and the scissors from the table with the other. "Hold him tight."

I flexed. One-handed, Howie pressed the scissors into the creases of the man's nose. Then a scream tore through the room.

Howie wiggled hard. "Hold him, bro!" He sawed with the scissors. They were dull, like he cut through a sixteen-ounce steak with kindergarten scissors. Blood poured out of the man's face, over Howie's hand.

The man shook, writhed, but the scissors kept sawing. Then they clicked, a sound that almost poured my birthday breakfast over the man's head, and a chunk of flesh splatted on the floor. From upper lip to boney bridge of his nose, there was a gushing hole. I tried not to stare at it, but couldn't look away.

Howie gripped Pretty Chang's collar and ripped at it, pulling and pulling until a strip came off. He pushed the piece of shirt into the man's new nose. "Show Mr. Chang to the car out front and grab the duffel bag out of the back of the van."

I gathered my strength, trying to show the noseless man a front of indifference. By his torn shirt, I dragged him through the cocaine room. Every woman had their noses to the ground. I rushed out the door and up the stairs. A black car with all black windows waited by the curb, and I tossed him in, nodding to the single Chinese man driving. It sped away.

My birthday breakfast made a puddle on the sidewalk.

"What am I doing, what am I doing, what am I doing?" I chanted as I opened the back of the van and pulled out the duffel bag.

Howie was speaking Cantonese in a soothing tone when I got back, and all the naked women were in a line on one wall. Standing, they were even more grotesque. I could see one woman's spine through her stomach. None tried to cover themselves.

"Give me the bag, bro. I'll pass out the robes. Put on this face mask and these gloves and start scooping the cocaine into trash bags. I'm sure Mr. Long will want it."

There was a lot of it, three trash bags full. Howie came back in from loading the girls. He grabbed two bags, I the other, and we fled that horrible place. The back of the van was filled with twelve women. They were eerily quiet.

"We're going to switch cars now, all right, bro?" I nodded. Howie tossed his keys and caught the ones from the man who had exited a familiar Audi. As we drove away from those women, I came back to myself.

Howie decided to start talking. "You did good, bro. Froze up a little there, but —"

"What was that!"

"A job."

"A job that Mr. Long gave you?"

"Is that hard to believe?"

"He ordered you to cut that dude's nose off?" I demanded.

His mirth vanished. "No." He refused to look into my eyes. "I went a little overboard."

"A little?"

"This kind of thing gets to me. Both of my parents came to America like those slaves did. The only difference was my father had skills. Useful skills. He had an opportunity to buy his and my mother's freedom.

All those women back there won't ever get that chance. Mr. Long tries to make sure they get treated right, but it's impossible to guarantee. If a person is property, eventually they get treated like property, no matter what terms are agreed upon."

Howie stared at the road, and the purr of the engine intensified.

"I know," he continued eventually, "that I didn't have to do what I did, but I don't feel bad about it. He was going to leave town without a blemish. After what he did to those women? So, I took something I knew he found important. Can't be Pretty Chang with a nose like that. And all that coke he was doing? Probably didn't even feel it."

I snickered. Knew it was wrong, but it was hard to stop. Howie's smile came back. "Howie —" I coughed, composing myself. I tried to file my thoughts into an order that I could push through my lips. "Howie, I can't stay here."

"What?" He squinted at me. "Stay where? in San Fran?"

"I told myself I'd be normal." Why I said it I didn't know, but I wanted it said. "I have to be normal for my brother."

"Then be normal. Just do it here."

"I can't. Look how easily I agreed to do what we just did."

"Bro, leaving won't fix you. Only you can fix you. There will always be opportunities to break your morals. Trust me. If you can't do it in one place, you won't be able to do it in another."

That was one of the truest things anyone ever said to me, but I was too young or naive or stupid to take it for the diamond that it was.

I'd ask for a business loan from Mr. Long then skip town, I decided. Tell him I want to open a restaurant or something. With that and all that cash I still had from Merdle's McDonalds, Pecu and I would live comfortably for years.

"I say we work off some steam," Howie said. "What do you say?"

I shrugged.

10

"Surprise!"

Pecu jumped into my arms as I was corralled into the living room by Howie. Streamers hung from the ceiling, all different colors. A *Happy Birthday!* sign draped over the walkway to the kitchen. A big, wrapped present took up the coffee table.

Song's face was priceless. His wife stared at him, smiling at his smile. Mr. Long Stood behind the couch. He was far overdressed in his suit. Then Song's daughters: Vanessa, Chelsea, and the youngest.

Jessy.

Her black hair was in two circular little buns on top of her head, and a thick bang curved to the corner of her mouth. Two dimples above each corner of her lips were the only features in her smooth cheeks. *Smooth like porcelain,* Song always told his wife. She seemed so fragile. Her hands, tapping away at a cell phone, were dainty things, each finger so distinct and small.

She looked up from her phone.

She smiled.

"Let me in, Jim." Howie pushed me out of the doorway. "The hell's the matter with — oh."

The bastard knew instantly. I tried to regain my footing. "This is too much, Song." I made it a point not to gawk at Jessy again.

"This is hardly extravagant, Jim," Mr. Long said. "I suggested a trip was in order. Europe, maybe. Puerto Rico. Song insisted that you would've refused."

"He knows me well. Thank you for the thought though, Mr. Long."

"You haven't got to meet my girls yet, have you?" Song asked.

"I've seen them." I stared at Jessy.

Her cheeks went red, and the room went quiet. I, grudgingly, tore my eyes from her. Everyone was looking to me, to her, and back.

"Uh-oh," Mr. Long said. "Lock up your daughters. Mr. Thompson's got the eye."

We all laughed. You did that when Mr. Long made a joke. I stepped to Vanessa; Song's oldest. "Vanessa, the dentist. Pleasure."

I took her hand in mine. "Thank you for saving my dad." She pulled me in close and kissed my cheek.

"And Chelsea the box lover." I smiled and we shook.

I went to shaking distance from Jessy. I almost choked on whatever witty thing I'd been about to say. "Pleasure," was all I could manage.

Her tiny hand was surprisingly strong. She yanked down on my wrist and touched my cheek with hers. I thought she was kissing my cheek, but then I felt her breath on my ear. I stiffened, body and all.

"You're fricken smelly," she whispered.

I snorted a laugh, and the effect was gone. "Just finished getting tossed around by that oaf."

She smiled with her eyes.

"All right, open your present." Song hopped from one foot to the other, then ran around the couch and sat in front of the present. "Open it!"

I smiled and sat next to him. The thing was huge, but when I lifted it it was light. "I think I'll wait until tomorrow, Song."

"You'll open that present right now."

I laughed and ripped the paper. It was my first time opening a present. The box was mostly empty space. Empty but for a book. It was homemade, the binding made from loops of yarn through holes in the paper. I flipped it open. Chicken scratches in neat rows covered every page.

"What is it?"

"A cookbook." Song slapped my shoulder. "All my recipes from when you were growing up."

"In Cantonese?"

"Just like old times."

I laughed. "Song, you're nuts. Thank you."

He rubbed my hair. "All right. Who wants cake and ice cream?"

"I scream!" Pecu squealed.

Everyone rushed for the kitchen except for me and Jessy. And Mr. Long. I smiled at Jessy, praying Mr. Long would follow the others. "Jessy, dear, would you give us a moment?" asked Mr. Long. She left without a word, and Mr. Long took a seat next to me. "How are you, Jim?"

"Doing good." I watched Jessy over the island to the kitchen as she grabbed a plate of cake. Her double dimples were so unique. They might have been ugly on another girl, but on her they were perfect. *She's perfect,* I thought. A porcelain angel in truth.

Mr. Long cleared his throat.

"I'm sorry, Mr. Long. What was that?"

He locked eyes with me, expressionless, but I knew this was the last time he'd repeat himself. "I said that Howie texted me earlier, praising how you handled things. I thank you."

"I — uh." I didn't want to think about earlier. I wanted to think about the girl in the next room.

I shook myself out of it. This was the perfect time to approach the idea of my business loan. "Thank you for giving me an opportunity." I hoped those words sounded sincere to him. To me, they sounded as phony as anything I'd ever said.

"You did well." He pulled an envelope from his jacket. "Exceptionally well, I'm told."

"What's this?"

"Payment, of course."

Of course. Payment for the crimes I'd committed. Payment for my principles. But who cares about those? You can't use them for anything. Not like cold, green cash. I grabbed the envelope and was shocked at its thickness. Thank him, then form the words to get a business loan. You know he'll do it.

Just say the words.

Everyone in the other room laughed at the same time. Jessy had frosting on her nose. Pecu was in her arms, and he was trying to get to her nose with his mouth. The giggles spewing from him as he chased her head around I had missed.

And the smile on Jessy's face. Beautiful. Beyond Beautiful.

She blushed.

"Thank you, Mr. Long." *Screw principles.* "I was happy to help."

"Perhaps I shall pay you through Howie next time?"

I nodded.

We ate ice cream and cake for a time. Eventually Mr. Long left. Then Howie. Ling put Pecu to bed. Song put Ling to bed. Vanessa and Chelsea settled onto the couch to watch a movie. Jessy had disappeared some time ago. I went to my room.

She sat on the foot of my bed. The top drawer of my dresser was open. My lotus flower was in Jessy's hand.

"What are you doing?" I asked a little forcefully.

"This used to be my room," she said, ignoring my tone. "I used to keep my jewelry box in the top drawer."

I went into the closet, got the jewelry box from a shelf, and brought it to her, staring at my flower in her hand. For some reason, I wanted to rip it away from her. "I moved it," I whispered as I handed it to her.

"It's so beautiful." She spun the lotus. "I didn't know you could get one preserved like this. How long have you had it?"

I shrugged. "As long as I can remember." I sat next to her and stared at the flower. I'd stared at the flower for so many hours that I knew every curve of every line. Barely noticeable but like a crash of lightning to my eye, one of the perfect petals was starting to wrinkle.

"In my culture," Jessy said, cradling the globe in delicate fingers, "the lotus means purity and perseverance. It grows in the filthiest of waters, but it is not stained by them. It rises above the filth, untouched and perfect. To me, it means no matter where you come from, no matter what you have been through, you can choose to stay clean, to be something beautiful. I've always loved the lotus."

I stared at her. She stared at the flower. Her words were a balm of sorts. It was like she'd expressed an emotion I'd had my entire life with nothing but words. I could find nothing to say.

"You want to go outside?" she asked.

"For what?" My mind was still on her words, and I had to force myself from them.

"To talk?"

The backyard was tiny, but green plants were everywhere. Ling's water fountain tinkled. We sat beneath the canopy. I stared at her like a fool.

"So... eighteen, huh?" she asked.

"Yup."

"Cool."

Say something, stupid. "How old are you?"

"Don't you know you're not supposed to ask a lady that?"

"Sorry. I —"

"I'm not a lady, good thing." She laughed. It was pretty and elegant. "I'm nineteen. Way older than you."

"I can tell."

"Gah!" She glared. "Thanks!"

"No — I mean — It's just. You don't have the beauty of a teenager. You have the beauty of a woman."

She blushed.

I swallowed. "So you're in college. What for? Where at?"

"For engineering at Stafford, but please don't make me talk about it."

"Why?"

"It's so fricken boring. I hate it."

"Then why do you do it?"

"Uncle Richard — Mr. Long needs me to."

"And what he needs happens."

"Yes."

"Well, what do you want to do?"

"I'd be a veterinarian."

"Animals are cool."

"They can just be. Don't have to worry about this and that."

"Be a veterinarian then. Mr. Long could make it happen, couldn't he?"

"He needs an engineer, not a vet. The dentist in the family handles most of the medical problems as they arise. Trust me, I've tried."

"Too bad Mr. Long isn't an animal." She looked at me funny. "Then he wouldn't worry. Wouldn't need an engineer."

"You're a nerd." She laughed. I already loved that too. "What are you going to do?"

I signed up to be the token white guy in a Chinese crime ring. "Whatever Mr. Long wants me to, I guess."

Her cheeks puffed up and she blew air out of her mouth. "He's a good man, you know. He's demanding, but he does care."

"Good to know."

"What happened to my dad?"

The question came hard and fast. "What part?"

"The my-entire-life part."

"What did they tell you?"

"I don't want to hear what they told me."

Her voice had changed from the playful banter I'd heard so far. I gazed into her eyes and found something there. Something about myself. I wasn't going to lie to her, not like I had in my last relationship.

"What do you want to know?" I asked.

"Where was he all these years?"

"With my family."

"Why?"

"He was captive."

"Your captive?"

"My mother's."

"And you stole him away from her?"

I nodded.

"Why?"

"Seemed like the right thing to do."

"Are you running from her?"

"I should be."

"Why don't you?"

I paused. "I met a girl."

Her eyes widened as she studied my face. A moment passed. Then her mouth split into a grin. "Oh, you're good."

"What?"

"You had me for a second." She made a silly face. "I met a girl," she mocked. "I was almost ready to fall into your arms and ride off into the sunset."

"What are you talking about?"

"Oh, give it up. It was one of the better shows though. I think I'll give you another chance."

"Another chance at what?"

"At swooning me into love. Or your bed. Whichever, try harder next time." She got up and went inside, mumbling, "I met a girl," in my voice.

I stared at the night sky and smiled. I don't know how long I sat there.

I was more interested in her than I'd ever been in anything, ever. She'd grown up sheltered, living with Mr. Long directing her actions, and she knew next to nothing about real life. If it was in a book though, she'd read it. Ask her how to fill a car with gas and she'd gawk at you like you'd sprouted another head. Ask her about a covalent bond and she'd talk until you had to make her stop.

She was nineteen and still a virgin, two things together that I didn't think were possible in America. The long beginning of a long courtship, I didn't kiss her, hug her, hold her hand, nothing. It was a kind of game she played: torture the boy with her teasing and see how long it took for him to give up.

And she did tease. Wearing skin-tight clothes, no bra sometimes. Talking in that voice, the one that is more purr than words. She was only like that when we were alone though. In public, classy as Michelle Obama. Straight-backed, conservatively clothed. What every mom wanted for their son. Well, normal moms.

I was determined to live through the teasing though. It would take more than months of wet dreams for me to give up the chance with a girl like Jessy. I'd never get another, for that I was certain.

I never knew what she was going to say either. At that point, I'd been around Howie enough to know about every thought that went through his head by the direction his eyes pointed. Not with Jessy. She was always new. I loved it. She was as easy to figure as a Rubik's cube with twelve sides.

The celibate thing did drive me a little crazy. She knew I wasn't a virgin, but said she didn't mind. "I'm the only person I know who doesn't spread her legs for anything swinging," she'd said on the subject. Somehow, she made something so vulgar sound PG. I'd asked her if she ever had urges. "Jim, you should see my panties after we hang out most nights."

What I would've given.

The knowledge that she thought of me like that made it easy to stay persistent. With Amanda, we'd started with sex. I'd liked her, but I hadn't respected her. What I was trying to accomplish with Jessy was different. What it was, I could only guess. But it was more than sex.

Comparing Amanda and Jessy I tried to avoid, but did in every way. Amanda won zero of the comparisons, but that wasn't to say she'd been a bad girlfriend. Jessy was just perfect. Any woman I would've compared her to would've lost.

Whenever I thought about my first girlfriend, the inevitable would happen. I'd start thinking about what had happened to her. Then I'd start thinking about why it had happened to her.

"This mood again?" Jessy asked from our hilltop out of town, the one perfect for seeing the stars. We were sitting on the hood of my car, feet on the ground.

"What mood?"

"The one where you can't decide if you want to keep trying or push me away."

She read me like a book. "What makes you —"

"Don't lie to me." She stuck a finger in my face.

"I don't."

"I know you don't. I love that about you. What happened that makes you go into these moods?"

I forced my eyes to the ground. It was blurry. "I don't want to —"

She grabbed my hand, our first touch. "I wouldn't make you."

Her hand atop mine, I spread my fingers, and she curled hers into the spaces. "I had a girlfriend. Her name was Amanda."

"Did she dump you?"

She moved closer. "I wish that was it. She was murdered."

"Oh, Jim." Her hand squeezed. "You don't have to tell me —"

The words came spewing out of my mouth. How I met Amanda. How I knew I should stay away from her, but didn't. How Stupro found out about her. What he did to her. It was the first time I ever spoke of it.

Jessy let me cry. I was apparently still dealing with the emotions. Maybe you never stop dealing with emotions like those. She pulled my hand until I was in front of her, pressing her against the car. She hugged me. "You realize how ridiculous you sound, right?"

"It's the truth."

"Your uncle killed her, Jim. Not you."

"But if I would've stayed away..."

Her fingers tickled at my neck hairs. Eventually, she whispered, "You think that you put me in danger by being with me, don't you?"

"How could I think any different?"

She stared into my eyes. I was all too aware of her body pressed against mine. "For one, your uncle isn't here anymore. Two, I can defend myself. I was raised differently than most women. And three, my uncle is bigger than your uncle."

My uncle would feed your uncle to my father. "That last couldn't be more untrue."

"He might be a little man, but I promise you he's capable of big things. If anyone were to hurt me... "

It was hard to keep hold of my depression, having the girl of my dreams pressed so tight against me. She had to bend her neck back to see into my eyes, and her silk hair flowed around her neck and shoulders, down her back.

"I'll be very careful then," I said, "not to make you cry."

She kissed me then. She tasted sweet, like berry lip gloss. My hands pressed into her back, squishing her into me, pressing a moan from her lips. I let my hands feel her back, and down. They got to her butt, and I squeezed gently.

She pushed my chest hard and slapped my hand. "The hell are you thinking?"

"I — uh — I —"

"You're thinking you can swoon me with sympathy, that's what you're thinking!"

"I didn't —" I swallowed. "I thought you'd like it."

She stepped up and got into my face, expression fierce. It took everything in me to keep my feet planted. Her arm reached around and she grasped a handful of my ass. She whispered, "I loved it. Now, take me home."

She was my nights; my days belonged to Howie. We did a lot of jobs like that first. Most of them violated my principles. At least now I had a reward for my sins. Sure, I'd kidnapped my little brother from criminals then jumped right into a real deal organization. But hey, look at the girl that kissed me. Was it a good enough excuse? No. Did I let it be?

Yes.

It might have been that Mr. Long believed me to have a good heart, but he seemed to only ask for my assistance if people needed help. Sometimes, Howie and I did breaking and enterings, but only if slaves needed repossessed. Other times, we'd be sent into some unsavory places to pull out members of the family. The family being the one Howie and Mr. Long were a part of, the one I could never truly enter, being white.

Mr. Long despised addiction of any kind, so a big portion of my job was to track down his men in gambling dens, crack houses, brothels, or the like and pull them out, give them a thorough beating, and send them back to Mr. Long. The irony? Mr. Long or his father owned about two-thirds of the establishments in which we found their men. It seemed to always be the same men we were tracking down, and I got to know a few of them. They all called me *gweilo*.

This job was different though. I knew from the moment Howie picked me up. For one, it was nighttime and we usually worked during the day. Two, his playfulness was gone. Here was a man that I'd watched carelessly charge into a room he knew killers were guarding, and now he was as straight-lipped as George Bush after 9/11.

"Mr. Long wants you along for this one, bro," he said. We sat in the Audi, positioned between two streetlights. The neighborhood was filled with typical, middle-class houses. Two stories, yards, fences. "But it's not like the other jobs we usually do together."

"What kind of job is it?"

"We have to go into that house and question a man."

"Question him how? politely?"

"We'll ask politely." His eyes met mine. "First."

I nodded. I knew what he meant. I'd been questioned once before. My questioning had just been resolved early. "What happens if I say no to this?"

"I don't know, bro. No one ever says no, but I've never met someone in your position."

"What, exactly, is my position?"

"You know. In the family but not. You're different. You're..."

"White?"

"Not only that. When I'm given a job, he tells me, 'Go here. Do this. This way.' When you're a part of the job, he says, 'Ask Jimmy if he'd like to join you.' I think you can say no, bro. I just don't know if he'd ask again."

By this time, I had spent many nights in my bed staring at the ceiling, imagining what my life could be. What I wanted it to be. I saw little half-Chinese, half-white kids running around with my eyes and Jessy's hair. I saw Howie flipping burgers on a barbeque in the backyard. I saw Pecu graduating high school and going to a fancy college. Uncle Richard and grandpa Song buying too many gifts at Christmas. Ling cooking too much food whenever we visited.

But I always returned to the same questions. Would the normality of that perfect life be worth the criminality of my work? How far would I go for normality? And what about Pecu? Would I be dooming him to be a criminal too? Growing up around the Chinese Mafia, what else could he become?

Those doubts were small though. My imagined life was close to normal, damn close, and I could live with being a hypocrite if it meant having it. Everyone makes small sacrifices toward their overall happiness. This was mine.

"I'll do it, Howie." *I have to.*

He nodded, silent and for a long time. "Let's go. This guy's white, so you knock. Get a James Lewis to the door, step out of the way, and put this mask on. It's important that only this James guy sees your face, and I don't know who else is in there." I nodded, pulled the door handle. "Jimmy." He held out my Ruger. "Just in case."

I smelled cooked onions as I rapped my knuckles twice on the door of the house Howie had indicated. Clattering plates hushed, then a man stood in front of me. "Sorry to disturb you, sir. I'm looking for Mr. Lewis. James Lewis."

"I'm him. We're in the middle of dinner. Can — oh."

Howie pushed by me and forced the man's wrist up and behind his back. A black zip tie bound the guy's hands together, and he smashed to the hardwood. I yanked the ski mask down over my face, twisted it until the stupid eyeholes were where they were supposed to be, and followed Howie into the house. His gun was up, pointed at a woman and two toddlers seated around their dinner.

"Not a word." Howie's voice was low and relaxed. "This is going to be nice and easy. I need to ask Mr. Lewis some questions then we'll be gone. Ma'am, do you have a coat closet?" She nodded. Tears fell from her eyes. "Would you mind taking the children there a moment?"

The closet was beneath the stairs, and the woman crouched into it with a kid on each hip. Howie closed the door and shoved a four-legged chair under the knob. The children's wails pierced the air.

"Bro, check the rest of the house."

I lifted my gun like I'd been trained to, left-handed with my right holding it steady, and searched the bottom floor. Howie took James into a room off the kitchen. The baby cries churned my stomach. Two masked men would forever be the nightmares of those children.

Three doors were in the hallway at the top of the stairs. One on each wall and one at the end. The last door rattled then swung wide, and a Chinese man wearing all black strode out. His eyes shot open when he saw the barrel of my gun pointed at his center; his arm came up, a gun in his hand.

I bolted down the stairs, slipped and slid on my ass, and was on my feet soon as I hit the bottom. I ran past the closet, through the kitchen, and slammed the door Howie had gone into behind me. My back pressed hard on that door.

It was an office. James was in a computer chair, blood leaking from a cut on his eyebrow. "We're not alone," I said, and my back bounced as my pursuer crashed into the door.

"Move!" Howie roared.

I rolled; two shots ripped through the silence. Light flowed through the bullet holes in the door where I'd just been. The man bashed into it again then was in the room, pointing his gun at Howie.

"Stop!" Howie reached his arm around James's neck and pressed the barrel to his head. "Don't move."

"Do what he says." James cried. "Please. Whatever he says."

My back was against the wall to the right of Howie. He made eye contact with me. They went wide then small twice. I shook my head.

"What was that look?" The man's hand shook. "You! Slide me your gun." Howie's eyebrows lowered the smallest amount, a scream that said, "Do Not Do That!" The man's gun went from me to Howie, to me to Howie. "Give me it. Now!"

I slid it across the carpet, to the man's feet.

"No one moves," he said.

It all happened at once. The man crouched down to pick up my gun, and Howie's gun fired once. A bullet tore through the man's cheekbone, and he fell to the ground. James cried out. I stared at the dead man and heard baby whimpers.

"Please, please, please, please, please." James's mantra was high-pitched.

"Tell me where he is, James." Howie moved around the man. He walked like he hadn't killed someone seconds before. "All you have to do is tell me where he is and we'll leave."

"I swear! I don't know. If I did —"

Howie shot him in the face.

In the hush that followed, Howie sighed and reached out his hand to help me off the ground.

"What — What the hell was that? Why'd you shoot him?"

"Not now. It's time to go."

On our way out of the house, I stopped in front of the closet. The woman was crying now too. "What about them?

"Cops will let them out." He pushed me out the front door and to the car. I gazed out the Audi's window as we fled the scene. "That guy could've killed us both, bro."

I focused on the passing city.

"Why didn't you shoot him?"

How do you answer that? "I got scared."

I could feel Howie's eyes. "You've never done it before." Both question and statement. I stared at him until he nodded. He took us around town with no direction. He spoke eventually, "I'm glad to see this in you. I was worried."

"Worried?"

"You seemed way too easy to convince. The first time, you said you had to leave town because you didn't want a part in crime, then you work with me day after day. I was starting to think you had no scruples."

I snorted. "You're the one without scruples. Hate to point this out, but you just killed two men."

"I've been at this a long time, bro. I killed someone even before I joined the military. Fifteen, I was. It was hard. Still is. But practice numbs the pain."

"That's what I'm afraid of," I said for some reason. "Exactly that. Being numb. Two years ago, you couldn't have got me to commit a crime if it meant my life. Now look at me."

I tried to read Howie. He stared forward. His eyes were a little wet, but his face was straight, straighter than normal. "Listen, I'm going to tell Mr. Long how excellent you did tonight. He will think you killed James because he ordered it and that you didn't even ask for an explanation. I think that is what all this is about anyway."

"Why?"

"He's testing you, seeing how far you'll go. He does it to all —"

"Not that. Why would you lie to him?"

He shrugged. "Seems like the right thing to do."

I was uncertain how to respond. "That James was going to die no matter what he told you, wasn't he? That's why it was fine for him to see my face?"

"It was a message." He nodded. "There's some shit brewing." He peeked over at me. "Not the best time to decide to join the family."

How true that was.

II

"All right, Paul," I said, leading Pecu and Jessy through the ringing bells of the pet store. "Let your puppy pick you, kay?"

His eyes lit so bright that I almost quit fidgeting. One side of the pet store, from floor to ceiling, was filled with different-sized windows. Within each window were rolling masses of puppies. The place was huge. Pecu was so happy.

Hopefully for the right reason. He pounded up to the first window.

Jessy pressed against my side. "You get nervous over some strange things."

I usually spent my weekends with Pecu. Mr. Long gave me those days off, and I only got to see my brother for a couple hours on weeknights. Jessy caught on to this and asked if she could hang out with us. "It makes me uncomfortable that you can read me so well."

"Don't deflect. I know you work with Howie. I know what he does for work." She pulled my arm until I stopped. "Why does buying a pet for his brother make that kind of man nervous?"

"I'll tell you later. Let's make this fun for Pe — for Paul."

We strolled the store, Jessy gushing over every window, me loving her smile. I was already trying to think of the explanation I'd give Song and Ling why we had two puppies instead of one, because I knew I would have to say yes if Jessy demanded one.

Pecu sat cross-legged at the last window, contemplating a puppy. It was an orange color, half the size of its brothers and sisters, and it lay curled in a tight ball away from the rest, back pressed against the glass. Pecu rubbed his finger back and forth like he was petting it. The runt brought its head up and stared straight into my brother's face. *A plea if I ever saw one.* Pecu's shining eyes came to mine.

"This one."

We purchased the puppy, took it home, and watched Pecu play with it on the living room floor. In its cage, the ugly little dog looked so miserable. On the car ride, it sat in Pecu's lap, making not one sound and moving hardly an inch. As soon as we got home, and after it sniffed every corner of the living room, it came to life, jumping all over Pecu, licking his face, running when he tried to catch him.

And Pecu. So gentle. So nice.

"You look like you're going to cry," Jessy ventured after Song and Ling had retired for the night. Pecu was still giggling uncontrollably on the floor.

I only nodded.

"Why? This is cute and all, but how can you sit here all day, all fricken day, and just watch Paul play with a puppy. I'm going nuts."

"You wanted to hang out with us."

"And I love it. But tell me why this is so important."

This single truth, the one she was asking me, was the reason for everything. It was hard to share that with another. But I wouldn't lie to her. And I wanted to share my life with her. This was a big part of it. The biggest.

"My family was messed up," seemed like a good place to start. She nodded.

"My uncle is a psychopath. He used to drown my little brother in this crazy rhetoric. I never heard him say anything, but I knew it came from him. He was trying to turn Pecu into him, and it was working.'"

This next was hard to get out. I didn't want Jessy to think Pecu was some kind of hell-spawn. *No lies though.* "He used to hurt animals. Pecu did. He tortured them."

She wrapped her arms around my neck. "It's the reason I left. The reason for everything. I had to get him out. I had to give him a chance to live a normal life. It's working."

The floodgates, the ones I'd been fighting closed, burst.

Jessy kissed my tears. Kissed my eyes. Kissed my mouth. "You're so beautiful," she whispered. "Such a beautiful, beautiful person."

What do you say to that? I appreciate it, but let me tell you the truth. Let me tell you about a girl named Amanda or a girl named Rachel. I'm garbage, done nothing but bad, except for one thing. I gave this little boy a chance.

Maybe it only takes one good act to be beautiful?

I kept quiet. We held each other for a long time, until Pecu was nodding in and out as the puppy snored in his lap. I carried Pecu, Jessy carried the puppy, and we put them down in Pecu's bed.

"You want me to drive you home?" I asked Jessy. She shook her head. Her face was tight like she was scared, but she said nothing. "Well, you can take my room. I'll sleep out here."

"I'm fine."

The silence was awkward. "I'll see you in the morning then."

"Night."

I crawled into bed and stared at the ceiling. The fish swimming in my stomach were impossible to ignore. It was a new feeling. People call it happiness. I associate it with normality.

My door clicked open. Jessy slid in. She stood there in a silken white robe tied tight around her, staring. I couldn't read her face.

"Everything all right?" I swallowed.

She nodded.

"Can't sleep?"

She shook her head.

Moonlight seeped through the window and illuminated half of her, the other touched by darkness. Her hair was loose, hanging in disarray around her face. Her eyes looked hungry. Her mouth looked terrified. She stepped forward. My entire body felt that step. She stood at the foot of my bed.

Slow, she untied the silk rope at her waist. The robe slipped from her shoulders. It was all she wore.

"I love you," she said.

And she came to bed with me.

❁

Two depressing, long, dreadful months and she was nowhere to be found. I called her. No answer. I went to her dorm. No one was there. I had to consciously take command of myself, lest I became a stalker, but I considered some pretty extreme ways of making her talk to me.

"She does this, you know," Ling told me one morning. "She's thinking. Never been good with people, my Jessy. Academically, she's a genius. Socially, she's retarded. But she'll come around."

I wanted to tell her to shut the hell up and mind her own damn business. The words never left my mouth, of course, but that was how I wanted to respond to everything, especially everything regarding Jessy. It made no sense to me.

We had shared a night together, possibly the best night of my life, and then she dropped me like it'd been nothing. An entire night of careful lovemaking mingled with the both of us sharing our truest, harshest feelings, and she disappears like it was nothing.

My first thought was that it was her. She was overwhelmed and terrified. She'd decided to break it off rather than try to figure out how to deal with it. That was all. She was scared. Typical response from a young woman who'd just given up her virginity.

My second thought was that it was me. The white man in the criminal organization she was associated with. A relationship with me would be frowned upon, and definitely never sanctioned. She had to distance herself from me, otherwise she'd be in disgrace.

Once I'd run through all the logical reasons, I started down the illogical. She'd been kidnapped. She'd run off with some other man. She'd decided she was a lesbian. She'd realized she hated me. She'd...

I thought of everything. Everything but the truth.

It was more difficult for me to commit crimes without Jessy sharing my nights though, even worse now that I'd been promoted to habitual violent offender. Rarely did someone need killed and when they did Howie did it himself and away from me, but I still had to be present for some vile acts.

I helped torture men. I helped invade homes. I even helped kidnap a woman. Only for a couple of hours while her husband came up with the money he owed, but try telling the police how nice you snatched a woman from her home, see where that gets you. Try telling your conscience.

The idea came back to me, the one I had before I had Jessy. Maybe it was time to leave. I'd tossed it around since about a month into Jessy's hiatus. Why not? I was breaking all my principles. Pecu was safe, doing well in preschool, and had a dog with all its appendages, but one day he would be in the very shoes I was in if we stayed. Without Jessy, there were more reasons to leave than stay. Plus, with all the money I'd made working for Mr. Long, leaving would be easy financially too.

Howie and I were driving home after a long day terrorizing followed by a long workout. I was trying to convince myself to forsake what I had with Jessy and just pack up and go.

We turned onto the block Song's house was on. "What the?"

Sirens and lights. Black and blue sedans. Men in uniforms. Howie slammed on the brakes at the end of the block. "Howie, they're at Song's. We got to —"

"We got to find out what happened, bro. We can't just roll up. What if they're looking for —"

"The front windows are shattered. Look! Bullet holes—"

I was out the car, running. I sprinted toward the front door, but an officer stopped me with his palm. "Hold on, son."

"What happened?"

Song came out from around a squad car. His face was straight but not frantic. "Song, what happened? Where's Paul?"

He stopped in front of me. "He went with Jessy to a hotel. Everything's fine, Jim. Calm down."

Bullet holes covered the front of the house. Dirt lay in piles on the ground under broken planters, flowers buried within. All the windows were shattered. Ling's wind chimes were tied in knots. Someone had spent a fortune on ammunition to destroy the house I lived in. The house Pecu lived in.

"It was a drive-by," Song said. "No one got hurt."

"Why us?" I asked.

"Same question I'd asked forty damn times," the officer said. "Mr. Ching Chong here says it must be random."

Ching Chong? "The hell did you call him?"

"Jim, go. I'll text you the hotel's address your brother's at. I'll finish here."

I jogged back to the Audi before I was in jail for police assault. "What happened?" Howie asked.

My phone vibrated. *Mr. Long's*, from Song. "Drive-by. We got to go to Mr. Long's."

He soared through the streets faster than he'd ever gone. My heart hurt it pounded so hard against my ribs. *He is fine.* Song had said so. But I had to see him with my own eyes. The neighborhoods changed; houses started costing more until they turned into mansions. We rolled up a long driveway and stopped in front of Mr. Long's house.

I leaped over the corner of a flower garden, ran up the stairs, and burst through the front door.

Pecu and Jessy sat on the waiting couches, beautiful smiles on both their faces, jointly holding Pecu's puppy. I rushed to Pecu and squeezed him. He grunted but squeezed back. "I love you, buddy. Love you so much."

"You too, Jimjim."

Reluctantly, I let go of Pecu. He jumped into Jessy's lap. Her eyes leaked a tear each. Words got stuck in my throat.

"Hey, Jim."

Hey, Jim? Two months and *Hey, Jim?* After a near tragedy! I almost cracked. I almost shouted the most obscene thing I could come up with. I almost picked up my brother and charged from the room. I almost decided not to talk to *her* for two damn months.

"I've missed you," I said.

She crashed into me, crushing Pecu between us. Her tears made her face slippery against mine. "I'm so sorry."

I pulled her head back and kissed her. "I forgive you." And meant it. "What happened?"

"I don't know. I just — I always told myself I'd save it for marriage. I held out so long. At first, I didn't call because I was so disappointed in myself. I didn't want you to see it and think I was disappointed in you. I'm not."

That was a much better reason than all of what I had been thinking. "You said at first you didn't call." She nodded, saying nothing. "What's that mean?"

"Well, by the time I was done analyzing myself, I..."

"You what?"

She turned away and shrugged.

"Jessy, say it."

Her face broke into a sob. I eased my knuckles under her chin and lifted her eyes to mine. Like Song had done for me once before, I tried to feed her strength through my expression. *Be strong*, I told her. *I'm here.*

"Jim," she whispered. "I'm pregnant."

I stared at her mouth, where life-changing words had sprouted. I didn't know what to say. Then I did. The words sprung from the depths of my mind like a shark out of water. There was no analyzing it. There was no stopping it. There was only living with the choice that my unthinking self had decided.

"Marry me."

"What?"

"Marry me, Jessy. Why not? You love me, I love you. You were saving yourself for marriage, this is the next best thing. It makes more sense the longer I think about it. Let's do it. Me and you. We could be a..."

"A family?"

"A real one. We could raise Pecu at the same time. It's perfect. I know this isn't the most romantic way to ask you, or a good time, but that doesn't mean that we shouldn't. I've known since I met you. It's the only thing that makes sense in my life. My heart's pounding. Come on, Jessy. Why not?"

"I..." She stared at her hands.

"You don't want to?"

"No! Not that. I do. It's just..."

"What?"

"I can't."

"You can. If it's what you want —"

"You don't get it. I can't."

"I —" I didn't understand. "Because I'm white?"

"It doesn't happen, Jim. Don't be upset."

"Then we'll run away."

"That's naive. Do you have any idea how much uncle Richard has already invested in my schooling? I don't. I know it's a fricken lot thought."

"So —" I swallowed, suddenly nauseated. "What?"

"I don't know. I love you, but —"

The door crashed open, and Mr. Long strode in, his expression stern. "Everyone with me." A trail of men followed him, all wearing the same expression. Mr. Long cut through the antechamber. "You too, Jim."

I waited until the procession passed. "If I can get permission, will you marry me?"

"Jim, you move that mountain, I'm yours."

I kissed her. Long and hard.

"Stop it!" Pecu groaned.

I ruffled his hair. "Stay with Jessy, all right?"

I followed Mr. Long's men to a massive living area filled with sofas, stools, and foldable chairs. There was a man in every spot, many I'd seen before. One of whom Howie and I had found in a pile of trash behind a strip club. Another we'd had to keep from killing his wife in a drunken rage. One thing had to be said about Mr. Long: he practiced compassion. He seemed to truly love these men. Why else would he put up with such nonsense?

I unfolded a chair and placed it next to Howie's. Every face was turned toward Mr. Long as he paced a short line, eyes to the ground. He stopped suddenly and looked up. "At the same time today, twelve locations were fired on by automatic weapons. As all of you are already aware, those locations belonged to people that I hold dear. Eight of those locations belong to men in this room. I —"

"Who do we have to kill?" someone shouted.

Mr. Long's chin dropped to his chest with a slow sigh. "No one interrupt me again. This is not the time." His head came up and he started to pace again. He looked like a military commander in front of his troops. "This act, this open defiance, it's war gentlemen. We war on men we used to call family. It was the Changs who attacked us."

As soon as he said it, I understood. The man from my first job for Mr. Long, the man Howie had taken a nose from, he was a Chang. His father, Lee Chang, was a man respected in the Chinese community. Respected in the way Mr. Long's father was respected. Howie had crossed a serious line when he'd done what he'd done.

"These are my orders. Every associate of the Chang's, known or suspected, is to be found and brought to my warehouse. Anyone belonging to that family. Killed. Their bodies are not to be found. Use the associates to learn of the made members' whereabouts, then do what you please with them. If their last name is Chang, I want them brought to me. I'll say it again, this is war. Mercy is for the dead."

This last he said with such a growl that my entire body cringed. His feelings were palpable. The anger. The pain. The disbelief. He reeked of it. I had the desire to leave this tiny man, the suddenly intimidating tiny man, and was happy when he told us we were dismissed. I followed Howie and stopped him outside the room.

"Did we do this?" I asked him.

"No. We might've made the spark, but this forest hasn't seen rain in years."

12

We, Howie and I, were part of the questioning team, not the roundup team. Neither team was a team I wanted to be on. Howie knew this though and did most of the questioning himself. I guarded the door. Sometimes though, I'd have to help. I never inflicted pain, I just held tight or held open or held down while Howie inflicted pain.

Our living arrangements had changed dramatically. Pecu, Jessy, Song, Ling, Vanessa, her husband and kids, Chelsea, and I, along with eight other families, had moved into Mr. Long's mansion for the time being. Once the war was over, we'd be able to go back to our homes, but Mr. Long wanted us all close. And safe.

Being in that house kept me from Jessy. Too many eyes. Mr. Long was much more sensitive to the propriety of a young woman than Song and Ling were, so it would have been impossible for me and Jessy to have another secret night together, even if she'd wanted to. Having her there, and not having her, drove me near insane.

"Have you asked yet?" She demanded one night as we sat on Mr. Long's porch overlooking the garden. It was vast and colorful and never died in the California climate.

"You know I haven't."

She nodded. "I understand."

A tear sprinkled from her eyelash. That tear was a razor blade through my chest. I was the cause of it. Some came from fear; she was pregnant, keeping the baby, and decency demanded she marry immediately, yet her family demanded she marry well. Some random white kid was not marrying well. But most of it was me. The way she kept her eyes on the garden, like looking my direction would affirm her thoughts, I knew it was me. She felt alone.

I stood. "I'll do it now. Yes or no. I'll find out tonight."

I stormed away as dignified as I could manage, but it felt like fleeing. I went straight to Song and Ling's room and tapped their door.

"Come in."

Song and Ling lay in bed, glasses on their face and books in their hand. "What happened, Jimmy?"

"Song, Ling, I need to ask you something. It's important."

Books went down and glasses came off. "What is it, Jimmy?"

"I —" This was it. "I want to marry Jessy."

They both went dumb. Their bottom lips curled over themselves and their eyebrows crossed. Slowly, they looked at each other. Ling spouted something in Cantonese. I'd picked up some, but it was too fast for me to follow. Song responded. She shrugged.

"Jimmy," Song said, bringing his eyes to mine. "I couldn't dream of someone better for Jessy." My heart stopped. His tone was apologetic. "But, as you know, I hardly know her. When your mother... took me, I didn't even know Ling was pregnant. I'd love to give you Jessy. But she's not mine to give."

My eyes drifted to Ling. And back. "Mr. Long?"

They nodded.

His study was on the third floor. Few bothered him there, and they did so only for good reason. This qualified, I figured as I tapped the door. "Enter."

He sat behind a huge desk, with dark, polished wood and jungle vines in low-relief. The right and left walls of the room were lined with shelves, the shelves lined with books. A massive window was behind Mr. Long, showing an expanse of night sky. Papers covered the desk in neat piles. He tapped some straight and set them down.

"Jim, have you found him?"

"Him," was Pretty Chang, the man who was mine and Howie's specific target. "No, sir."

His forehead crinkled like he was irritated. "How can I help you?"

"Mr. Long, sir." I took a deep breath. "I'd like to marry Jessy."

He nodded slow, but took it as though it was expected. "She is a wonderful young lady. I could see why you would." He went quiet. Horribly quiet. "Have a seat, Jim." Mr. Long leaned back in his chair and rubbed his eyes. My knees wobbled as I lowered onto the seat opposite him. "You've heard of my father?"

I nodded. Everyone had heard of his father.

"You've heard of him, but you don't know him. He came to this country with nothing and climbed to where he is now with little help, forbidden to do so by the triads. He's a stubborn old bastard who would do anything to progress. Honestly, Jim, my father's a nasty man. But because of his nastiness, my family is where it is."

He stopped and waited. I kept quiet. "Think on this. My father knows of my distaste for the slavery business, has known my entire life, but what does he do? puts me in charge of it.

"I have to do as he says. Everyone does. I've told him of my ideas. I've advanced my identity business so far that I can have identities made. Not fake ones. Actual identities. Jim Thompson has a valid social security number, birth certificate, everything.

"I want to stop selling my own people, Jim. I could sell them identities. Then instead of slaves, I'd have loyal friends. You know how much a salve will do for you?" He waited until I shook my head. "As much as can be forced. You know what a loyal friend will do for you? as much as he's capable. I've even produced a business model that makes it more profitable than slavery."

He turned red-faced and his volume climbed. "My father tells me no. We'll do it as it has always been done. We're making money and we know the risks. Be happy with what you have. That is my father. A man stuck in his ways because his ways work."

I had no idea what this had to do with me marrying Jessy, but I knew he had a reason for sharing all this with me. "I like you, Jim. I see a Long in you. That is why I offered you work. I felt you struggling with choices, so I showed you an option. And in my opinion, you're perfectly suited for the work. I could see you being family one day, Jim. I would love to call you family. But my father, he would not."

I stared.

"I'm sorry, Jim," he said. "My father would not condone such a marriage. I already know what his response would be if I were to ask. 'Look at Pretty Chang. The result of Chinese and *gweilo* fornicating. No honor. A disgrace.' Jim, I would love for you to marry Jessy. But you cannot."

I'd been here before. It was like waking up in a van, knowing I'd ended Amanda's life. Jessy was still alive, but everything was ruined. Because of me.

"But! Though I hope he lives forever, father will not. A lot of things will change once he dies, Jim. It may be another thirty years, but when he is dead, then you may marry my Jessy. This I promise you."

That did nothing for the half-white baby growing inside of Jessy. "Thank you, sir." Dazed, I stood to go tell Jessy. In the hallway, I fell to my knees and put my face in my hands. No tears came though. I was numb. I'd done it again. I'd ruined another life.

"Get up." I turned toward the voice. Howie. "We have to talk to the boss."

"Why?"

"They found him."

"In my own fucking place?"

It was strange hearing Mr. Long curse, and that had been the third time. No one had answered the first two times either. I sat in the back seat of the Audi next to Roy, a man whose house had been shot up like Ling and Song's. Howie drove. Mr. Long sat the front passenger. Two similarly arranged vehicles followed us. Two led.

"He must not know it's mine." Mr. Long said through clenched teeth.

"Everyone knows it's yours," Howie responded.

"The gall of the man. The idiocy. The... The gall!"

"You shouldn't have come, sir." Also not the first time that had been said. "We are perfectly capable —"

"I'm going to be the first to slap this little bastard in the mouth."

Howie stared at our boss. "Yes, sir."

We stopped in front of a building I'd visited once before, the massage parlor where I'd demanded a meeting with Mr. Long. A half million dollars worth of Audis parked in a lower-class neighborhood was a sight to see, and I stared as all the men climbed out onto the sidewalk. Their suits made me feel official since I'd been ordered to wear one myself. Their guns made me nervous.

"Jim!" Howie whispered. I was the only one left in the car, and he was leaning in. "Let's go."

I climbed past the folded-down seat and out the passenger door. Twenty or so armed Chinese men, and one white guy, crowded the steps leading up to the business. This all seemed a little excessive to catch one noseless cokehead, but Mr. Long had to make a statement.

Mr. Long put his foot on the first stair leading into the parlor.

"No." Howie pulled the back of his shirt and pushed in front of him. "Sorry, sir, but I can't let you go in first."

He went up the stairs. Like an idiot, I jumped to second in line. One receptionist was behind the counter in the closet-sized waiting room. She looked like she'd collapse as everyone smashed into the place. "Which room," Howie whispered.

She held up four fingers.

Gun up, Howie glided around the woman and clicked open the door behind the desk. I followed, mimicking his movements. Doors lined both sides of the long hallway. A deep grunting and a phony moan came from the first we passed. The second, a female cried loudly while a man laughed. More sex noises from the third. The fourth was silent.

Howie signaled to go right on three. He stood square with the door, ready to kick it in. I peeked behind me. Twenty men were impressively silent. Howie lifted his hand. One finger... two.

Tat, tat, tat, tat, tat!

Holes crashed through the door and kept coming. Howie went down. I dropped to my hands and knees, grasped Howie's collar, and started scooting back down the hall. Shots sprayed out of the door and the cheap drywall of room 4. Howie was too heavy, he hardly moved each time I yanked, but my hand stayed firm around his collar. I'd die before I let go.

Mr. Long's hand was suddenly next to mine. "Pull!" I heaved and he slid easily. We passed a forest of legs and were in the waiting room. "Check him, Jim. I'm going to kill this son of a bitch."

I ripped open Howie's shirt as Mr. Long ran back toward the hallway, shouting indecipherable words. The hole in Howie's shoulder was survivable. The one six inches to the right of his belly button was sketchy. I tore myself out of my jacket, yanked off my shirt, and ripped a strip from it. I pressed it to the stomach wound. Howie moaned.

"You're fine." I made another bandage for his shoulder. "Hold tight."

Gunshots roared, and whores in varying degrees of nakedness sprinted past me and Howie. Mr. Long drug another man from the hall. "Jim, help me get these two outside." We dragged Howie outside, laid the front seat of the Audi back, and set him in it. The gunshots sounded like a war from the sidewalk. I ran back in.

"Take these two back to my house, Vanessa will be there," Mr. Long shouted. The gunfire had faded to tap taps. "Drive fast."

I nodded.

I dragged the man to the Audi's driver's side and shoved him into the back as gently as I could then climbed in behind the wheel. It was difficult to make sense of the car, like I'd hopped into a space shuttle, but I found the pedal and floored it.

"Hold on, Howie."

Men waited outside Mr. Long's, and they pulled the wounded from the car. They carried them into a room off the kitchen. The maid stopped me at the door with a palm. "You'll only be in the way."

I pushed forward.

Someone put a hand on my shoulder. "I'll take care of him," said Song's daughter Vanessa, sliding past me. "Go."

The door slammed, and I stared at it, thoughts whirling. *A dentist can't save a man who's been shot. Howie is going to die. He's my friend.*

Arms wrapped around my waist.

"Come with me," Jessy whispered. I nodded and let her lead me through the house. We stopped outside my room. "I know this is a lot right now, but you have to talk to Paul. He woke up and won't stop crying."

Pecu's face was puffy. Snot ran from his nose. Tears on his face reflected the night light. *This is the last thing I need now.* "What's the matter, Pecu?" I sat on the bed and put my hand on his foot.

"I want mama." He pressed both his fists into his eyes, sniffling. "When's she coming, Jimjim?"

"Pecu, she's not." The words just came out. Pecu's feelings seemed petty, petty with my friend bleeding downstairs.

"Wha — why?"

I'd thought about what I would finally tell him a thousand times. None of the options were good. I chose the worst. "Pecu, mom's not here anymore. She's... She died."

"No." His head shook hard and tight. He was confused. "No!"

I hugged his head to my chest. His sobs shook us both, and his tears, snot, and drool soaked into my undershirt. I held him, but my mind was downstairs with Howie. Pecu would survive the lie. Howie might not survive the night.

Pecu cried until he slept, then I left him. In the hallway, Jessy climbed to her feet from sitting with her back to the wall. "Jim, why would you —"

"I know. I —" I pulled her to me. "I was thinking about Howie and. And I don't know. It just came out."

"My sister's good, you know. She's removed more bullets than teeth. If Howie can be saved, she'll do it."

"Let's go check on him."

She held me from leaving. "Jim, did you talk to Mr. Long?"

"He said his father won't allow it, but he would say yes."

Her eyes filled.

"I won't give up on you, Jessy. I'll be here whether we're married or not."

"Will you?"

"Of course."

"Look at what you're doing. You could be in Howie's place right now."

I stared at her dimples. They weren't so beautiful when she cried.

13

He lived. The other man I'd driven home, along with three others who'd stormed the massage parlor, died. It had been a well-organized trap. Six men had been waiting in that room for us with automatic weapons. They'd silently taken the place over and forced the call to the Longs indicating that Pretty Chang was there. He'd never been there. They had hoped that Mr. Long would feel angry enough to show up there himself. The trap had worked. Perfectly.

Well, almost. Mr. Long had survived. It was a scary thing, watching that man realize the truth of what'd happened, of what he'd fallen for.

"All of them. I want them dead."

"The whole parlor, sir?" one of his minions responded.

"If they were working in the building when those men called and they work for me, they die."

It was a ruthlessness I'd not expected. He caught me staring at him and sighed. "Father ordered it, not me. I hate it, but it will prevent it from happening again. Hopefully."

Pecu had been sullen and silent since that night. For days, he stumbled around in a daze. Now that Howie's immediate death was no longer a thought, Pecu's feelings gnawed at me. I could have thought of something else to tell him. Anything else. She's on a trip to Africa.

She's in rehab. She's on the goddamn moon, even. Her being dead crushed him.

I think it changed how Jessy looked at me too. She always told me how much she loved that I didn't lie, then she witnesses me tell a lie that demoralized the person I held closest to me? I knew what I would think if I was her. *How long until he lies to me like that?*

And outside my personal life, the gang war was raging. Mr. Long considered me to be Howie's partner so if he was out I was out, but people were being massacred daily. It wasn't a struggle for territory or money or drugs. It was a struggle for vengeance. It would continue until one side lost enough men to choose surrender.

"We've got to find a way to end this." Mr. Long said. He, Howie, and I were in Howie's recovery room. Howie was making intense progress. Already he could walk but weeks after the shooting. The bullets had gone straight through, something I was told was more desirable in the event that you're shot, though it sounded less desirable than anything I'd ever heard.

"What ideas do you have?" Howie asked.

"Get every Chang in the city into one building and burn it down."

"Lovely in theory."

We fell silent, smiling over the most unfunny of jokes.

"What you want is the Changs, right?" I asked and they both nodded. "And they're holed up, much like you and all the Longs have been since this started." My mind, the part I'd inherited from my mother, twisted around some thoughts. "Many people must know where they are, and not only people in their family, same as many know where you are. What we need is to find someone not in the business."

"What do you think we've been doing, bro? Almost anyone who has ever worked for the Changs we've questioned. No one will —"

"We need to stop thinking about people that've worked for them, at least from the family perspective. Think about your maid, Tamara, she knows where Mr. Long is. I'm talking about people like that. The Changs have to have gardeners, maids, mailmen. Some of them probably don't even know what kind of work the Changs do."

"Are you suggesting," Howie said, "that we start kidnapping and questioning innocents? The cops would be on us like white on rice."

I tried to put myself in a brighter light. "Maybe we wouldn't have to question them, in the traditional sense. We could just ask."

They both stared at me. For too long, they stared.

"It's a stupid idea. I —"

"No," Mr. Long interrupted. "It's worth pursuing."

Three days later, I sat in front of the TV in our room, watching Pecu kill zombies on his game. He still had a zombie look about him himself, like he just pushed through the motions.

Mr. Long charged into the room and grabbed my face in both hands. "You're a genius, Jim." He kissed my cheeks and wiggled my face. "A genius!"

Pecu glanced at us, but only for a second. He turned back to the TV. "What'd I do?"

"We found Lee Chang. Would you believe it? My gardener and his gardener work for the same landscaping business. Just like you said. Told him how much better my gardens are than his, and the other man had to prove him wrong, took my man straight to his home."

"That's great, Mr. Long. What happens now?"

His smile disappeared. "Death, Jim." I got up to get away from Pecu. He'd heard enough. "Howie will not be coming, so neither will you. I've got a plan anyway, and I won't need but a few men. I wanted to thank you. You've ended this war."

The metaphor that if you cut the head from the snake then it dies was the furthest from the truth in this case. Mr. Long's men, with inspiration from a single unfunny joke, using explosives and gasoline, put fire to Lee Chang's home. Every entrance was covered by a man, and anyone who tried to escape was shot dead. Our side lost zero; their side lost many.

But it was hardly a victory. We cut the head from the snake, but it worked like kicking the beehive.

Where the Longs' most thriving business was slavery, the Changs' was guns. We carried pistols. They carried M16s. It was ugly. Our men would be shot while eating dinner or shopping or getting gas. Usually all the bystanders around them would be killed too. The heat from the police this caused added to the stress. A month after Lee Chang was killed, the Long family and associates were scattered all over town, unable to show their faces.

That was when I finally met Mr. Long. *The* Mr. Long. He was a wrinkled copy of the son. Tiny in stature, massive in presence. The differences came from age. Daddy Long's hair was stark white and thinning. The lines on his face told a story of long hours of frowning. His worst feature though: he hated me.

Mr. Long, his father, his sister, and his two brothers would move residences on a weekly basis, all to different homes. The locations were random and different. They kept two or three armed men with them. It was our defense against what had happened to Lee Chang happening to us. Mr. Long, Richard Long, was the only man who knew where every person in his family was at any time. Two guards would stay with that family member until it was time to move, then two more would show up, transfer them, and stay until the next week.

Howie and I were in the rotation. We'd work a week on, a week off. Pecu stayed with Song and Ling at a hotel while I worked. Jessy stayed with us all when I didn't. It was no way to live. The uncertainty of when it was all going to be over, if ever, hung over us and no one was sure of how to go about their life.

The somewhat normal life I'd provided for Pecu was gone. He was being raised in a hotel room.

That wasn't even the worst of it. Jessy was starting to show.

"What am I going to tell everyone?" she asked one night next to a shabby hotel swimming pool.

I had no answer.

"What do we do?"

No answer there either.

"You have to do something, Jim." Jessy's voice was tight. "Help me."

Two days into our week guarding Daddy Long, I approached him. He slouched in a leather chair in the upstairs bedroom, glaring at the wall. Smoke trailed off his cigar.

"Mr. Long, sir. I need to speak with you."

His cigar pressed to his lips. He puffed.

"I'm not sure if you know her. Jessy, Jessy Chan, she's —"

"Ngo sun neui." *My granddaughter.*

"Yes, sir. I —" It felt like I was speaking to a Supreme Court justice. "I wish, with your permission, to marry her."

He choked and coughed out smoke. "What you say?"

"I love her, sir."

He spoke through a locked jaw. "Come here." I stopped in front of the chair. "Lower." I went to one knee, and his palm crossed my cheek. I touched the spot with the tip of my fingers. "Get foul notion from your head! Because my son, I let you work. Now overstep. You think I want a Pretty Chang in my family?" He slapped me on the other cheek. "Go!"

I stood and stared down at that man. The tiny man. His legs were so short that they stuck straight out from the leather seat. His arm I could've broken over my knee like a twig. I took a deep breath, then I left.

"What was that about?" Howie asked from the couch downstairs.

"Nothing."

"Whoa, bro. Just a question."

I sighed and told him what happened.

"That was stupid," Roy said, the extra man guarding Mr. Long with us.

Howie glared. "Shut up."

He continued anyway, "He'd never let the *gweilo* marry any of his people." At some point, I'd evolved from *gweilo* to *the gweilo*.

The door pounded. It wasn't the secret tap.

Howie ripped out his gun and spoke with his hands. *Go upstairs.* Roy and I hurried up the stairs as fast as we could without making a sound and closed the door to the smoke-filled room after we entered.

"I tell you once —"

"Shush!" I put my fingers to my lips to silence Mr. Long. His eyes almost fell out of his head.

All went quiet, then something clicked, then Howie's pistol emptied, the whole clip gone in a breath. Another clip. Feet pounded on the stairs. Automatic gunfire followed. I aimed my gun at the door as Howie fell through it.

"Damnit!" His ankle was red. "Shoot through the wall. On my count." He paused. "One. Two..."

They shot. My gun was up, aiming where they aimed, but I never pulled the trigger. I squeezed my eyes shut and tried to do as Howie had explained about pulling the trigger and only seeing to the end of the barrel, but I didn't. I couldn't.

"Roy, check around the corner," Howie ordered. "Four came in, two I shot downstairs."

Roy put his back to the wall next to the door and pushed it open. No gunfire. He swung his head out and back in, then his posture deflated. "Two bodies."

"Bring me one of their guns." Howie winced as he pulled up his pant leg. His sock was saturated with blood. "Been shot more times in the last few months..."

"What's this for?" Roy passed Howie an M16.

Howie fired twice before I could finish blinking. Faster than I could think. After, I couldn't think.

"It's for the best, Jim. Think about it." I gawked at the hole in Roy's chest, wondering when he'd fallen to the ground, then at the hole in Mr. Long's temple.

What happened? Why?

My eyes went to Howie.

"You need to listen to me. Go outside and spray into this room. Aim high. I'm sick of being shot."

"Howie. What —"

"Go!"

I took the M16 and went into the hallway. I emptied the clip at shoulder level, crossing the wall twice over. The gun fell from my hands as I stumbled back into the room. My thoughts wouldn't order themselves. "What the fuck, Howie? What — What did you do?"

He was wrapping his ankle in his shirt. "We were the last up the stairs. We were on the ground, so the bullets missed us."

"Why, Howie? Tell me!"

He sighed. "For me. For my people. They've been suffering for years. It helps you too though, if you'd stop and think."

"Are you saying..."

"Think, Jim. You know it's the right thing."

"No," I whispered. Then louder, "No, Howie. You killed Roy."

His eyes fell. "He wouldn't have stayed quiet, Jim."

"How do you know I will?"

"You will."

That made me think of who I had to keep quiet to. "Mr. Long's going to kill us."

"He will feign anger for a time, then it will be like nothing happened."

"Feign anger?"

He nodded. "Think. How many people knew where we were."

What? "He wouldn't."

"No? You don't think he might let slip our location while I'm here? It's no secret my feelings for his father."

"So this is all some elaborate plan, is that it?"

Howie shrugged.

"But —" Things tumbled into place. "We all could have been killed."

"Did you think you weren't dispensable?"

No. I guess not.

"Jim, bro." We made eye contact. "You were on the ground when they fired into this room. It's how you survived." My eyes narrowed as I tried to discern what he was getting at. "Why were you on the ground?"

I didn't get it. Until I did. "Seriously?"

He nodded. I sighed.

In the hallway, I got a rifle and shot myself in the foot.

"Is this how obsessive you're going to be over everything."

Jessy smacked my shoulder. "It's our fricken wedding. I have every right to obsess."

Her eyes were radiant. They had been since she found out we could get married. She flipped a page in some magazine then asked my opinion about something. I agreed but kept my eyes on her. She was by far the most beautiful thing I'd ever seen, and her pregnancy only enhanced it. She obsessed over the wedding; I obsessed over her.

"It's all settled, babe." She called me that now. "I'm putting the date in the newspaper. Are you sure you can't think of anything else?"

"I still think we should have a Chinese wedding," I said.

"Will you be serious?"

"Jessy, you've thought of everything down to the phony rice people are going to throw at us."

"I just don't want —"

"The pigeons, I know. You told me. There's nothing in my head that hasn't run through yours fifty times."

"I don't see how you can be so nonchalant. There are so many things. It's all so much to think about."

I squeezed her waist. "There's only one thing I need to think about."

She kissed me.

"Stop it!" Pecu shrieked from the end of the bed. "No more kisses."

"Get used to it, little bro." Howie leaned on the door frame to our room. We had matching boots on our legs. "Jim, you got a second?"

I hobbled out after him. He kept limping. "Sup, Howie?"

"You'll see in a second. Come on."

It had gone exactly as Howie said it would. Mr. Long had been livid with us when he found out about his father's murder. He put us on restriction, which felt much like being grounded would have had I a mother to do such a thing. Neither of us was allowed to leave the Long residence, which Mr. Long said was now safe because the Changs had got their target, and no other members of the family were allowed to see us.

It was for show though, I knew. The mystery of mine and Howie's disappearance caused the rest of the family to conjecture. No one knew the kind of punishment we were experiencing, but it had to be the worst imaginable. In reality, we sat and played video games with Pecu.

Now that Mr. Long had a firm grip on his empire, he treated us like nothing even happened. Not once did he question us about the nature of his father's death. You'd think he would've wanted to know how it happened and why we'd survived but not his father. He didn't. It was strange to me.

But what really bothered me was that I knew the world was better with the man dead. Already, Mr. Long had stopped slave trading. Anyone he owned at the time was given a new ID and let go. He lost a lot of money, but I think he was high off the power.

Howie tapped on the door to Mr. Long's study and entered without waiting for a response. "Ah, Jim, how are you?" He looked tired around the eyes, but within them was a smile that radiated.

"Perfect, honestly."

"Have a seat, Jim, Howie. I want to show you something. Then I want to talk. This package showed up today. Let me read you the note.

"Mr. Long, please take this gift. It is a symbol of our sincerest apologies. We all pay deference to you and your family. Signed, the Changs, now the Wongs.

"I suppose that two bosses in a short span is enough for everyone. This letter puts me in control, Jim. I couldn't have done it without you and Howie." We'd only done our job. Unless he was talking about... "Take a look at the gift."

Howie and I rose. A cardboard cube sat on Mr. Long's desk. Wrapped in plastic, wrapped tight enough to discern all its features, was a human head. It was missing a nose.

"Jim, you've been through so much with us. I'm elated that you're marrying into my family, but I believe you deserve to be recognized more than that. I want you to be a sworn brother. The first white man. Do you understand what I'm offering?"

I nodded.

"Welcome to the family."

"That's it?" I asked. "I don't have to drink wine with all our blood in it?"

"No, Jim." Mr. Long laughed. "Those days are over."

"Am I still the *gweilo*?"

They both laughed, and Howie said, "Forever and always."

There were only two white people at my wedding, me and Pecu. I didn't care. There were many there that had similar opinions to Daddy Long regarding a *gweilo* and Chinese marrying, and they scoffed at Jessy's western wedding. I didn't care. I still walked with a pronounced limp. Didn't care. My side of the seating arrangement was empty. But I didn't care.

The only thing that mattered to me on that day was Jessy. And she was perfect. More than perfect. Indescribable, unbelievable beauty, inside and out. It was the happiest day of my life.

And the night could only get better.

It was the only wedding I'd been to, but it seemed to be everything it was supposed to be. We, said vows, kissed, then danced and feasted and drank. All I could think about was the woman next to me and getting her to our very own home. Multiple times, people had to repeat their comment after I'd snapped out of staring at her smile. I was trying to figure out how you could take a perfect pregnant woman, throw her in a fifty thousand dollar dress, dip her in glitter, and somehow make her more beautiful. Perfect was supposed to mean perfect.

That day, and into the night, was a haze. Eventually, I was cuddled within the folds of dress in the back of a limo. Pecu was with Song for a week. It was just me and her. My heart thudded so hard I could feel it in my eyes.

"I love you," Jessy whispered, staring into my eyes.

"I know." I kissed her. "I love you."

The limo stopped. I helped Jessy out, then lifted her into my arms. She squealed. It was just like the movies. Man carries wife into their new home to start their new life together. I slammed the front door closed with my foot, and she leaped out of my hands. Her legs wrapped around my waist, lips pressing against mine furiously.

I carried her to the bed and laid her down soft. She stared at me with the most seductive smile I'd ever seen. It was hard to believe that I was finally getting to sleep with her again. We hadn't since I got her pregnant. I crawled on all fours to her belly and set my cheek against it, listening.

I pressed my lips to her belly. "I love you."

"Love you too," Jessy said out the side of her mouth in a baby voice.

I crawled a little farther up, kissing her body until I reached her mouth.

"What was that?" she demanded. Her eyes went wide.

"What?"

"Listen."

I froze, projecting my hearing out. "I don't —"

Jessy scrambled backward, her eyes wide, and pointed a finger at the doorway. I followed her finger.

"Miss me, Jimmyboy?"

Her face was more sunken than I'd ever seen it. Black circles made tiny islands of her eyes. Her teeth stubs poked through the crease in her lips. She waved a gun at us.

"Jessy, run as fast —"

Mom pointed the gun at the bed and fired. "Ah, ah, ah, no, no, no, no one's running anywhere, let's go have a talk, a nice little chat with the newlyweds, talk yes, just a talk."

Neither of us moved. "Mom —"

She fired into the ceiling. "Now! We'll talk now, in the dining room, get up, up!"

I stood and limped toward her. "Mom, she has nothing to do with anything. Leave her —"

The barrel of her gun crushed into my temple. White zapped through my vision. Jessy screeched. "Shut the fuck up, Jimmy, shut your chink up too, shut up, both of you in the dining room, now."

She ushered us into the living room.

"Oh, Jimmy, Jimmy, Jimmy." Stupro's tone was friendly. Two of the dining room chairs were set in the middle of the room. He stood behind them. "Never were very smart, were you? The date in the newspaper, really? Come, sit. Two chairs for the newlyweds."

"Mom, please, you have to listen."

"Both of you in the chairs, if I, me, I —" A shiver ran through mom's entire body, and she gasped air. "If I have to repeat myself, pretty gets a, Gnah! A bullet."

I gaped at mom, at Stupro. I could go for mom's gun. They'd overpower me, or I'd get shot, but it would make time, hopefully enough for Jessy to run.

"Sit, Jim," Jessy whispered. She sat in a chair herself.

She had no idea. It was either one of us. Or both.

Stupro forced me into a chair. He started with the duct tape. He circled tape around my chest then taped my arms to the armrests. Mom squatted in front of me as he started on Jessy.

"How we —" Twitch. "How we do this, Jimmy, long or fast?"

"Let her go."

"No problem, sure, Stupro, untape her, he said let her go, the great fucking Jimmy, Gnah! Got to listen to the great Jimmy." Her gun caved in my nose, and I might have passed out. When the room coalesced, I felt warm blood on my chin. "Don't be stupid, Jimmy, you want her let go, give me my son."

"I don't —" She hit me in the exact same spot.

I wailed.

"I'm not fucking around, we'll be here until I have my son, get him, Jim, get him here, get him here now!"

"Why?" I cried. "Why can't you leave us be? You don't care for anything. He's better off without you!"

Staring hard into my eyes, she folded her arms, unfolded them, and folded them again. "I do care. He's a baby. He's my baby. You were a baby once. Now look."

"He's better off, mom. Think about it. Maybe he'll not be ruined if you leave him —"

"Stop! No more, we're not debating, arguing, no, no, you're telling me where he is, now!"

Jessy's eyes were circles. She shook in her bounds, teeth clattering. Stupro stood above her, petting her hair, smirking.

"If I get Pecu, does she go free?"

"When, not if, I get Pecu, both of you go back to your wedding bed."

"Jim, don't," Jessy said. "You can't."

"You can, gnah, you have to, last chance."

"All right, just —"

"Jim, if you tell her, I'll never speak to you again. Don't do this."

I stared into Jessy's eyes. Instantly, I saw Song's strength. She meant what she said.

Mom must've seen what I seen. "Fine, you win, fine, Stupro, you're up."

He crouched in front of me, and we stared into each other's eyes. My eyes were leaking. His were dead. His lips curled at the edges. "We're going to get him back. And when we do —" His smile broadened. "I'm going to teach him all I know."

I yanked on the tape. It was too tight.

"Now." The legs of a chair screeched across hardwood until Jessy sat across from me. We locked eyes. "This is how this'll go. I'll start with her. Then you. When we have Pecu, I'll stop. Got it?"

"Don't tell him anything, Jim. I'll be fine. Don't! Okay, babe. Promise."

"Jessy, no. I can't. We —"

"Promise! If you tell them. You'll lose both of us."

"I... I'll try."

"No." Her look was penetrative. "Promise."

I cried. "I —"

"Don't bother," Stupro interrupted. "This is all very nice." He flipped open a butterfly knife. The tip traced Jessy's jawline. She cringed and whimpered. Stupro ripped her head back by her hair. "Last chance, Jimmy."

"Don't!" Jessy fought against her restraints. "Don't. You can't tell him."

"Jessy, I have to."

"No! Don't you fucking do it."

Stupro sighed.

The knife dug into her bottom lip. "Stop!" She tried to wiggle away. Stupro held her jaw in his hand. The knife went deep, dead center of her lip. It passed completely through. He stopped at the end of her chin.

Two flaps of flesh hung from her chin. Someone was screaming, then I ran out of air. "No. No!"

She cried. Blood drenched her wedding dress.

"Well, that was fun. I'm glad you didn't crack, Jimmy. I've got something good planned for you. Your mom says I can't kill you, but I thought of something almost as good." He moved behind me. I heard rustling. Jessy blanched. The strength was gone from her face.

Something loud turned on behind me. Jessy's eyes shot wide. "Mno!" she bawled, spitting blood. "Mno. Ndon't. Mstop."

Stupro strode around my chair. He held high a buzz saw.

I pulled at my bounds, yanked. "Stupro, don't." He held it forward in both hands. "Please." The blade blurred. "Stupro, stop!" I could feel the sound of it in my bones.

"Stop?"

He pressed the blade into my right wrist. Blood splashed my face before the pain hit. I screamed. Jessy screamed. The blade vibrated into bone, stopped. Stupro pulled it up, back, forth, until it started again. It sunk, found bone, and came to a grinding halt.

I shrieked. Stupro wiggled and pressed hard. I jerked, pulled, frantic. It jumped off the bone then found soft meat between my wrist and hand. It soared through the easy flesh, tendons giving the least resistance.

My hand flopped on the floor. Blood gushed twice with my heartbeat.

Mom was there. She pressed something into my wrist.

A frying pan, I realized. It was hot.

I lost consciousness.

14

The first time I woke, my fingers itched. I scratched them, found nothing but pain, and passed out. Next, I was awake long enough to recognize I was in one of the recovery rooms in Mr. Long's house. After that, wakings and sleepings blended.

A night came when holding my eyes closed wasn't enough to bring the void. A house that large makes a thorough kind of silence, and I listened to it. Eventually, I brought both my hands up and held them inches from my face. An IV hung from my left arm. My right arm was shorter. I cried until I slept.

"I can tell you're awake."

I peeled an eye open and was blinded by piercing sunlight. Howie sat next to my bed, a familiar man with a bruised face sat at the end. It might've been the following morning or three weeks later. I didn't know. "How long have I been out?"

He stared.

"That long?"

A nod.

I wiped my eyes and a surge of pain jolted from my right hand. Except... "I lost my hand."

"It wasn't lost," Howie said. "Someone took it."

The anger in his voice stirred me. "Where's Jessy? Howie! How — Where's —"

"Jessy's fine. Calm down or you'll have Vanessa in here."

I groaned. My hand hurt like someone was crushing my fingers and hand in a vise, but there were no fingers, there was no hand. I wanted to scratch it, but it wasn't there. My breathing came faster. My hand was gone. That meant it had all actually happened. That meant Jessy was hurt. My heart thudded in my chest. I squirmed to get up.

"Jim, stop!" Howie put a hand on my shoulder. "Don't think right now."

I studied the bandage encasing the end of my arm. I tapped at the bandage with my fingertips; jolts of pain coursed through my body each time, and my hand tingled. My right hand.

How the hell does it tingle?

"Listen to me, bro. Focus on my voice. That's right, breathe."

I listened to him as he lied in a droning tone but stared at the man at the end of my bed. I tried to imagine him without the swollen, ruined nose and the black bruises spreading from it, but his identity was lost to me. I'd seen him before though, that I knew.

His eyes stabbed into mine and glistened like he could burst into tears any moment. We stared like that until my breathing slowed then I turned.

"Jessy's fine?" I interrupted Howie's soothing rant.

"She... looks different. But she's recovered."

Stupro had given her three lips. "I want to see her."

"She's coming." Howie rubbed my shoulder. "Jim, the most important thing is that you guys are both alive. That trumps everything. Understand?"

"Howie, I — Everything. It's my fault."

He flicked my forehead. Hard. "Don't say that. And don't you dare say it to Jessy. Blame isn't what you two need right now, bro. You need each other. Be happy, be very fucking grateful, that you still have each other. Any other way, you two'd both be dead."

He was right. My mother and uncle were more likely to kill than show mercy, and I should've felt blessed to only have lost a hand and not my life. My new wife's life too. I was lucky. "You're right, Howie. Now, who the hell is that?"

"You don't recognize me, Jimmy?"

I knew instantly. "Dad!" *No.* "You've got to be kidding me. You're — You're..."

"I lost three hundred pounds."

His features were different without the roundness. His bulbous nose, bald pate, and huge ears were exactly how I remembered them. The rest of his face sagged like the drapes over a window.

Howie said, "We found him on the floor in your living room after. I'll give you guys a minute." He stared at dad until it was uncomfortable then left.

Dad wiped his eyes. "After you took Pecu, I realized. I have something to live for. You made me realize that son, by showing me. My kids need me. That, and eating myself to death wasn't working."

He said that last like a joke. I didn't laugh. "I haven't been gone that long. How did you lose so much weight?"

"Surgeries. I used what I'd managed to hide from your mother of my inheritance on surgeries. Liposuction and gastric bypass."

"Why are you here?"

"My kid needs me."

"All of your kids have needed you for years."

"I'm horrible. I know. I let you see terrible things. It's different now though. I swear. I want to help."

"And I should believe you?"

"I'll prove it."

I was exhausted. I closed my eyes.

"I've already done some good, Jimmy. You and Pecu got away, so I worked on Coitus and Coitum. They both moved away from their mother. Coitus lives in Nevada, and Coitum lives in Texas."

"So they're not..."

"No."

"How?"

"Coitum fell in love with someone else. It ended badly, but it was enough to piss his sister off. She wouldn't take him back."

"God, who could possibly?"

"A prostitute. I had to pay her a salary, but it worked."

I snorted.

"I mean it, Jimmy. I want to help. I'll never make up for my past. But I'm here now."

"Why were you like you were? I don't get the change of heart."

"When my parents died, I decided to eat myself to death. You going through what you did to save Pecu —"

The door swung open.

The stitches in her face had recently come out; I could tell by how red and angry the wounds still were. Not wound. Wounds. From the center of her forehead to the corner of her mouth ran a curved cut as vicious as the one that split her bottom lip. She winced when she saw me looking at the cuts, then winced at the way the wince pulled at her face.

"Jessy, no!" Vanessa was right behind her. "He shouldn't have company now. He — Who is that? Howie! I told you no. He's not out of the woods yet. The infection —"

Jessy stepped in.

"Dad," I said, "get out."

He scurried out, and, alone, we stared at each other. I had no idea what to say to her. I wanted to apologize, but I knew that'd anger her. I wanted to tell her she was still beautiful, but that'd anger her too.

She sat in the chair next to the bed and whispered something.

"What?" Tears rolled over her cheeks, down her healing face. "Jessy, don't. Please, don't." I felt tears on my own face. "I know it's messed up, but at least we still have each other. We'll get through this. What's important is that we're still alive."

She looked away from me and sobbed.

"They would have killed us. Jessy, you have to know that. We are lucky to have survived. I love you. I'll always —"

"The baby's dead!"

My thoughts crashed into a wall. That should have been my first question. After I saw she was alive, I should have asked about the baby. Our baby.

I couldn't speak.

"And Paul. I had to give them Paul. I'm sorry, Jim. He had the saw. You were unconscious, but he cut my face again anyway, said it was the rules. He was going to cut off your other hand. I couldn't watch, Jim. I had to give them Paul. I'm sorry, Jim."

I settled into my pillow. I could only think of one thing.

"No. I'm sorry."

My arm got infected, and I almost died. Apparently, when you amputate a hand a lot can go wrong. You have to be very careful how you cut. Stupro hadn't been careful. When he sawed, he hit bone, and tiny fragments shredded my flesh, causing a thousand tiny wounds within the massive one. The perfect breeding ground for infection.

If I wasn't spinning through nightmares of death, I was wishing for it. Everything hurt. My body. My hand. My insides. *My heart.* The poor, unborn child. The poor helpless brother. My disfigured wife. My hand. I wished to die.

"It looks good, Jim," Vanessa told me the first time I was coherent.

It looked like my hand had been cut off with no reason or form. It looked like burn scars stretched tight over the two gnarled bones.

"No," I told her. "It doesn't."

"You healed though. If you weren't so young, that infection would have killed you. You're lucky."

Those words had lost their worth. Lucky people hardly get called lucky. People who go through dreadful things get called lucky to ease the pain. It doesn't ease shit.

"You are healthy enough to move back in with Jessy. She needs you right now. She shouldn't have taken time from school."

I should have gone to her. I should have swallowed my emotions and made everything better for my wife. Instead, I sat in that bed and did nothing but stare at white walls, sleeping when I could, eating when I had to.

But she came to me.

She sat in the chair, and the coward I was stared at the wall. I felt tears leak from the corner of my eyes and I heard her mouth open and close a few times. She soon left.

It was harder than after Amanda, harder than after Rachel. I'd given this woman that I loved the hope of a beautiful future, then had been the cause of that future ripping away. Her face was ruined. Because of me. Her baby was dead. Because of me. She was married to the cause of all her problems in life.

Me.

And Pecu. I'd lost him. I'd lied to him about his mother. Why would his older brother, his one true caretaker, tell him such a lie? He must've hated me. I'd have hated me.

There came a time when I was healed. I still lay there in that bed. People came to visit me, Howie, Jessy, my dad, but they left once they realized they'd get no more than a grunt out of me.

I don't know how long it was that I stayed there after I was able to leave. Long enough to draw the attention of my boss.

"It's time, Jim," Mr. Long told me. "You're moving back with your wife."

I wanted to argue. I didn't. Shakily, I got dressed, pissed, and let a man drive me home, where I climbed into our unconsummated wedding bed and continued my sulk.

Jessy played the dutiful wife. Forced meals, forced showers, forced sleeping pattern, she forced me to remain human. A thousand things I wanted to say to her, anything to bring the passion back, but I didn't. I should have held her, kissed her, made love to her, something. She was hurting too. She needed comfort. But all I did was wallow.

Jessy manned up for the both of us though.

"Enough." She ripped the blankets off me. The clock read noon. "We have to do something."

"Do what?"

"Anything but this. Look at us, Jim. You haven't touched me since our wedding. I know I'm not as beautiful as I used to be, but you should still feel something. We're dying, Jim."

I clenched my jaw. What could I say?

"You want to know how I feel? There's only one way to fix this. One fricken way."

I waited. "How?"

"Paul. We have to get him back."

"Easier said than —"

"So you just want to stay like this!" she yelled. "They ruined my face, ruined your hand, killed our baby, and took your brother, our brother. Are we going to let them ruin our marriage?"

I stared. Then I got out of bed.

Howie flipped me to the mat in the gym. It was empty but for us. "They could be anywhere in the country, bro."

"I know." I climbed to my feet.

"They are probably on the move too. I would be."

I shook my head. "They moved somewhere secluded, somewhere random, and they're living as they always have."

He grabbed my left wrist and pulled me toward him. I was sick of it. All he had to do was incapacitate my left hand and I was helpless. I jammed my nub into his ribs as hard as I could three times, then ripped my hand away. The jabs left him breathless, and they hurt like nothing I'd ever felt. I wrapped my arm around his neck and threw him over my hip, landing across his chest.

He groaned. "That nub hurts." I shoved it in his face, rubbing it all over. "Ah! Stop. It's so disgusting. Get it off me!"

I pushed down with my legs so he couldn't wiggle free.

"Really, babe?"

I looked up at Jessy and blushed. "What are you doing here?"

"Was headed to my mom's, thought I'd peek in and see what you meant by getting your strength back. I would've never guessed it meant cuddling with Howie."

I helped Howie to his feet. "He was trying to convince me that saving Pecu is a lost cause."

"That's not what I said at all, bro. I'm just being realistic. This shit isn't going to be easy for us."

"Us?" Jessy and I said at the same time.

"What, you thought I wasn't going to go? It'll be me and you."

"And me," Jessy added.

"No," Howie and I said at the same time.

"Yes, I have every right —"

"It's not about rights," Howie interrupted. "It's about getting Paul back. I don't mean this offensively, Jessy, but you'll only get in the way. And distract, Jim. It will be better with just us two."

Inwardly, I praised Howie's name. I could tell by Jessy's face that he'd won a battle I could never have won on my own. Jessy understood logic. She would have only heard emotions had it come from me.

"Maybe you're right," she mumbled. "How long you going to be here, babe?"

"I could leave now if you need me."

"I don't need you... It's just..."

Two minutes later, Jessy and I were in the gym's shower. All those long months of our courtship then that long period after our disfigurements had to be made up for. It was better than I ever could have imagined. I won't go into detail, she's my wife after all, but she made love like a professional.

Since I'd realized what needed to be done, enjoyable things like sex became possible. Though I wasn't tracking Pecu yet, I knew I would be. I knew what had to be done. Knew it would be done. That knowledge made life possible. I didn't feel ashamed to laugh or exercise or make love. I would do what I needed to when it was possible. I had a new wife, and I'd enjoy her as much as I could while I could.

Somehow, in a way I find difficult to explain, that wife was more beautiful to me because of her scars. She'd received them because of me, in my war, and she never complained or blamed me once.

"I almost left," Howie said as Jessy and I came out of the shower in towels. "I thought you'd be quicker."

"I'm going to pretend that wasn't an insult."

"I've been thinking. About Paul. You've got your strength back."

"You want to leave now?" Jessy sounded panicked.

"No. There's something we need to do before we can leave though."

"What?"

"Ask Mr. Long."

I hadn't even thought of that. Howie had been working the entire time, and he'd told me that Mr. Long would give me as much time as

I needed before coming back to work. I'd almost been able to forget about the career I'd chosen.

"You're right," I said. "Let's go now." Howie and I sped to his house. After a lengthy sit in Mr. Long's waiting area, we were admitted to his study.

"Ah, Jim." It was the first time I'd seen him since he'd kicked me out of his house. "Good to see you."

"You too, sir."

"Please, have a seat. Both of you. You must be ready to get back to work. I'm sorry for everything you've been through, Jim, but I'm thrilled to know you're through it."

I glanced at Howie.

"Thank you for your concern, Mr. Long," I said. "But I'm here for something else."

His eyes bored into me. "I was the one who gave Paul to your mother. Did you know that?" I shook my head. "We came to an agreement, she and I. No more funny business. She leaves with her son and everything is forgotten. She goes away for good. No one follows."

"Sir, I can't just —"

"I refuse to allow her back into my life. Do you understand?"

"No, sir. I don't."

He leaned over his desk. "I'll spell it out. No one, you Howie, or otherwise, will be chasing after her. She took back what was rightfully hers and that's the end of matters. Put it behind you, Jim."

"After everything she put me through?" I stood so fast that the chair tipped over. Howie put a hand on my arm. "Put me and Jessy through? I'm to let it go?"

"You have to, Jim."

"Have you seen my wife? Have you seen this!" I shoved my nub close to his face. "My baby's dead. Let that go? You're out of your mind. What about family, Mr. Long?"

The words hit him like a blow. He flinched then the muscles on the side of his face flexed. This man had preached to me the importance of family and how you treat family. Now he wanted me to abandon mine to people that hurt me and my wife so viciously?

"Jim," Howie whispered. "Sit down."

I was leaning over the table and over the top of Mr. Long. I stood straight, patted the wrinkles from my shirt, picked up the chair, and sat. I almost apologized, but instead I stared at Mr. Long. He held the eye contact until he sighed. "I can't let you go."

"You can," I said.

He shook his head. "I made a deal, Jim. So let me make this easier. I forbid you —" His eyes turned to Howie. "Or anyone else from chasing after those people. They are a cancer on my family that I've removed once and for all. You've been ordered, Jim, Howie. Put this behind you. It. Is. Over."

We left without another word.

"We're still going," Howie said. We were parked outside my house. "Doesn't matter what he says."

"It does matter, Howie, and you know it."

"All right, it matters. But we're still going."

"I am." I put my hand up before he could speak. "Howie, we don't even know where they are. I appreciate your willingness to give up everything for me, but I won't let you throw it away for nothing. Maybe I should forget it."

He flicked my forehead. "Shut up, bro. We'll figure something out. There has to be a way to find him. We'll figure this out."

"See you later." I got out of the Audi.

Dad was sitting on the couch watching Jerry Springer. The scene was eerily familiar. I still was not used to dad's new role in my life. He wanted to help me, I wanted to let him, but neither of us could figure out what he could do.

"Have a seat, son." I sat and he muted the TV. "Everything all right?"

"You know it's not."

"It hasn't been for a while, but you managed to keep the look you have on your face away."

"My boss ordered me to give up on Pecu."

"Any that's not what you're going to do." It sounded like a question.

"Maybe I should. It is her son. And look at me. I turned out all right. Maybe Pecu —"

"Do you remember that cat in Nevada? before Spinny and Stupro robbed those Mexicans." I'd found a cat's head in Pecu's room. How could I forget? "Or that dog, the city before Nevada?" Pecu had got hold of a staple gun. The poor thing had looked like a croquet course. "Do you remember —"

"I get it."

"You weren't ever like that, Jimmy. We can't leave the boy with them. We can't. They'll ruin him. Do you know what happened that night? the night they took Pecu back." I shook my head. "I was there, waiting in the car. They tried to make me stay at the hotel, but I got in the car and refused to leave it. I was there to make sure no one got hurt."

I opened my mouth.

"I know, Jimmy. I failed. When Spinny and Stupro got out to follow you into the house, Spinny put a gun in my face. Me. Her husband. The man who took her in when she was running from whatever she was running from all those years ago. The man who asked not one question about the slave she had. The man who let her spend his inheritance."

His chin fell to his chest, and he shook with sobs. I rubbed his back with my nub.

"I was forced to wait in the car, son. I could help no one if I was dead, and there was no doubt that your mother would have killed me."

"If you were in the car, how did you end up with a crushed nose?"

"I heard the saw. I heard your scream then Jessy's scream. I couldn't listen. I ran in. I was hit with something as I came through the front door. Everything was over when I woke up with my hands tied behind my back."

He went quiet. I could imagine the thoughts he was having. His son, whom he'd decided to save, had lost a hand while he lay unconscious but feet away. Some words came to mind to ease his guilt, but I kept quiet. This was something he had to learn to live with on his own. There was nothing anyone could say to make it better. I knew the feeling well.

Dad sighed and lifted his head. "I'm telling you this to show you. I have to get Pecu away from those people. If they'll do what they did to you, do what they did to us, they'll do anything. We can't let there be three people in this world like that, not if we can prevent it. If you're not going, tell me. I'll leave alone."

"Leave alone?"

"I've been waiting for you to heal. I'm going no matter what."

"We don't even have a way to find them."

"You don't."

My mouth fell open. "The hell does that mean?"

"It means you don't have a way to find them. I do."

"Why didn't you say something?" I demanded.

"Why didn't you ask?"

I stared at dad. Then I decided. I ran to my room and went straight to the closet. Jessy jumped as I came in, and I told her I was leaving. One-handed, I tore clothes from my closet and stuffed them into a suitcase.

"Move, babe." Jessy pushed me away from my suitcase and started folding the ball of clothes. "Do you have to leave right this instant? Slow down."

I dashed into the bathroom. "I have to leave tonight." I tossed some razors toward my wife. "Before I see Howie again." Threw some soap. "He'll know I have a plan the next time I see him." Toothbrush, toothpaste. "I can't hide anything from him."

I ran out of the bathroom, straight into Jessy's palm. "Stop." She wrapped her arms around my waist and placed her head on my chest. "You're not going to run out of here without telling me what's going on."

"Sorry." We sat on the bed. "I have a way to find Pecu. Well, dad has a way."

"Thank god. Why can't Howie know?"

I stared at her for a long time. If I told her, she'd want to use her own solution to the problem. I knew what that was. I wanted to use my own solution. It was safest for everybody. "I want —"

"Don't you dare lie to me," she interrupted.

"I hate how you do that. Look, Howie can't come with me. Mr. Long forbade us from chasing after Pecu, and I'm not going to ruin his life for mine."

"It's not only for you though. It's for Paul. It's for me. Howie won't let you leave alone."

"That's why I have to leave before he finds out."

"Well, why don't I —"

"You can't go to Mr. Long," I interrupted.

"You're right. That is annoying."

I snorted. "If you go to him, he'll forbid you from letting me go too."

"I can make him see though. Uncle Richard has too big a heart."

"No, Jessy. I've already decided."

Challenge sparkled in her eyes. I prepared myself to accept defeat and try it her way. "Fine," she said. "But you're not going to just run out of here. Who knows how long it will be until I see you again. You're going to give me a proper goodbye."

With my nub, I traced the scar on her forehead down her cheek. Then the scar on her lip. She was still the most beautiful thing I'd ever seen. I gave her a proper goodbye. That time was different than most. I could say a thousand corny things about the experience, but I won't. We made love for the sake of each other, not for pleasure or release or to make a child. It was the closest I'd ever been to someone.

It was near three in the morning as I drug my suitcase from our bedroom. I stopped in the living room.

"Sup, bro."

Howie sat on one end of the couch, dad on the other. A Jerry Springer rerun was on the TV. "What the hell's going on?" I demanded.

"I could ask you the same thing." He smiled. "Looks like you're all packed. About time."

"Why — Who — How —"

"Sorry, Jimmy," dad said. "I get that you're being honorable for his sake and all that, but we need all the help we can get."

"Howie, Mr. Long —"

"Screw Mr. Long. If he doesn't see that saving this little boy is the right thing to do, then I don't want to work for the man anyway. I'm going, bro. Get used to the idea."

I stared at Howie. I stared at dad.

"Fine you bastards. Let's go."

15

The place was eerie as they come. A thick brick wall, some ten feet high, stretched left and right from the gate as far as I could see. Atop the wall was barbed wire running jagged in two lines, both rusted and full of plant debris. The gate was a tunnel of stone with two black, steel gates keeping it barred. A weather-worn sign topped the gate.

Mental Hospital.

Over the wall, a hill dominated the scene, a hospital dominated the hill. A dirt road bordered by dead or dying old oaks wound its way from the gate to the hospital, zig-zagging strangely across the property.

The hospital was as run-down as the rest of the place, with rusted bars over the windows and bleeding color down the bricks. It seemed taller than it was wide, some five or six stories, and each roof came to a sharp point like an old cathedral.

It'd taken days of driving nonstop to reach this place outside some hick town in Nebraska. Dad had been tightlipped enough about where we were headed to send me and Howie into brooding silence more than once, and now that we were here I had a million more questions than I had while we drove.

"Why are we here, dad?"

"Stupro."

"He's here?"

"He'll come here."

"Why?"

"He always comes here."

"Why, dad? Who is in there?"

He shook his head.

My gaze left him. The dirt lot beneath the hospital's wall was hardly more than a shoulder off the highway that had brought us here. Four other cars were parked facing the wall, each with a nameplate in front of it. They all looked like they'd have a hard time starting, let alone driving. The new Taurus we'd rented for the trip was as fancy as a Mercedes next to them, and only highlighted the poverty I'd seen since we arrived.

"So, your plan is to sit here and wait for Stupro to come, then put the tracker on his bike?"

"Pretty much."

"What if he doesn't come?"

"He will."

"What if he doesn't?"

"He will."

"Dad! You've got to give me more than that. How long are we —"

"Bro," Howie interrupted from the back seat. "He doesn't want to talk about it."

"He'll be here, Jimmy. He comes every year around the same time. You know he does. Don't you remember him being gone when you were growing up?" Of course, I did. "We just got to keep an eye out for him. He should be here soon."

"Well, where we going to park?"

"Yeah," Howie said. "We're suspicious as hell right here."

"What about there." Dad pointed behind us, across the highway. A little cove of willows was nestled in a field this side of the tree line. I put the car in drive and crept past it.

"Perfect." I pressed the gas. "Let's go into town for the night. I'll start the watch in the morning."

"Here" Howie pressed forward a little black box, the GPS tracker. "See the magnetic side. Stick it on the bike. Make sure he can't see it."

The highway went straight through the town, one of those blink-and-it's-gone types of places littering America. I turned onto a side street, drove for three blocks, and the pavement turned to dirt. We shared a look. I turned the car around and parked at the café we'd seen at the beginning of the settlement, the only place that looked public.

"Anyone see a hotel or something?" I asked.

"Haven't seen anything," Howie said. "This whole place is creepy, bro."

He was right. The town was as shabby as the hospital. Weeds instead of grass. White walls faded to yellow. Picket fences with paint peeling and whole planks of wood missing. *And the people*, I realized. We hadn't passed a car, pedestrian, anyone since we'd got here.

Tap, tap, tap.

I let slip a squeal and drew my fist back to swing. A man stood outside my window with his thumbs wedged behind a square, golden belt buckle holding up a pair of starched blue jeans. I rolled down the window. The man bent at the waist while removing a bucket-sized cowboy hat.

"You boys lost?"

Scraps of greasy, grey hair were stretched tight over a bald pate in mockery of a comb-over. Deep pockmarks freckled his cheeks and deeper lines surrounded his eyes and mouth. Sun damage gave the face the hue of rust.

"Cat gotcha tongues? What you all doing here?"

Dad recovered first. "Looking for a place to stay, sir. Is there a hotel or something around?"

"Why for? Nobody comes to stay down around these ways. What you people doing here?" He stood tall and took a step back. I noticed the pistol on his hip, which his hand settled on, and a star badge next to the lapel of his red and white flannel. He glanced at me like I was all that was wrong with the world. "Calerforner plates don't much get seen these ways neither. You boys drug running? What have you? One of yous best start talking."

"Look, sir." Dad leaned over my lap to talk to the man. "We got family in the hospital outside of town here. We're going to be visiting him for a while. Need somewhere to say."

"That hospital ain't got nobody new in years. A fistful of years, I'd say."

"He's been in there a long time."

"And you just now coming?"

"It's been too long," dad said. "I'm past due."

He made a noise. Might've been contempt, but I think it was a laugh. "A man's got to respect another man's guilt, I suppose. Look boys, we don't get tourism these ways. No motels, hotels, or the like. But if you all got money, I'm sure I could find you a place to lay your head. Long as I can assure no trouble from yous. You going to be trouble, there Chinaman?"

Howie's teeth grinding was audible. "No, sir."

"Good. Go in now, get yourself some grub. I'll get you all a place to settle. Tell Betty Anne Jack sent you."

Betty Anne was the oldest person I ever met. Her eyes were glossed with a white film, and she hollered when she spoke, demanded you holler when speaking too. Her café had two booths and a bar. We took a booth.

"What you all want!" she screamed. "We're only serving chicken-fried steak and eggs today."

"We'll take three plates then."

"What?"

"We'll take three plates!"

It was damn near the best breakfast I ever ate. Betty Anne kissed my face after I told her as much too. Bells jingled, and Jack stomped into the café. "Found just the place. You boys ready? Follow me up."

He led us down a dirt road through thick forest. Ten minutes we drove, then came upon a cabin. It was the end of the road, like it led to this place's front door. The cabin was square and a stream of smoke drifted out a chimney dead center of the roof.

"This here's Russel," Jack said as we closed our doors and moved up to the man who'd come out of the cabin. "He don't usually take on visitors, but he needs the cash."

Russel looked like he wore the same set of furs every day. He did. Russel smelled like he had been covered in blood for weeks. He had. Russel seemed like he could outlift me and Howie combined. He could. I'd never met a man like that, someone living off the land, and I was as intrigued as I was terrified.

Jack hopped in his truck without another word and sputtered back down the road. Russel stared at us. We stared at him. "Thanks for taking us in," dad said. "We shouldn't be here long."

Russel grunted, turned his back to us, and left the door open after going into the cabin. I gagged as I entered. A huge carcass hung from the rafters in the back corner of the single room. An elk or deer or something, it was split open down the center of its chest and stomach. The fur was gone. The red meat glistened, reflecting the fire in the open fireplace.

Russel pointed to a pile of blankets on the dirt floor opposite the dead animal. "For you." He sat on a stool and picked up a knife. "Hunnerd a night."

"A hundred dollars?" I exclaimed. I scowled at the soiled blankets, at the hanging carcass. Russel grunted and sliced a long chunk of the animal.

"Dad." I turned away from the sight. "How long are going to have to be here?"

He swallowed. "Hopefully not long."

It was long. Much, much too long. Living with that man was horrifying, and I grew up in a house with Stupro in it. Russel almost never spoke. When he did, you'd wished he hadn't.

"Last night was a bit cold, huh Russel?" I said one morning in an attempt to increase the fuel added to his fire.

"It was once so cold on a hunt, I slept inside my dead prey."

That was the end of that conversation. I would have rather slept outside, away from that man and his hobbies, but the late summer air was too cold for me after living in California for so long. You never get used to sleeping in a room with a body hanging from the ceiling. I'd hoped that once he finished butchering that first beast it would be the end of the experience, but he had a new one up the very same day he took the remains of the last down. It made shifts of watching the hospital very appealing.

Staring at a dilapidated mental hospital was better than sharing the day with Russel by a thousandfold, and all three of us were willing to throw fists if another tried to steal our turn, which still we tried to do. We'd agreed that only one person would go at a time. In case Russel decided one of us was to hang from the rafters instead of some game, two of us had a better chance of fighting him off. Not much better, to be honest, but enough to keep a team at the cabin.

We rented an ancient Ford truck from Russel, one that he never used but cost more than it would've been to buy it outright, and parked it in our willow spot outside the hospital. Every eight hours, two would drive out to the spot and pick up the other. On the way back to Russel's we'd stop and eat at Betty Anne's. That was our life. Russel's, Betty Anne's, and the hospital.

I loved my time in that Ford truck. I spent the hours writing to my wife. Learning to write left-handed was a challenge, but I'd never had very good penmanship anyway. Everything I could never tell Jessy in person was suddenly easy to share. All the personal, darker things I wanted my wife to know but had not the courage to say poured out. It was actually during this time that I first contemplated putting my life into a chronicle.

I started with my earliest memories, which were of school and how I always desired to achieve the highest marks. I wrote about the period when Pecu was born and how I finally felt like I had a companion in this world. That was the extent of things positive to write about. The rest were the things I knew made me different.

The man that mom had buried after he overdosed. The Mexicans my mother and uncle had murdered for drugs. The animals in varied degrees of torture I'd ripped from my brother's hands. The way sunlight had reflected off Amanda's bloody ass when I'd found her; the haunting I'd been left with forever after. The robbery in Sacramento. The innocent Christian girl, Rachel.

Everything came out in those letters. She had no avenue to immediately respond — when she tried to talk about it on our nightly calls, I told her it wasn't the time — but I think that was what made it so easy to share. Her disgust in me was thousands of miles away.

I read through the letter I was writing. I'd run out of things to say about myself, a feat for any man to achieve, and had started blabbering. "Dad isn't telling us what this hospital thing is about," I read in a whisper. "He and Stupro know someone in there. It's obvious. Dad told me that his parents were dead. He said he has no other family. Just us kids and Stupro. It's family in there though, I know it."

I set the letter on the seat and stared at the hospital. Dark clouds formed behind it, and a wind blew the willows into a percussive cacophony. *Why does dad get so weird about this place?*

"Who's in there?" I whispered.

A car door slamming popped my eyes into focus. A man wearing a short-sleeve button-up and slacks approached the gate. Shift change at the hospital was 8 A.M., 4 P.M., and 12 A.M., not 7 P.M., which my watch read. The man pressed his finger to something on the wall beside the metal gate and leaned his mouth close to it. Hands in his pockets, the man hopped from one foot to the other.

The golf cart that I'd seen the staff use to get from the gate to the hospital came down the winding dirt road until I couldn't see it behind the wall. Moments later, I saw the cart through the bars of the gate. A man unlocked it and let the visitor in.

A visitor.

The next day, at the same time, I jogged to the gate and pressed the circular button beneath the circular speaker. "Yes?" came a woman's voice.

"Yes, hi," I said. "I'm here to visit a relative."

"Did you schedule an appointment?"

I pushed some dirt with my toe. "No."

Silence. "Who's your relative?"

Dad had said *him* to Jack the sheriff. "Mr. Torquere."

"Oh, Stupro? Why didn't you schedule?"

"Uh —" I checked the highway both ways. "This isn't Stupro."

The speaker went dead for a full thirty seconds. "One moment, I'll send someone down."

The summer air was hot, but my teeth clattered.

The chain rattled and clattered to the ground. A man in a grey uniform swung the gate open far enough to let me through. He mumbled something I took to mean get in the passenger seat of the golf cart.

We stopped at the bottom of a wide, stone staircase leading up to double doors just as wide. I climbed out of the golf cart and craned my neck back. A crow cawed and landed on one of the lower turrets, hopping, turning in place, until it looked me in the eye. It cawed again.

"Come on, son."

The man was at the top of the stairs holding one door open. I looked back up but the crow was gone. I marched up the stairs and squeezed by the man. Inside, everything was white and clean to a shine. A stainless steel, waist-high desk stood opposite the door, two metal chairs were left and right of me, and two tall doors were left and right of the desk. A woman smiled and came forward.

"Hello, my name is Dr. Rasheed." She was of Indian descent, with tan and flawless skin. She must have been on the far side of fifty but was still good-looking. Her hair was in a tight bun, and she wore a white, knee-length lab coat.

We shook. "James Torquere."

"Another Torquere? What a surprise."

"Yes, you've met my father."

"Stupro?"

I shoved down the urge to cringe. "Yes."

"He's been coming here for twenty years, never mentioned a son."

I broke eye contact and studied my feet. The moment drew out.

"Course, he doesn't talk about much. Pleasure to meet you, Mr. Torquere."

"Please, call me James."

"I have to say, you look like your uncle. The resemblance is striking."

"I — uh." *Uncle?* "Thank you."

She giggled. "You'll see what I mean. Follow me."

We went through one of the doors behind the desk. It opened into a long hallway, white as the rest of the place. Lining the hallway were doors like none I'd seen before. They were massive, steel, and almost featureless. At eye level, there were covered slots that were slidable. A large handle extended from each, a keyhole beneath it. Those doors could keep in a demon.

"Peter loves this time of year, I can tell." Dr. Rasheed led me down the hallway. It seemed impossibly long; the building hadn't seemed so large from the outside. "He knows he has a visit coming. He'll be tickled to get two this year."

"I've always wanted to meet him, my uncle Peter. But father has never allowed it. I'm eighteen now though. Figured I could come alone."

"Ah. Stupro probably wouldn't be too happy about that, would he?"

I looked away, feigning admonishment.

"I won't tell him, James. I'm happy Peter gets to meet his nephew. I grow close to everyone here."

"How long have you worked here?"

"Oh, thirty some years."

"No?" I looked at her again. "You're too young."

She smiled. "A charmer." She stopped at a door. "Here we are." There were no identifying features, numbers, names, or marks, on the door. She slid open the eye slot and peered in. "He's not lucid. You can go in."

"Not lucid?"

"Right. We couldn't allow you in if he was. He can get violent. Just go in and talk to him. He hears you, though he won't respond."

"Can't he talk?"

"I'm sure he can. When he got here, he called me a vile bitch." She said it with a smile. "That was over twenty years ago though. I haven't heard him say a word since. Go ahead. Introduce yourself. I'll be right outside the door."

She unlocked it and pushed me in. I heard it lock.

Peter Torquere's back faced me. He stood over a four-legged foldable table, whistling a melody, which sounded like some kind of child's song, a note or two different from twinkle twinkle little star. On the table were three or four little play pots and pans, each a different color. The only other piece of furniture in the room was a twin-sized bed. The walls, floor, and ceiling were pillowed.

"Hello, Peter," I said.

His tune cut mid-note. Slow, he turned.

Our eyes met.

"Dad?"

We both flinched at the utterance. His eyes went wide. Dark eyes, dark hair, round facial features, we truly did look identical.

"Dad! I've missed you." Two long strides and the man hugged me. "I knew you'd be here in time for dinner. I told them so. Sit, dad." I sat on his bed as he went back to his table and tinkered with his toy cookware. "Helluo and Stupro tried telling me that you weren't going to come to eat, but I knew you would eventually. I wish they were here. When are they coming, dad?"

"I — uh. I don't know."

"We'll eat without them then. I've been cooking all day. I'm the best cook in the family, huh dad?"

"Sure."

He scooped invisible contents out of a red frying pan with a yellow spoon. The bed bounced as he plopped down next to me, our legs touching. I stared at his face. Even with the age difference, we could've been mistaken for twins. The only difference was our eyes. They were the same shape and color only his were off, like they were missing something.

"Well, try it."

I took the plastic plate he offered me without taking my eyes off him. He stared back, but he obviously saw something other than myself. I remembered what the doctor said a moment ago. Not lucid. I pretended to eat.

"This is very good, Peter. Thank you."

"Why do you keep calling me that?"

"What should I call you?"

"Perire. Don't you always say Peter is the name dumb people call me because they can't figure out how to say my real name?"

My grandparents had come up with odd names. Stupro, Helluo, Perire. "When's mom going to be home," Perire asked. "Should I start dinner for her too?"

"It's all right Pa — Pe — Perire. We'll wait until she gets here. I want to ask you some questions."

He set down his plate.

"Why are you here?"

"We live here."

"Look around you." His eyes left mine. "You're in a hospital. What happened to —"

The lock on the door cranked. "That's enough," Dr. Rasheed said. "Come with me, Mr. Torquere."

I stood. Perire's arms wrapped around my neck. "Love you, dad. Next time, I'll make steak, your favorite."

It took some time to gather myself in the hallway, and Dr. Rasheed kept quiet while I did.

"You must look like his father," Dr. Rasheed said. Her smile was large and genuine.

"You said he doesn't speak."

"He hasn't in twenty years. You triggered something good, James, but I had to stop you."

"Why?"

"You were drawing attention to reality."

We walked toward the entrance. "And that's a bad thing? I would think that it'd be better for a person to live in reality than some fantasy they made in their head."

"Normally, yes." We walked in silence until we got to the door to the reception room. "In Peter's case —" She stopped from opening the door to look me in the eye. "It isn't better. It's far worse."

16

At Dr. Rasheed's encouragement, I visited Peter every day. She told me that in all the years she'd known him, never had so much improvement been made. He not only talked to me, but had started talking to the staff. He slept entire nights. He'd even been allowed to go outside.

I needed it too. We might've just met each other, but Perire was family – real family like dad and Pecu and Jessy, not Stupro, mom, and the twins. If my visiting him made his life even a tiny bit better, it was my duty to visit.

Most days, we would sit in his room, and he'd cook for me or we'd play cards. Sometimes, we walked the hallways. Perire them as some sort of shopping center, where he'd buy food. On two occasions, I was allowed to take him outside. He'd smiled so large that I felt like I'd managed to atone, at least by a fraction, for some of my dreadful sins.

Dr. Rasheed had set some ground rules. For one, I had to get used to him calling me dad and was instructed to treat him like a son. She said the father-son dynamic had something to do with his initial psychosis, and that if it could be repaired it might do something toward making him better. Another rule was that I could not draw attention to reality.

"If you want to be in his life," Dr. Rasheed had told me, "you'll have to live in his world."

I managed to learn some small scraps of information about his, dad's, and Stupro's childhood during our time together too. It came in bursts.

"Can I play football like Helluo, dad?"

"Sure, Perire. If you —"

"If you don't want me to, I won't," he sputtered in one breath, flinching away from me. "I'll do whatever you say, dad. I'm not like Stupro."

Or another time.

"I like when you're happy, dad."

"You too, son."

"It doesn't hurt."

When he'd start talking about events in his past, I tried to nudge him on, but it was difficult to keep him going without being too direct. Dr. Rasheed had thoroughly warned me about driving Peter into lucidity. I had to be careful to stay in character, which was sometimes difficult when Peter spoke of memories I, as his father, was supposed to have shared with him.

"You remember the Christmas when you got us a puppy, dad?"

I nodded.

"How old was I?"

"Oh," I drawled like it was hard to remember. "Five or six."

"I thought eight. He slept in the room with me and Helluo, remember? Stupro was mad."

"Why was he mad?" I asked. Stupro had no feelings, of this I was sure. "Why do you think?"

"He told me why. Told me why he did what he did too. But he said I can't say."

"Perire, you better —"

His face scrunched and he jerked away from me. "Don't! I'll tell you. Stupro said we shouldn't take gifts from a man like you, is why he... did what he did."

"Killed the puppy?" Wasn't too hard to guess.

Eyes brimming with tears, he nodded.

"Perire," I said. "Why did Stupro say you couldn't take a gift from me?"

"His words, dad, not mine!"

"I know, son. Tell me what he said."

"That you're weak. You and mother both. That you had kids to fit in because society demands it. He said..."

That was it. He jumped to his feet and pretended to cook, humming his nursery rhyme at a frantic tempo.

I'd pieced together a narrative of their childhood from the things Perire shared and what I already knew about dad and Stupro. Their parents had been wealthy. Stupro, being the psycho I knew well, was in a constant power struggle with them. My dad was the favorite. Perire was the baby. Their father beat the shit out of them, seemingly often. Their mother allowed it.

None of that did anything to explain how Perire ended up in an insane asylum and dad ended up a worthless glutton. Stupro, I believe, had always been the person I knew, but I had the feeling that Peter and dad had once been normal.

"You're early," Ron the groundskeeper said as he unlocked the gate with a giant set of keys. Howie, dad, and I had traded shifts to switch up the monotony. I watched Stupro from seven to three now.

"Have some things to do later."

He slid his keys into the golf cart, and we started up the hill. It was beautiful out. Birds sang all around us. The sun was warm on my face. The sky was a perfect blue. All the eeriness of the hospital had disappeared. It'd become familiar.

Ron left his keys in the cart and followed me into the hospital, where he picked up a mop and went to work. Dr. Rasheed escorted me to Perire's room. "Good morning, Perire." I sat on the end of his bed. "Ready for breakfast?"

He scurried to his table-stove. "Take me two minutes."

He tinkered then brought me a blue plate. "What is it?"

"Grits."

Plate in my hand, I pretended to spoon it in my mouth with my nub. "Mmm."

Perire's fingers snapped around my wrist, grip so strong it hurt. He brought my disfigurement close to his face. His eyebrows came together.

"Dad —" He choked. His eyes met mine. They were different. "Who are you?" He let go of my hand. "Where am I?"

"Perire, be calm." I stood slowly. "Everything is fine."

"Not. Not fine." His hands went to his head, fingers gripped hair, and he pulled. "I didn't want to. I didn't want to!"

I rose and backpedaled to the door. "Perire, listen to me. Hear my voice. It's all right."

"It's not!" he screeched loud enough to hurt my ears. "Kill me." He paced, pulling his hair. "You have to kill me."

"Listen —"

"AHHHH!" He pulled his fingers from his hair, shoved the soft part of his wrist between his teeth, and clenched his jaw closed. Blood sprayed from his mouth. He spit, spraying red. "The only way!"

He moved his wrist then bit a new spot. The door behind me crashed open, and I was shoved out of the way. Ron and two others tackled Perire. Pools of bright blood soaked into the pillowed floor.

"Someone, please!" He cried as his arms were secured. "I have to die." Little whimpers. "Please."

"James. Out!" Dr. Rasheed rushed in, pressing a bandage to Perire's wrist. My feet stayed planted. "Out. Now!" I went into the hallway. Dazed, I found my way to the reception room and sat in a chair. I was there a long time, maybe hours. Dr. Rasheed sat across from me eventually.

"Is it always like that?" I whispered after the silence had gone long enough.

"No." She sighed. "Usually he doesn't say anything."

"He just..."

"Screams and tries to kill himself? Yes."

"Is he better now?"

"Yes. We've treated his wounds and put him in a secure place."

I imagined a straitjacket in a padded closet. "How long will he be like that?"

"The longest was a week. The shortest a few hours. There's no way to be certain. James, how did you trigger him? It must be documented." Eyes to the floor, I held up my right arm and let the sleeve fall away from my nub. "I see. You should go, James. You won't be able to see him again today. I'll get Ron to drive you down."

My head was so full of Perire, of what I'd caused, that I noticed dad and Howie too late. "What the hell was that?" dad demanded. He was in the passenger seat of the Taurus. "What were you doing in there?" I stared into his face for a while then shrugged. "Get in the car!" We sped from the gate. "Jimmy, what was that?"

I didn't have the energy to lie. "What did you expect? I had to know."

"Leave him alone! I mean it."

"What happened?" I asked.

"I said leave it alone."

"Tell me why he's like that."

"Leave it alone!" He sounded like a hysterical little kid. His face was scrunched tight, eyes leaking streams, mouth drooling. "Please!" He snorted snot. "Just leave it alone, Jimmy."

I'd never seen him act like that. I left it alone.

❦

Russel burped, smiling at me from his side of the cabin. We'd made him rich in our time staying with him, and the man spent all the money on one thing. Every night we'd give him a hundred, and every night he'd come back with a mason jar full of clear liquid.

He winked at me and blew a kiss.

"Come on, dad. Howie's probably ready to trade."

The sun was still hours away, but I had to get out of there. All night, the man had been giving me looks. The only thing I could think about was our size difference. Russel was the size of a bear. Bundled up in all that fur, smiling at me with those predator eyes. I'd have rather faced Stupro. And having dad with me instead of Howie only made it worse.

I drove and took my time, making my mind stay focused on the road and the waking forest. We got to the hospital about the same time the sun crested the horizon. "Screwing me out of an hour?" Howie greeted me, hopping out of the truck.

"Russel's drunk again."

"Scared he might try you this time?" Neither of us laughed.

"I'll see you in a few hours."

"Listen, bro. Your dad is really stressed about this whole thing. Whatever's in that hospital is his past. Let him bury it."

I nodded because I didn't know what else to do. I hadn't gone in since the incident, not because of anything Howie or dad had said, but because I was still shaken up. The man had opened his veins with his teeth, for Christ's sake.

The first couple hours of that shift, I tried to explain to my wife what had happened with Perire the week prior, attempting to explain how I felt about it all. After the fourth crumpled piece of paper, I gave up. I settled my head back to catch up on some sleep.

A rumble jerked me awake. The sun was high. I shifted up, rubbed my eyes, and listened for the noise. It grew louder. From the west, a motorcycle appeared. The bike rolled to a stop in front of the hospital gate. He stood off the bike, stretched, and lowered the black bandana covering his face.

Uncle Stupro.

He pressed the button and leaned in front of the microphone. My hands tightened around the steering wheel. My pulse thundered in my ears. My palms sweated. I could hardly breathe.

Ron appeared on the other side of the gate and let Stupro in. The golf cart made its way up the road, then they went inside the hospital.

I ripped open the glovebox and pulled out the black GPS device. I ran across the street bent at the middle, making myself as small as I could. Once I was close enough, I dove, landing in the dirt beneath his tires, peeling the skin from one side of my body.

I placed the GPS on the underside of the gas tank. Crouching, I circled the bike, making sure it wasn't visible from any angle. It wasn't. I sprinted back to the Ford, jumped inside, covered myself in the blanket we kept there, and listened.

Everything was silent. For another three hours. I spent the time wondering what to do. I'd accomplished what we had come there for, we could now follow Stupro anywhere he went, but leaving was betrayal now. I'd met Perire, couldn't unmeet him, and felt like I owed him something. Was I going to abandon him to live forever hospitalized?

Stupro came out, got on his bike, and left. Just like that. Mission accomplished. I could have started the Ford, driven to Russel's, and left that place behind me to do what I sought out to do.

But I stayed in the truck and waited.

Lying on the ground, staring at the stars, I wondered what I was supposed to do. I'd been wondering all day. I needed to save my brother before he turned into our uncle. The feeling was urgent, but for some reason I stayed.

The cabin door slammed shut, and footsteps came from behind me. They stopped a few feet away.

I spoke. "Dad, I want to help Perire. What if we can help him? What if all he needs is family? We could talk him through his lucid moments. It would take time, but maybe we could heal him. He's family."

He stayed quiet.

I sighed. "We have to try, dad."

Still quiet.

"Dad? What do you think —"

A huge hand wrapped around my neck. My back, then my feet, left the ground. He brought our faces together. Russel's mouth reeked of alcohol. "No more thinking." He wore that sick smile. "Just acting."

I kicked, clawed at his fingers, and jerked my body. His grip was tight. My scream came out as a croak. With his free hand, he ripped at my jeans. He turned me and put me in a chokehold.

"No —" I gasped. "Stop."

"Shush..."

My pants came off. He dug at my underwear. We lowered to the dirt. I thrashed in earnest, trying for anything, an eye to dig my finger into, flesh to bite. I felt him wiggling behind me, knew what he was doing, but was helpless to stop it.

He took off his own pants.

I felt it on the back of my legs. He was four hundred pounds and proportionate. I shrieked despite the arm crushing my windpipe. I reacted, grabbed a fistful of testicles and squeezed. Squeezed hard.

He roared. Releasing my neck, trying to jerk away, Russel scooted on the ground. I squeezed harder and scooted with him. "No! Oww. Let go. Leggo!"

I jammed my nub into his throat then his eye then his throat again. His hands grabbed for his neck. I hit him again. He fell back and curled up, trying to dodge my swings, and I released his testicles. I postured up and stomped. Anywhere I could find with my foot, I stomped. Head, ribs, neck, stomach, again and again.

"Jimmy!" It was dad. "Jimmy, stop!" Russel was flat on his back, sprawled out. I was out of breath and unsure how long I'd been jumping on his head. In dad's hand was the pistol we kept in the car.

Russel moaned and tried to sit up. I ripped the pistol from dad's hand and shoved it into Russel's face. His eyes were swollen shut, but they widened as he saw the barrel at his nose.

"Jimmy, stop!" Dad placed a hand on my shoulder. "Jesus, son, look at you."

I stood above the man. His head was as large as a pumpkin. Blood ran down his face and tears mixed with it on his cheeks. He stared into the gun in my hands and whimpered.

"Don't take that step, son," dad said. "You won't come back."

"This piece of shit doesn't deserve to live," I whispered.

"Who gets to decide that?"

I could. I could decide right now. Easily. One twitch and the decision was made.

I lowered the gun and Russel fell backward. "Let's go," I said. "You're driving." We got in the car, and Russel was in the same spot when the headlights illuminated him.

We drove in silence for a few minutes. "You did the right thing, Jimmy," dad said.

"Shut up and stop here."

"Why?"

There was a creek running alongside the road. "I need to rinse my hands."

"Hands?"

"Fuck off."

"I'm done arguing with you about it."

We three sat in the Ford. The Taurus was parked beside us. I'd explained my plan, and spent the next hour arguing with dad over the whole thing. The sun was well up. I was sick of that truck. It was time to get the hell out of Dodge.

"What happens when Stupro shows up and Perire isn't here?" dad demanded. "Haven't thought of that, eh?"

I sighed. Howie, having that damned sixth sense against me, reached over us and popped open the glove box. "Damn it, Jim. How long have I been sitting here after you did it?"

I shrugged. "Couple days."

Dad, sitting between us, rocked his head left then right. "Did what?"

"Stupro already came, dad. I put the tracker on his bike."

"You what? Why the hell are we still here?"

"I've been telling you for the last hour! I don't want to leave Perire. You'd think you'd want to help him. What's the matter with you?"

"There's no helping him, Jimmy." His voice was quiet. "Trust me. You don't know what I know."

"Then tell me." He shook his head. "Fine."

I jumped out of the truck and pushed straight through the willows. Dad shouted for me to stop. I ignored him.

I pressed the button, told Dr. Rasheed who I was, and waited. "How are you, James?" Ron asked a moment later.

"Doing fine."

He drove us up the hill and left the keys in the golf cart. "I'm glad you returned," Dr. Rasheed said as I entered the waiting room.

"Figured I'd give Peter some time to recover."

"He was only lucid for a couple hours. By bedtime, he was cooking me spaghetti." I smiled at her. "Come on, I'll take you back."

"It's a beautiful day out." There was tension in my voice. I forced myself to ask, "Do you think Peter would be up for a day outside?"

She stared at her feet and chewed her lip. "Let's see how he acts with a walk in the hall. If he went lucid outside, we might not get to him in time." We stopped outside Perire's door. "Ask him if he wants to go for a walk. I'll wait here."

"Good morning, Perire," I interrupted his whistling. "How are you?"

"Hey, dad. Just making breakfast."

I moved behind him and patted him on the back. He smiled at me. "Listen, Perire. We're going to go on a trip today. Would you like that?"

He nodded.

"We have to be quiet about it, okay? Dr. Rasheed can't know."

"What — Why?"

"It's a game. Trust me all right." At the irritation in my voice, he flinched away from me.

I stuffed some of his toy pans into my pocket. I'd have his sanity on me at all times. "You ready, Perire?"

"Let's go."

Dr. Rasheed's smile seemed sincere. "I'll leave his door open," she said and started walking down the hall. "When you guys are done, put him in and knock on the front door."

"Yes, ma'am."

"I thought —" I quieted Perire with my hand and listened hard. Dr. Rasheed passed through the door. And locked it.

"Come on. Let's walk some laps." We walked up and down the hall a couple of times before I worked up the nerve. "All right, Perire. Dr. Rasheed is going to tell you to stop, but it's part of the game. Keep with me."

"She says I always have to listen to her."

"But who is your father?"

He flinched. "I'll listen. I'll listen. Sorry, dad."

I rapped my knuckles on the door. My foot tapped a rapid beat. Keys rattled on the outside. The lock cranked. I grabbed Perire hard. "Ready to —" I pushed by Dr. Rasheed and she tumbled, papers scattering. I moved past her, but Perire's hand got heavy.

"Come on, Perire. Let's go." I put authority in my voice. The effect was instant. He followed without a word. I pushed on the door to the outside.

"Peter, stop!" My arm jerked back. I was outside; Perire was still inside. He stared at his feet, shivering. "Peter, come to me," Dr. Rasheed said in a calm voice. "Let's go back to your room."

"Don't listen to her, Perire. It's time to go. Remember what I said. It's a game. Come with your father."

Her voice was calm. "Don't you want to cook for me, Peter?"

My voice was steel. "Perire, you come with me right this instant. I'm not going to tell you again."

He squeezed his eyes shut, covered his face with one hand, and prepared to take a punch from me. "Sorry, dad. Sorry. I'll go. I'll go."

I jumped in the golf cart. Ron dropped his rake as he saw Perire hop into the passenger side. "Hold on, Perire." I drove the cart over the grounds, ignoring the zig-zagged road. Between trees, in and out of shallow ditches, over twigs and shrubs, the five-minute drive took thirty seconds.

"Stop!" Ron's shout was distant. The chain of the front gate rattled as I twisted the key into the lock. The chain clattered to the ground. Howie had the Taurus waiting. I ushered Perire into the backseat next to dad and hopped in the front.

"Drive!"

Sometime later, my pulse had found its regular rhythm and my breathing had slowed. The car was as silent as a car can be on the highway. I checked the backseat. Dad's eyes were saucers, pointed at Perire. Perire's eyes were just as large, and they held something I'd seen before.

Lucidity.

17

It was like looking into a mirror, had I done so during one of the many tragedies I'd lived through. Short, shallow breaths he sucked through his mouth. A high-pitched whine squeezed out his throat. His body flexed, and his head swiveled from me to dad and back like he couldn't decide who terrified him more.

His breathing came faster, faster, and shorter. He pressed his back higher in the seat and pulled his knees to his chest. Tears streamed down his face. He was going to do something stupid. I reached out to him. "Perire —"

"Shush!" Dad shoved a hand at me. "Perire, look at me. You see me? Who am I?"

"He — He — Helluo?"

"That's right." Dad's voice was calm. "It's me. Your big brother."

Perire rocked back and forth then lifted his head. "Why are you so old? Why's dad so young? I don't get it."

"That's not dad. He's my son. Perire, you've been gone a long time."

"Gone?" he shouted. Then whispered, "Gone where?"

Howie's eyes were fastened to the road ahead, and his knuckles were white on the steering wheel. What could you tell a man who had more than a twenty year lapse in memory? The truth? An extravagant lie? "Perire. After... what we did, you snapped. You haven't been right."

"After... After?"

"Stop. Pee, look at me. Don't think about it. You can't think about it. It's the only way."

There was silence then. They stared at each other. Dad burst first, pulling Perire in by his arm and pressing his head to his chest. They sobbed. "I didn't know, Helluo! I wouldn't have done it. I didn't know."

"I know. Quiet now. It's not your fault. Shush. Quiet now."

The hum of tires on the road was the only sound beneath Perire's low cries. Eventually, they quit and were replaced by long, smooth snores. I gazed at the passing world outside my window, a brighter world suddenly. Things were coming together. I had a real father and a real uncle. I'd make children for them to love. A real family was taking shape. Only one person was missing.

"Howie," dad whispered. "Pull over." He slowed then stopped. "Pop the trunk. Jimmy, help me find some clothes for Perire." The hospital clothes were little more than pieces of paper sewn together. I walked around the back of the car.

Dad's palm struck my cheek. "What were you thinking?" *Whoom!* a car passed. "I told you not to! You have no idea —"

"Look at him already, dad. You know what happened when he went lucid at the hospital? He —"

"I know exactly what happened." *Whoom!* "Why do you think he was in the hospital?"

"We can help him, dad. We have to try."

He slapped me again. "You think I haven't tried?"

"Don't slap me again. I mean it."

"Oh yeah? or what?" *Whoom!* then silence. Dad deflated. "Jimmy, you don't know what I've been through."

"Because you won't tell me." He said nothing. Eventually, I accepted it.

We got the clothes out for Perire then got back in the car. We drove in silence for hours. Eventually, we switched positions. Dad drove, Howie next to him. Perire was in the back with me, his moist eyes stuck on the window. I decided to write my wife.

He's been lucid for eleven hours, I wrote. *He looks sad, but it's the type of sadness that everyone goes through, nothing manic looking about it. I think we are helping. To think that he's been in that hospital all these years when all he needed was a family hurts my heart. I'll make up for it though. We will, babe. Over the next twenty years.*

"It's going to be a long drive," Howie broke into my writing. He stared at his phone. "He's still moving."

"Same way?"

He nodded. "North and west."

I closed my notebook. It was dark out. The sway of the Taurus was relaxing. I closed my eyes.

A sniffle woke me. Rays of light peeked through the rear windshield and landed on Perire. Tears dripped from his chin into his lap. His face was red and puffy. Hesitant, I squeezed his hand.

"Don't touch me, dad!" His hand shoved into his mouth, and he stared at me with wide eyes. "You're not my dad."

"No," I said.

"You're Helluo's son." I nodded. "My nephew. What's your name?"

"Jimmy."

He stared at me. "Do you know what I've done, Jimmy?"

I swallowed. "It's in the past."

"My past," he mumbled, "is always today." Dad's eyes met mine in the rear-view mirror. He shook his head. Eventually, we stopped at a gas station.

"I got to use the bathroom," I said.

"Me too." Perire opened his door.

Dad moved to follow, but I stopped him. "I got it, dad."

The bathroom had two stalls and a urinal. Perire went into one, I the other. "Perire, we all have regrets. Most of us have regrets that no matter what we tell ourselves keep us weighed down with remorse. I could have saved my first girlfriend's life. She died. I have my regrets too, Perire. They're hard to live with, but what other choice do we have?"

Silence came from the stall next to me. "What I do is look to the future, try to dream of a better life, then take steps to make that life. I see myself in you, Perire. If I can go on with life, you can too."

Still no response. "Any thoughts on that, Perire?" He was silent. "Perire?"

Something heavy hit the floor in the stall next to me. I ran out and threw open Perire's door. He lay on the ground, face blue, belt around his neck. "No, no, no, no, no." I worked at the belt I'd given him. "Howie!"

He'd pulled so tight that the leather broke skin. Blood made the clasp slippery. I worked a finger in, wiggled the clasp loose, then ripped the belt from his head. His eyes were closed. His chest was still.

"Move!" Howie pulled on Perire's legs until he was flat then pumped on his chest with both hands. I stood back, fingers in my hair. Dad put a hand on my shoulder.

"Ghah!" Perire sucked in air. Another hard breath. He looked me in the eye. "What —" He coughed, sputtered, sucked in another breath. "What happened, dad? Where am I?"

A crowd was peeking into the bathroom. "Come on, son," I said. "I'll explain in the car." Howie and I put one of Perire's arms over each of our shoulders and carried him. I sat in the back with Perire. Dad stared at me as we sped away from the gas station.

His stare was the saddest *I told you so* I'd ever seen.

"Damn," Howie said. He stared into his rearview. "This isn't good." I whipped around in my seat, and my stomach dropped. Highway patrol. The lights flicked on.

"What do we do?" I demanded.

"We can't run," Howie said. "This piecer won't beat his."

"So we stop?"

"Keel meh! Pwease, Keel —"

"We get it," Howie snapped. He'd been ranting the same thing since we left the gas station. It'd been Howie's idea to gag him. "Bro, we can't hide him." The highway patrolman pulled up next to our car, pointing to the side of the road. Howie slowed. "Take the tie off around his mouth and hide his hands."

"With what?"

"Figure it out!"

I ripped off my shirt, worked it down over Perire's head, and started on the knot to his mouth tie. It came off at the same time we stopped. "Kill me!" Perire shrieked.

I pinched the back of his arm hard. "Shush!" He glared at me. "Be quiet."

Click, click, click. Howie rolled down the window. "License and registration, please," the officer said.

"Why'd you pull me over?" Howie demanded.

"License and registration, sir."

"You can't just pull me over. I know my —"

"Kill me!" Perire slapped his head off the seat. "Please, help. I must die!"

"What's wrong with him?" The patrolman snapped open the clasp on his holster.

"He's retarded." Howie smiled. "Sorry about that."

Perire's head struck the window so hard I thought it'd break.

"Where you all coming from?"

"Why?" asked Howie.

"Nebraska?" How'd he know that? He drew his gun. "Step out of the car." The gun was on Howie. "You first. Nice and slow. Let me see your hands." Howie put both hands where the officer could see them. "You're not under arrest," the officer said as Howie got out of the car. He forced Howie's hands onto the top of the car. "I'm only restraining you." One arm went behind his back, and the handcuff clicked into place.

Howie's elbow crashed backward. "Help me," he shouted.

I jumped out of the car. The patrolman was on the ground, trying to focus his eyes. I picked up his gun and aimed it at him. "What do we do?" Howie crushed his fist into the cop's chin, and the man went limp. A truck slowed to a stop at the sight. I leveled the pistol at it and roared, "Keep moving!" It sped off. "We're screwed. We're so screwed. What're we —"

"Grab a leg!"

We drug him to the side of the road and let him settle in the long yellow grass there. "He's going to wake up soon, Howie. Should we do more?"

"Kill him?"

"What! No. Here." There was a handcuff key on the patrolman's belt. I unlocked Howie, wiggled the cop onto his stomach, and handcuffed his hands behind his back. "Go get in the car."

I threw his radio as far as I could and went to follow Howie. The sight of the patrol car stopped me. With its lights still flashing and it being empty and there being no one in front of it pulled over, it would be investigated by a good Samaritan, damn them all. I ran to the patrol car and got in.

The seventh button I pushed turned the lights off, then I tossed the car into drive. *This is so stupid*, I thought as I drove past our car. Howie fell in behind me. *So damn stupid.* I took the next exit and searched for somewhere to hide the car.

With a burst of inspiration, I slowed and yanked the wheel toward the ditch on the side of the road. I smashed into the steering wheel, knocked the air from my lungs, and smacked my head into the windshield. I sought the door handle with my hand, but couldn't focus.

Howie pulled me out by my arm. "You crazy bastard." He threw me over his shoulder, feet off the ground, and carried me up the hill.

He set me next to Perire, then continued driving us down the dark highway.

"Kill me! Please, just —"

"Oh, shut up already!" I screamed.

My doubts turned to certainties. I'd messed up, messed up bad. What had I been thinking? To take a man who had been hospitalized his entire life away from his comfort zone and shove him into the real world with people he hardly knew was a great idea. Good job, Jimmy.

We tried to stay on the highways but eventually had to get back on the interstate. It was the only route to where Stupro had stopped. Darkness still held, morning a distant promise. Perire's slobbery mouth tie had gone on shortly after the patrolman incident. Over the music, I could still hear his pleas for death.

"Turn here." Dad's voice was hard yet quiet, but it was more powerful than if he'd yelled it.

"The GPS tracker has stopped moving," Howie said, lifting his phone. "We have to hurry."

"I said turn." His tone brooked no argument. Howie turned off the interstate onto a road to nowhere. Huge mountains yawned around us, but they were miles away, separated by yellow grassland. The mountains loomed like shadows on the night sky, and the grass we could barely make out in the darkness. "Stop the car."

"Dad, what're we —"

"I said stop!" We pulled to the shoulder. A ditch ran on both sides of the highway. We were the only souls for miles. I heard dad digging in the glove box then his door was open. Then Perire's door was open. Dad yanked him out.

"Dad wait." I followed him. "What are you doing?"

"What I should have done years ago."

"Keel meh," Perire begged.

Dad petted the side of his face. "I love you," he said. "I was a coward before, Pee. For that I'm sorry."

His arm went up.

"I love you," dad whispered.

The gun exploded.

Perire rolled to the bottom of the ditch.

The ringing in my ears slowly faded, replaced by chirping crickets, and I fell to my knees. Dad was on his knees too. I couldn't see his face. His body shook.

Then a melody floated over the night quiet. Dad whistled Perire's tune.

Long yellow grass danced in the wind. The song was all there was left. It was beautiful to listen to but contrasted the moment: a nursery rhyme twisted into a dirge.

"My mother used to whistle that to us," dad said after a while. His words were low. "I was her favorite. Dad's too. They told me that. Told us all that."

There was silence. I let it be. Dad eventually stood. "That whistling was the most affection we ever got. Dad taught us strength, strength above all things. The best way to teach strength, he told us, is to show it. We got lessons most days.

"Stupro and father were always at each other's throats. It did something to Stupro. Being weaker than father affected his brain."

Dad cried into his hands. "Our parents went on a trip and never came back. Stupro told us not to worry, he'd take care of us. We never went to the police. We didn't tell anyone. We were strong enough to live without them. Stupro kept us clothed. Housed. And fed."

He choked on the last word.

"It was them, Jimmy! Perire, he cooked. Every day for three months, every meal, he cooked. Then Stupro told us, told us what he'd done. Mom into hamburger, dad into steaks. We ate them, Jimmy. Ate them until they were gone."

Everything jolted into place. The glutton my father had been. The psychosis from which Perire had suffered. Oh, God. *Dad's favorite food*, Perire had said. *Steak.*

"The police found out they were missing when our aunt came to visit. We told them that they would come back. We pretended to be clueless, innocent children. I inherited everything. A year later, Perire snapped. A year after that, I gave up on him, sent him away. A year after that, I met your mother. That's when I decided how I'd atone. I had to eat myself to death."

"I wish." He finally looked at me. "I wish I had a brother to put me out of my misery."

Now was not the time, but I had to ask anyway. "How could you live with the man after he'd done such a thing?"

He looked into the ditch and winced. "He's my brother. He thought he was protecting us."

"By feeding you your parents?"

"They beat us."

"Are you defending him? My whole life that man's been feeding you. What about that? You think that was some juicy cow?"

He flinched. "I suspected, but didn't care. I wanted to die."

"Dad, you're fucked up. Your mind's as twisted as Perire's is — was. But you're not to blame for this." I waited for him to look at me. "Stupro is."

I sat in the front seat and cradled the lotus flower. Its pure white had turned a weary beige and its lines were ragged and depressed, not the sharp perfection I'd known. It looked as tired as I felt.

Jessy had said that it meant you could rise above your past, that even something beautiful could grow from filth. *No matter where you come from you can choose to stay clean.* It was a blossom of hope floating above rot and ruin.

Jessy had not known waters as dark as the Torqueres though. How could anything possibly emerge beautiful from something so sick? My mother had killed her father. My uncle had killed both his parents. My father and Perire had helped dispose of their body. That was the waters beneath me.

How could anything beautiful grow from that?

"It's about time to throw that thing out," Howie said next to me. He stared at the globe and the wilting flower within. "It's going to turn black."

I nodded and slid it into my pocket.

We drove in silence the rest of the night. My mind was stuck on Stupro, the problem in all this. For generations the man had been ruining lives. Mine, my father's and uncle's, their parents', my wife's, my unborn child's. The problem with the Torqueres, though mom had her place, was Stupro. He should've been the uncle lying in a ditch.

Howie checked the phone, nodded, and pulled off the interstate. It was a huge truck stop, a little city of its own. Semi-trucks fueled up everywhere. Cars filled with families and trucks pulling campers weaved to parking spots. I didn't see any motorcycles.

"The GPS says he's here," Howie said. "On the other side of the building, I think." Dad had been in the back seat pretending to sleep since he murdered his brother. I left him alone. "It says he's right there." Howie glanced at his phone and pointed at a dumpster.

I sprinted for it and dug through the trash inside. The tracker was buried beneath a pile of wet toilet paper and sprinkled with coffee grounds. It had a note on it.

Fuck the police.

I crumpled. "No!" I screamed. "Damn you. Ghah!" I squeezed the tracker until it shattered and screamed again. Howie's arms lifted me from beneath my shoulders. I pushed him away and stood on my own. People stared.

"Come on, Jim. Get in the car."

I threw what was left of the tracker at the ground as hard as I could and went to the car, slamming the door behind me. "Damn it!" I punched the dash. "Damn it!" Again. "Damn it!"

"You done?" Howie asked as he drove us away from the truck stop.

"Am I done?" I shouted. I punched the dash. Something popped and my pain ran up my arm. "Damn it!"

"Helluo. Tell him."

"I know where he's going," dad whispered.

I stopped. "Excuse me?"

"I know where Stupro's going."

"Why didn't you say something?"

"Been a little preoccupied."

"Well, where's he headed?"

"Montana," he said. "Where Pecu was conceived."

18

Whitehall, Montana, a tiny town nestled under the I-90 with a giant green interstate sign the only betrayal of its existence. I remembered the place. We'd never lived there, but we'd stayed in the area for a couple of weeks after that guy overdosed in mom's car. It was in a huge valley beneath some of the biggest mountains I'd ever seen. A quaint, quiet kind of place. Perfect for drug addicts.

The house had been easy to find. We just followed the traffic. Mom had moved from a place where drugs were cheap, California, to a place where drugs were expensive, Montana. In her mind, there was only one reasonable thing to do.

I watched another bone-thin man scurry from his car into the front door. We were put up in a field, Howie and I, across from the house. Long, yellow grass kept us concealed and itched like fleas. The wind was chilly. A rock was stabbing into my hip. I wanted my little brother back.

"What kind of sick..." I trailed off. Now that I had an idea of what family should be, the love I shared with my wife, this selfishness from my mother made me shiver. Bone-thin men and women were in and out of that house all day long. They were around my little brother. "All right, here's the plan," I whispered to Howie. "We're going to rush in there and —"

"Shut up and watch. That's all we're doing today."

"All we're doing?"

"You want to rush in there? For what? You don't even know if your mother is in there. We're not rushing it."

So we watched the whole town come to that house over the next few hours. Even a sheriff's car came at one point. I thought he was there to arrest everyone, and I was ready to swoop in and claim guardianship over my brother. He disappeared inside and came out five minutes later, eyes shining and jaw spinning.

A man came out of the house. His eyes were open as wide as they would go, but the rest of him looked exhausted, mouth droopy, shoulders slouched, like he'd been awake for a week. He started down the road. "Go get the car," Howie said. "I'll follow him."

We'd parked on the other side of the field, past the train tracks. Dad was at the hotel, the only hotel in town, a single-floor line of rooms. He'd been an invalid since Perire. I hopped in the car and turned the key.

Howie was a block behind the man when I stopped to let him in. "Did he see you?"

Howie lifted an eyebrow.

"What's the plan?" I asked.

"Pull up next to him and match his speed."

The man looked over at us as soon as we came close. Howie rolled down his window and stared. No words. No expression. We drove like that for an entire block. The man wiggled in his skin, eyes darting to us and away, to us and away. His steps gained speed until he almost ran. He mumbled something to himself.

Finally, he stopped. "What!"

"Get in," Howie growled.

The man thought for a moment then got in the back seat. "I didn't do nothing. Nothing at all. Pay my bills. No games. Not ever. Don't know —"

"You're in some trouble," Howie said. "Big. Ugly. Trouble."

"What? No. I've not. No."

"Too late to deny it," I said. "You're in it deep."

The man's eyes touched the door handle. I made a point of pressing the lock button, though they were already locked. I heard the man swallow. "Do you know who we are?" Howie asked.

"Nah. No. No, sir."

Howie paused and took a deep breath. "We're with the FBI. And we've been watching you a long time."

"The what? Cops? Oh, no. No, no, no. I knew it! I've done no wrong. Nothing, sir. Nothing at all."

"We'll be the judge of that. Answer my questions and maybe we'll send you on your way."

"I ain't got to. You got nothing on me. Done nothing wrong. Nothing for the feds to be noticing."

"You're right. We'll have to let you go. That is, after we process you into jail." That shut him up. "Good," Howie continued. "Just some quick questions. That house you left. Who lives there?"

"This going on paper? If it is, I ain't no snitch, man. Not no snitch if it's on paper."

"No paper," Howie promised.

"I ain't no snitch. Don't count if there's no paper." That couldn't have made sense, even to his riddled mind. I kept silent though. "Woman named Spinny lives there with some creepy fella."

I nodded at Howie. "Who else?" I asked.

"Nobody I saw."

"You sure? Think hard. You didn't see any kids or anything like that?"

"No. I'd remember that. What's this about?"

"We ask the questions," Howie said. "How's the house laid out? the floor plan."

"Can't you find that out yourselves? Damn cops got fancy puters—"

"Answer the damn question or I'm taking you in."

"Walk in, a living room, that's where everybody stays, two doors off it, one to the kitchen, one a bedroom, never been there, bathroom off the kitchen."

"That's it?"

"Yes, sir. I think, sir. Can I go, sir?"

"Do you know the sheriff?" Somehow, his eyes grew larger. "You tell anyone about this conversation, I'll tell him you told us how Spinny gets her drugs from California. I'll even say you told us who the connect is. You think the sheriff would tell her?"

He swallowed, nodded, then swallowed again.

"Get out." He snapped the door handle back. As he unlocked it, I pressed the lock button. His fingers scrambled at the mechanism. I locked it again. Twice more. He finally got it open and sprinted down the street.

"They must keep him in the bedroom," I said.

Howie nodded.

"What do we do now?"

His eyes went out the window. "Let's wait and see if we can get in without force. Maybe they'll leave him there alone."

"More waiting?"

He shrugged "We've done enough for today. Let's go eat something."

We went to the gas station, Whitehall's' version of a market, and got some donuts, chips, and soda then went to the hotel. We were still laughing at what we'd done to the tweaker as we walked into the room. "Or the look on his face when you said you were the FBI — Dad!"

I crashed through the hotel door. He was spinning a slow circle from a rope tied around his neck, the end tied to the light fixture. Howie was to him the same moment I was. He lifted his legs, and I climbed onto the bed and worked the knot. The springs to the bed whined as dad landed on it.

He gasped.

I stared at him as he recovered, wondering what the fuck. Then I straddled him, gripped his collar, and bashed his head onto the bed. "The hell's the matter with you!" I choked on my tears. "After everything... You coward. You son of a bitch coward. Why would you —"

"Jim." Howie pulled on my shoulder. "Bro, ease up."

I collapsed on the bed next to dad. We both whimpered. I just couldn't understand. "Why dad?"

"It's all too much. I'm done with it."

"What about me? And Pecu? What happened to helping us?"

"I've done all I can for my kids. They'll be better off without me."

"What about Pecu? Is he better with mom? with Stupro?"

"He's not — He's not in any more danger than you were."

"Thought you said he wasn't like me."

"Just —" He snorted snot. "I want to die. Everything I've done. I can't ever make up for it."

"I'm not doing this again." I got off the bed, wiped my tears. "You want to kill yourself, do it. I'm done. I'm responsible for more than you are in this life and I can go on living. Hear that word? Responsible. You didn't do it, dad. You want to be a coward and take the easy way, be my guest. But do it knowing you're a coward. Do it knowing that you're killing the wrong man. Stupro should be on that noose, not you."

I stormed into the bathroom and slammed the door.

❦

Dad waited in the car, while Howie and I watched mom's house from our field. He'd said nothing of the attempt since he'd made it, but I think my words touched something in him. He was active in our planning now, asking good questions and seeing points we might've missed. I had the feeling it wasn't for Pecu that he had such renewed vigor though. He had another brother to kill.

"We know they're in there," I told Howie, not for the first time. "Let's just storm the place."

"The easy way first, Jim. Your brother could get hurt." There was no argument against that. It was just difficult to sit there and stare at the house my brother was in. He was so close. I needed him.

The front door to the house flung open, and a flood of the most despicable-looking people poured out of it, six in all. Bloody scabs covered faces. Grease-saturated hair to the point that it looked wet. Crimson eyes. Pale skin. The four days that we'd been watching the house, I'd seen none of those faces, which could only mean they'd been in there the entire time.

"We'll be back." Mom came out of the house, followed by Stupro, screaming to the crowd. "Don't worry. Mama will be back."

Everyone laughed like their queen had made a joke then dispersed. I held my breath as one started toward our field. If we stood, we'd be seen. If he stumbled on us, we were caught. I buried my face in my hands and prayed he chose a different direction.

"Stupid bitch thinks she's something," he mumbled. "Thinks she can come into my town, she doesn't know, just doesn't know, she'll see, just wait, I'll show her, she'll know…"

His feet crunched gravel a couple feet away. I dared a glance. The man was walking through the field, already past us, mumbling his rant. If I would've reached out my arm when he'd gone by, I'd have grabbed his ankle.

"Idiot," Howie whispered.

Stupro's bike roared as he took off down the block. With stringy hair whipping around her face, mom snuggled her arms in deep around Stupro's waist. Dad's part in this plan was simple. If they left the house, he'd follow.

"Now," Howie said once the bike's engine faded.

The front door was locked. I moved back to kick it in. "Wait!" Howie took out his wallet and found a credit card. It slid into the crack. He wiggled, jerked, the card wedging into the lock mechanism. It popped and the door cracked open.

"Easy way first, bro."

Song's absence in mom's life was obvious at a glance. The once-white carpet was a tie-dye of black and yellow stains. Every inch of the coffee table was littered with beer cans, with cigarette ash and butts scattered on their tops. Glass pipes and syringes fought for their own right to the table. Two long couches, missing all the cushions, sat at lopsided angles.

Gun up, Howie surged into the house. I pulled mine and followed. It was strange, holding the gun steady with a nub instead of a hand, but at least Howie had forced me to learn to shoot with my left. The living room was clear. We checked the kitchen. Clear. Bathroom. Clear. That left the bedroom. The door was closed.

Howie held up one finger. Two.

His foot crashed through, and we squeezed past the doorway. The room was empty. The cushions missing from the couches were tossed about on the floor. A safe dominated one corner. That was it.

No Pecu.

"What the hell?" *Where is he?* My stomach turned a cartwheel at the possibilities. I'd been watching the house for days. If they'd taken him somewhere, I'd have seen.

"Not now, bro," Howie interrupted my thoughts. "Let's go."

On our way out, we closed all the doors exactly as they'd been. Howie started for our field. "Hold on," I said. "I want to check the back."

It was a tiny yard. Weeds grew up a six foot, timber fence. A single gate led to the alley.

"Do you remember seeing a door to the basement inside the house?" Howie asked. He pointed to two doors. They leaned against the house and when opened led under.

"Howie, wait." He stopped with his hands on the door handles. "Pecu's not down there."

"How do you know?"

"I just do. Let's go."

"We have to check." He flung open the door and went down old wooden steps. I followed. A familiar smell hit, and I gagged. Howie pulled a beaded chain. A light came on.

It made no sense. Some kind of art, like a painting. He'd built a square wooden frame: four feet by four feet. It hung from the ceiling by a single wire, rotating slow. What was inside the frame was hard to comprehend.

Three points on the sides, two points on the top and bottom, connected the frame to material like canvas by rusty wires, pulling it tight. *Skin*. The frame spun slowly. A head sagged over the stretched flesh, hair hanging limp.

We bolted, making it to the top of the stairs at the same time.

"The hell, bro —" Howie covered his mouth with a hand. "What the hell was that?"

I ignored the question. "Did you turn the light off?"

"What? I — no." I went back down. The skin rack had kept spinning. It stared through hair with wide eyes. She'd been young, in her early twenties. Her eyelids were gone, forcing a look of eternal surprise. Her mouth had been sewn shut by the same metal wires that stretched the skin of her back.

Is this what happened to Amanda?

"Bro!"

I shook my head, turned off the light, and ran up the stairs. I walked back to our spot in the field and collapsed, eyes pointed at the sky.

<hr />

There were two main routes over the massive mountains next to Whitehall, the interstate or the highway. The highway wound up and between the mountains like a fish swims. Fragrant pines crowded both sides of the road most the way. When they didn't, it was because a near-vertical cliff fell from that side. It was one of those highways where you drive with your seat forward and both hands on the wheel. Mom and Stupro had gone to the top of the pass yesterday.

"Why won't you tell me?" I had asked dad.

"I don't want to," he responded. "It has nothing to do with Pecu. Can't you trust me?"

The day prior, after we'd found Stupro's art, dad picked us up and brought us to the top of the pass. He'd pointed at a pull-off, told us that was where mom and Stupro had gone, then brought us back down the mountain.

I waited until we were all back in the hotel room. "You need to tell me why they went up there." He stared at me with blank eyes. "Dad just fucking tell me. After all we've been through, what could possibly be so –"

"They went to fuck!"

"What?" My mind froze. "What?"

"I knew when they started up the pass." He sighed. "It was a long time ago. We stopped at that spot in the middle of the night. You,

Coitus, and Coitum must've been sleeping. I looked out my trailer window, saw them... you know. We stayed in the area while your mother sold her drugs, and they kept leaving together. We left when Spinny was pregnant."

Spinny was... "What?"

"You were old enough to start having thoughts on your own. Spinny says that's when they're no good no more. Kids. They only love you, truly love you, when they're babies, when they need you. Something happened to her. She's never told me what, but she's only happy when she's got a baby. She had to have one, Jimmy. We tried. Well, she tried. I was too fat to do anything. So she found someone else. Stupro's sick sense of loyalty won't let him deny her."

"Why's he so loyal to her?" Howie asked.

"Stupro's brain works different. He's got principles, but he chose those principles because father beat them into us, not because they feel right. Loyalty's one of those principles.

"Spinny took care of me after... after I sent Perire away. She handled everything for us. Plus, your mother lets Stupro do whatever he wants in her house. Stupro owes her, at least in his twisted mind he does."

None of that mattered to me. "Pecu is Stupro's son?" Dad's slow nod brought tears to my eyes. "That's why." I sat on the bed and put my face in my hands. "That's why Pecu kills animals. That sick bastard is his father. That's why..."

"It won't be long before he starts giving him the lessons father gave us," dad whispered when it was clear I had no more words. "Pecu won't come back if that happens."

I stared at dad, chewing his words. I clenched my jaw.

"Everyone out," I said. "I want all eyes on that house at all times. We've got to find him."

No one moved.

"Now!"

19

The alley was almost completely black. Without the moon, it would've been. I was wedged between two trash cans across the way from the back gate. My knees and back throbbed from sitting in the same position for hours.

Howie waited in the car in case they left the house. Dad was in the field. It'd been hours of waiting, but I didn't care. I'd stay until they led us to Pecu.

The gate rattled, and Stupro squeezed through. He wore an all-black jumpsuit and a stocking cap with his hair tucked into it. His heavy boots crunched down the alleyway away from me.

Holding my breath, I waited until he disappeared around the corner 'then pushed out of my hiding spot. Stupro wasn't going to visit Pecu dressed as he was, I knew, but I had to follow him. I pulled my ski mask the rest of the way over my face and jogged to catch up.

As I pressed myself to the corner fence, Stupro turned into the next alley. My instincts told me to creep to the next alley, but my heart was beating too fast, sending adrenaline through me quicker than a bullet, so I ran. My back crashed into the corner of the garage before the alley, and I bit my lip. I peeked around the next corner.

Two trails cut through high grass from where car tires had driven. The alley was narrow, with high fences or garage doors running the entire length, and Stupro was stepping up a metal frame used to hold trashcans off the ground. Hands to the six-foot wooden fence, Stupro swung his legs in one motion up and over and was gone. I ran to the spot and up the metal frame.

The yard was a small square covered in green grass. A large pink doll house, one of those massive things a father builds over a period of weekends, and a swing set with a seat ripped from one chain and dangling to the ground took up most the yard. Dolls and dolls' clothing were scattered.

On the other side of the yard, against the back of the house, was a low porch with handrails enclosing it. Stupro stood on the porch, his back to me. To his right were sliding glass doors made black by the darkness on the other side. In front of him, where his hands cupped over his eyes, was a wide bay window that shimmered from a nightlight on the other side. Flowers were printed on the wallpaper within.

My gun hand came up, as though of its own accord, and the barrel pointed at the back of Stupro's head. I felt my trigger finger tighten.

But I stopped.

Not for the little girl on the other side of that window. Not for the family that would wake up with one less person in it. Not for anything to do with the crime unfolding in front of me. I hesitated because I had no idea where Pecu was.

But what about this family's Pecu?

I tilted the gun back and fired at the same time, the crack like thunder before the rain. The window in front of Stupro shattered.

Stupro turned.

His eyes found mine.

Frozen, heart slamming in my ears, I stared back. A light turned on in the house behind him. Shouting came from within. That fractured second felt like an eternity. My mask was down and there was no way he could know, but the scared little boy in me, the little boy who was aware of the wicked capabilities of this man, knew. He saw straight into me.

We reacted at the same moment. I jumped off the trash holder. He moved for the fence. I hit the ground running and was out the end of the alley, across the next street, and into another alley without thinking of the direction I was going, away from mom's tweaker house, away from Howie and dad. Away from help.

I ran through yards, hopped fences, kicked away a dog, and dodged a speeding pickup truck. I needed to find the train tracks that led through the entire town, but I could only concentrate on my feet moving.

I was lost.

My lungs burned. I dove into a shrub wall that surrounded a yard. It was thick, green bristles brushing the sidewalk, and I tucked myself into it completely and turned so I could watch the sidewalk. I focused on slowing my heaving breaths.

Footsteps hammered down the sidewalk. I brought my gun up. I could only see in front of me. Feet stopped in my view. They turned. Black boot-toes pointed at me.

Separated bodies in a basement. Stretched skin over a metal frame. An innocent little girl sleeping in her room. Amanda's bloody ass.

I pulled the trigger once, then twice. Ringing in my ears replaced everything. Stupro fell forward and landed on top of me. I swung the gun like a hammer, over and over. I tried to push out of the bush. Stupro was too heavy. The butt of my gun connected with hard bone. A huge hand gripped my shirt. I kicked, and I whacked.

I rolled free of the bushes.

And ran.

❊

"We're done with the easy way," I told dad and Howie. We sat in the car at the end of mom's block and had been quiet since I got back and explained what had happened. The sun was well up, but my lungs still burned. That was the extent of my injuries. Stupro had fared much worse than I.

"Jim, bro, I don't think —"

"We'll storm in, Howie and I, and we'll find Pecu while dad waits for us in the car. If he's not there, we'll make mom tell us where he is."

"How you expect to make her?" Howie asked.

"I'll torture her if I have to!" I screeched, heaving, tears falling down my face. "I'm done with this. I want my brother back. I want to go home to my wife. We're ending this."

"Guys —" Dad pointed from the driver's seat, but Howie spoke over him from the back, "I just worry that we haven't found him yet. If he was here, then we would've seen him by now."

"Guys —"

"If he's not here, then we'll take mom instead. She knows where he is."

"Guys, you need to —"

"I don't like it, Jim. It seems —"

"Look out the fucking window!" dad shouted, pointing out the windshield.

A flood of tweakers ran across the front lawn, doubled over like the kids of Columbine, and mom stood in the doorway. She waved a pistol, pointing it without pattern. All the twig-people jumped into a rusted Dodge, some in the cab, most in the bed, and the tires sprayed dirt as it sped away. Mom disappeared back inside the house.

"This is it," I said into the silence after. "Now's the time."

"I don't know, bro."

"Howie, this is our best chance and we're taking it."

Dad's eyes went to the rear-view mirror, staring at Howie. I held Howie's attention. He nodded to dad.

I turned in my seat as dad put the car in drive. "All right, dad, drop us off and drive around the block. This will be quick."

His jaw wormed and his eyes looked anywhere but at me, but he nodded. The car stopped. Howie and I got out without a word. We crossed the weed-speckled yard. The car sped off behind us, and Howie's foot crashed into the front door. Our guns came up at the same time.

"Grab her!" Howie shouted as he moved through the living room, pistol high. Mom's eyes widened and she scrambled toward the table, but I was closer and kicked her pistol away. The end of my gun touched her nose.

"Sit." I twitched the gun toward the cushionless couch. Her hands went up and she waded through beer cans to sit. A commotion came from the direction Howie had gone.

Stupro limped into the room, hands above his head. He wore basketball shorts and nothing else. His left leg was wrapped in a cut-up piece of sheet. Blood saturated it. His head was lumpy and swollen. Wounds leaked from where the butt of my gun had connected.

I smiled.

"Say the word, Jim," Howie said as he pressed his gun into Stupro's neck. "Let me end this sicko."

"We'll let him live," I said. "If he tells us where to find Pecu."

"No time," mom said. "None. I got to get and go." She tried to get up, but Howie drove the butt of his gun into her forehead. After everything, I still flinched. She gripped her head in both hands. "You don't understand. I got to get!"

On the floor next to the table, a massive safe lay on its side. Deep gouges in the hardwood trailed behind it from being drug.

"We're not going anywhere without Pecu," I said, turning back to mom. "So tell us —"

"Ah!"

Dad rushed in.

He howled and ran straight for Stupro and fell on him, a knife high in his hand. Howie yanked him up, but the tip of the blade was red.

"What're you doing, dad?" I cried out.

"We don't have time for this!" Mom was hysterical, wiggling in her seat.

Dad yanked against Howie's hold. "He ruined everything. Mom! Dad! Perire!."

Stupro laughed.

A boom came from outside, and the window shattered. Tatters hit the house. *Gunfire!* Everyone dropped to the floor.

"Jim, to me!"

Howie was behind the safe, trying to push it. I army-crawled to him. When I put my shoulder to the safe, it slid up against the wall under the window. Howie put his gun up and fired a few shots toward the epicenter of the noise coming from outside. The bullets hesitated, and I dared a look.

The rusted truck had returned. It was full of tweakers with guns. Hunting rifles, a few handguns, an AR-15. As the guns came up, my head went down.

I fired out the window until my gun clicked. Howie did the same. Bullets slapped around us.

"What do we do?" I yelled to Howie.

"Pray they quit!"

The only prayer I ever heard answered, the gunfire died. A roaring silence came, and I could just make out debris settling to the ground. Then came a voice, "Give us the damn safe!"

"Don't you fucking dare," mom said behind us.

I looked at Howie. He looked at me. I shrugged. We put our shoulders to the safe and it tumbled out the window.

"No!" mom shrieked.

Clattering came from outside. A stringy man in nothing but a holey pair of jeans ran to the safe and wrapped a chain around it. He padlocked it closed and ran back to the truck. They sped off, the safe dragging smooth down the street behind them. The tweakers pumped their guns like a scene out of a Western.

"Time to go, bro," Howie jumped off his hands and knees, then threw mom over his shoulder. "Before the cops get here."

I got up. Dad was on top of Stupro, trying to punch down but Stupro had hold of his wrists. "Dad, let's go." Howie was already out the door. "Now!"

"He doesn't get to live. He killed them!"

The car horn sounded. I pulled dad off of Stupro. "We have to go." I pulled dad's shoulder "Get up!"

He crawled toward Stupro who was trying to use the couch to get up. Dad grabbed a bottle and smashed it onto the table.

"Dad, let's go!"

They both stood. The car horn wailed. Stupro half-stepped, half-limped toward dad. Dad brought up the bottle. "Just go, Jimmy."

Cop sirens echoed through the small town. "Dad, enough. Let's go!" He didn't even acknowledge my words.

I stared.

I bolted out the door.

The passenger side door was open, and the car started to move. I jumped in and looked back.

"Wait!" I told Howie. "Give him a second."

"We can't, bro. We got to —"

"Just one second!" I held my breath. The sirens were louder now. "Come on, dad."

They came out onto the front porch. Stupro had dad in a choke-hold. Dad's face was bloody mush. Stupro let the hold go and took dad by the hair. Stupro and I made eye contact.

"No!"

Howie hit the gas. Stupro held the knife dad had brought. It sunk into dad's neck hilt deep, spraying red. I stared at the fading scene as Howie turned the corner. Blue and red lights appeared behind us.

Dad lay at Stupro's feet.

20

We drove in mostly silence. Occasionally, a thump or yell would come from the trunk. I ignored it and stared out the window, forcing my mind blank. After living through so much trauma, I'd developed techniques to deal with it. Not thinking, though the hardest to learn, was the best. I watched Montana pass.

"You all right, Jim?"

I shrugged. Howie stopped on the side of the deserted highway. His door opened, then the trunk opened. A moment later, mom was thrown into the back seat. A herd of cattle grazed beside the car. Howie drove.

"These ropes are pointless," mom said. "I won't run."

"Promise?" Howie scoffed.

"Listen here, you little —"

Howie climbed over the backseat and started slapping her. "How dare you —" *Thunk, thunk.* I put a hand on the wheel to keep us between the lines. "After all you put us through —" *Thunk.* "Talk to me like that —" *Thunk, thunk.* Eventually, he sat flat in his seat and sighed.

"Feel better?" I asked.

"Not really." His eyes went to the mirror. "Where we going, Spinny?"

"You stupid punk. Think you can —"

"Shut up. Tell us where Pecu is or I'll come back there again."

"Doesn't matter where Pecu is."

Something in her voice made me look up. "What's that mean?" She glared out the window. "Mom!"

"It means it doesn't matter where he is." She looked me in the eye. "He's dead."

My shoulder banged into the dash and head spidered the windshield as we screeched to a stop. Howie's hand threw the gearshift up, and he was out the car. "Howie, what are you doing?"

The back door opened. "Stay in the car, bro."

"Aye!" mom blurted out. Howie dragged her out by her hair. "Stop!" That's when I saw the gun. I jumped out. I caught up to him in the field next to the highway. He tossed mom to the ground and lifted the pistol.

"Wait!" I yelled.

"Get in the car, bro. After all this? No. She's done. You don't need to watch."

"No. Wait! Please, listen." Mom shuffled to her knees. "Don't. Listen. Just —"

Howie cocked his gun.

"Not dead!" She yelped. "He's not dead."

I wobbled at the knees. "Liar," Howie and I said at the same time. He continued, "You better keep talking."

"Vegas. Went to Vegas after getting Pecu. I knew if Jimmy lived he'd be after me, was going to keep Pecu with Coitus for a while. They got me when I got there."

"Who got you?" Howie asked.

Wind whistled through high grass around us.

"The Mexicans," I whispered as mom said it. The gangbangers mom had killed and robbed. She knew she couldn't go to Vegas. Stupid woman knew how dangerous Vegas would be and brought my brother there anyway.

"The Mexicans," she continued. "They knew about Coitus, knew she was mine, been watching her. They jumped us and took Pecu."

And killed him for revenge, I thought. Howie must've had the same thought. His gun pressed into her face. "Wait!" Mom put her hands up like she was praying. "You won't get Pecu back without me."

"He's not dead?" I demanded.

"No."

"Then why'd you say that?" I demanded. "And why the hell are you in Montana trying to make a baby when those people have my baby brother?"

"Make a baby?" She looked away then back when it dawned on her. "Stupro? That's not why I came. Been trying that for months, wanted to see if it would work where..." She went quiet.

"Where you two made Pecu," I finished for her.

"Nah, not in Montana for that. Came for the price of dope. Taunter gave me one chance. Said if I get his money, Pecu will live. Have to pay interest, but he gave me the dope to move."

"Taunter?"

"That's his name. Well, his gang name. Probably his real name is Francis or Gilbert. Nobody's scared of a Francis. Got to be something tough. Like Taunter or Lucifer or —"

"We get it," Howie said. "So you're up here getting Taunter's money?"

"Was." She looked up at us. "Until you threw it out a window."

Howie and I shared a look. "He'll give you Pecu back when you get his money?" I asked.

"That's what he said."

"How much money?"

"A lot."

"A lot isn't a number."

"More than we can get."

"How much is it, mom?"

"Two hundred and fifty grand."

A low whistle pressed out of Howie's teeth. "That's how much you stole from them? Jesus, mom, what were you thinking? You can't let that kind of money go. We're lucky they didn't find us all sooner."

I sighed

Howie dragged mom by her ankles and looked at me. "Vegas?"

"Vegas."

The meeting spot was beneath a huge rock formation with nothing else but cacti for miles. A perfect place to murder someone, I couldn't help but think. We showed up while the sun was still high, and in a moment of vindictiveness I forced mom back in the trunk, out of the AC. She could suffer a little, plus I didn't want her seen by Taunter.

I'd kept mom in the trunk the entire drive from Montana and only brought her out to get Taunter's number. He'd been reluctant to deal with me, but no one ignores a two hundred and fifty thousand dollar opportunity. He'd told us to meet him here at sundown.

He rolled up in a black Suburban well after dark. Howie and I were leaning against the hood of our rent-a-car with arms crossed. The driver and passenger side doors opened to the Suburban. Two big, bald Mexicans got out, wearing Dickie pants and shirts buttoned all the way to the top button, untucked. One opened a back door and out stepped Taunter.

He was dressed exactly as his homies were, but he had a pair of pure black sunglasses on, wasteful but for the look. He couldn't have been an inch over five feet tall. All three came forward.

"Where's Spinny?" Taunter demanded.

"Don't worry about her," I said. "Deal with us now."

"Deal with you? I didn't want to deal with her. Bitch convinced me. A quarter million for three keys is hard to turn down. I don't see a bag of cash in your hand though. You playing me?"

I took a deep breath. "I don't have your money."

"You what?"

"I don't have it. I wanted —"

"Then why we here?" One gun came out, and two followed. I put my hand on Howie's arm. "Where's my money, fool?"

"Put your guns down. Let me talk."

"Talk with the guns up."

"I know what Spinny did to you." He went to talk but I put my hand up. "I Can't make up for that. I don't have a quarter million to give you. But I need that little boy. Work with me."

"Work with you? Fool, I've been working with Spinny, and look where I'm at. Looks like I'm out three more kilos on top. I should kill you, kill the kid, then find Spinny and kill the bitch too."

"Do that and you get nothing. Possibly a murder beef along with it."

He laughed. "Wouldn't be the first tourists to disappear on vacation."

"Still, you'd have nothing."

"And what do I got now? You're steady telling me it won't get me nothing to kill your ass, but you ain't telling me how letting you live will. What you got for me?"

"Nothing tangible. Not now. We could work for you though. I don't know what you need that I could provide, Taunter, but I'll do whatever you want so long as I get my brother back." The night slowed as I realized what I'd done. I swallowed.

"Your brother?" Taunter smiled. "Mean's you're Spinny's too?"

"I hate her as much as you do."

"I doubt that. That explains why your dumb ass'd come here with nothing though. What makes you think you could work for me?" I told him what Howie and I did for a living. "A white guy in the Chinese mafia?" He snickered and his guards laughed too hard. "But if that's the kind of skills you think you have, I might have something for you."

"Anything."

His smile was devious. "I've been watching this truck. Came up with a little job with a big payoff."

"What kind of truck are you —"

"We'll do it," I interrupted Howie. He glared at me.

Taunter laughed. "Eager?"

"I just want my brother back."

He nodded. "Truck stops at the same places every time. Only two dudes in it, one pistol between them. You who you say you are, should be easy. Bring me everything in that truck, you get your brother."

"Deal." He told us the details he knew: where the truck would be at what times, when to hit it, and what to expect inside. "That sounds like more than a quarter million," I said.

"Cost of putting me through this bullshit. Tell Spinny when you see her that she's back on the list. Don't show her face."

He turned to leave. "Taunter!" His sunglasses pointed at me. "Did you bring Pecu?"

"Of course."

"Can I see him?" He stared at me a long time, like he had to think about it. I nudged him. "To make sure I'm not doing this for nothing."

"For nothing? Should feel lucky I'm letting you leave here." He popped open the back door.

"Jimjim!"

He ran to me and I ran to him.

"Ah, ah, ah." Taunter swung my brother into his arms. Pecu's baby blues shined in the moonlight, and he reached both arms toward me. They had him dressed up exactly like them. "You see him? Just fine. Hit that truck, bring everything here tomorrow night, then you can hug and cry together all you want. Otherwise, kid's mine."

They got in the Suburban, and Pecu was gone.

He walked past the man with the gun and tossed two duffel bags into the back of the armored truck. We were parked across the street, Howie silently watching, me violently shaking. His calm excited me more than relaxed me. *What kind of man is calm watching a truck he's about to rob?*

We'd rented another car, left mom in its trunk, and parked it off the beaten path. I could have felt guilty, leaving mom in the trunk as we had, but all I had to do was think about dad. However evil this woman was, dad had had some kind of feelings for her, and how'd she repay him? by sleeping with his brother. It wasn't her fault that Stupro had killed him, but I blamed her anyway. She deserved much more than a few desert hours alone in the trunk of a car.

The guy with the gun said something to the other man, and they both laughed. Just another day on the job. Nothing out of the ordinary. "I don't like this," Howie said as the man went back into the side exit of the casino. "Don't like this one bit."

My teeth clattered. "You look like we're about to do some gambling, not a reckless heist."

"This is the kind of shit you stay away from, bro. We don't do this type of shit."

The man threw two more heavy bags into the back of the truck. That made four. I tried to do the math but had no idea how much cash it took to fill a duffel bag. I figured it had to be worth about a life sentence. Gunman closed the door. Duffel bag man locked it. They both climbed into the truck.

"Here we go." Howie's words almost made me puke. We followed the truck, staying three cars back, as they pushed into traffic, and I went to pull down my ski mask. "Not yet." Howie shook his head. "Two guys in masks behind an armored truck? We can't have the cops called too early. Relax, bro. I'll tell you when."

Relax? Seems like the perfect time not to be relaxed. If there is ever a damn time not to be —

"Jim, calm down. Win or lose, all we can do is stick to the plan. Worry and fear will only make you sloppy. Breathe." We followed them. The truck turned. It was off-route.

"The hell they going?" I asked. Howie turned and stopped as the truck had. "This isn't where Taunter said..."

"This is bad." The men were out of the truck again, gunman on the back door, duffel bag man going into another casino. Two more bags went into the truck. Then two more. That made eight.

"That's a lot of money, Howie."

He coughed. "Too much to lose."

"Taunter said they'd only stop at the first casino, and the one we'd hit them at."

He nodded.

"What do we do?"

"Four bags are as bad as eight." I wasn't sure that was how it worked, but it didn't matter. Whether eight bags or eighty, this was how we got Pecu back.

The truck continued. All through the center of Vegas it drove, never veering again from the route we'd traced the night prior. The closer we got to where we'd hit it, the more difficult it became to sit still. This wasn't like robbing a little old lady behind a McDonalds. This was the real thing.

The casino appeared up ahead. With my nub, I cocked my gun. "Can I put my mask on?"

He pulled down his own. "Win or lose, bro." The truck missed its turn. "What the fuck?"

"They're not stopping."

"No shit, bro."

"Keep following?"

"What else can we do?" He looked at me. "Unless you want to..."

Pecu in those silly gangbanger clothes, surrounded by cholos swearing and drinking and whatever else they did on the street corner. Pecu crying, begging for his Jimjim. Pecu tossed aside to lay face down like I'd seen my father but days ago.

I pulled down my facemask. "Drive."

We followed for five minutes in silence. Either Taunter knew this would happen and gave us the job anyway or he was an idiot who hadn't done his due diligence. We had to meet him that night though, whichever it was. Had to meet him that night with the contents of that truck. "Their next destination is going to be the bank," Howie said.

"How do you know?"

"Because that's how life works. How determined are you?"

"Completely."

He nodded. "Put your seatbelt on."

My back pressed into the back seat, and we soared through a right turn. The engine roared. Left turn. I got my seatbelt fastened. Left turn. Howie's foot had the pedal to the floor. We headed straight for traffic. "You get the driver, get the key!" Howie bellowed. "I'll get the gunner."

The armored truck appeared in front of us. Howie roared something guttural. I closed my eyes. The impact slammed me into my seatbelt and the airbag slammed me back. My ears rang. Dizzy, blurry, I dug at the latch, unfastened myself, then fell out the door. On the ground. I coughed and moaned. Blood dripped from somewhere. My hand pressed into broken glass, gun still in it.

Suddenly, I could differentiate sounds. I could focus on my gun. Then came the adrenaline. I jumped to my feet. Our hood was smashed to the cab, engine gnarled. The armored truck was dented at its hood. The gunman jumped out of the truck, gun drawn but wobbling.

"Put the gun down!" he screamed, pistol pointed at me. I lifted mine, and he fired. I dove behind the corner of our mangled hood, heat burning me where my skin touched metal. Shots hit the car. I put my gun over the hood, eyes closed, and shot. Bullets quit slamming into the car around me.

I peeked over. Howie was on top of the man and threw a fist down. Gunman went limp. I sprinted over them both, opened the truck's door, and shoved my gun into the driver's face. "The keys!" His eyes were round and he stayed still. "Keys to the back. Now!"

They hit me in the chest and fell to the seat. I scooped them up with my nub, pressed them to my chest. "Don't you dare move." I put the gun under my armpit to take the keys in my hand, and the guy grabbed for my neck. His fingers got my collar, and his fist hit my face.

With my nub, I jabbed and jabbed and jabbed, hitting something hard each time. Then I hit something soft. He squealed and grabbed for his eye. I fled around the truck.

I shoved the key into the back door, and Howie cried out, "Wait!"

The door opened.

Tat, tat, tat, tat, tat...

Air whooshed by my ear. I fell to the ground. Each bullet crashed into the cars behind the truck. The gunfire stopped. Howie dove around the back of the truck and fired once.

The world stilled.

"Come on, bro!" Howie was digging in the back. A man, some kind of assault rifle slung across him, slouched against the back of the cab. One bleeding hole decorated his cheek. *A man just working, working to make a living. He probably has a wife, kids.*

"Not the time, bro. You hear the sirens. Get the bags!" I snapped out of it, grabbed four, and headed for the car. "This way, stupid." Howie opened the back seat of a red Chevy directly behind the armored truck and tossed his four bags in. I had the door of the passenger seat opened when Howie pulled a man from the driver's seat. He flopped to the ground without moving.

"Was he dead?" I sat next to Howie. He floored it, and we scraped alongside the truck we'd just robbed. "Was he?" I screamed. Howie looked at me. His eyes were wet.

Two dead.

A cop car almost crashed into us from a side street, drifting around the corner to follow. Two more made the turn right after. Howie floored it, and we hit the back of another squad car on the next side street. It spun three times. "Howie, this is bad."

"Not the time."

"What do we do?"

He flung the wheel right, and I fell into him.

When two cars were too close together he crashed into them, forcing a gap. When it was impossible to do that he drove on the sidewalk, sending pedestrians screaming. I held onto the seat and prayed we were fast enough. To get caught at this point wouldn't only damn my brother. It'd damn Howie too. The cops stayed close behind, not letting us gain an inch.

"Look out for a parking garage, bro."

"Why?"

"I'll drive through it. You can get out with the bags. I'll lead them away."

"No." He went to speak, but I cut him off. "Absolutely not."

"Don't make this for nothing."

"I won't do it, Howie. Think of something else." The streets became more crowded. Every red light had cars backed up ten, fifteen deep, four wide. Howie tried to use the center divider, but we still rammed vehicles. People walking between dived to get out the way. "Why're we going toward the strip?"

"Plan B," Howie said. Our tires screeched around a corner. Then another. I looked back and counted. *One. Two. Three. Four.* Five seconds until a squad car made it around the corner. We turned again. Seven seconds that time. "When I say run, grab some bags and go. I'll be right behind you."

Howie turned the wheel, this time onto the sidewalk. People dove and ran and screamed. The crowd grew thick, panic growing with it. Howie turned again. A huge screen was above us, giving a light show. Someone soared past on a zipline. Buildings crowded in tight all around us.

"Ready?" Howie said. "Try to blend in."

"Take your mask off then." I removed my own.

"Right." Howie pulled his up. The lunatic had a smile on his damn face. "Ready?"

Eeeeeeeeaaaaaarrrrrch!

People swarmed away from us and we jumped in with them, the only difference between us being the four duffel bags of cash in our arms and not theirs. We followed where the crowd was thickest. I dared a look back and saw no cops. It was hard to stay close to Howie in the press, but he was taller than most the crowd by a head, as was I, so it was easy to keep sight of him. He led us around a corner. I stopped for a final look.

Cops surrounded the Chevy.

Around the corner, people were walking, not knowing yet why the panic. We matched pace and turned again. A bus was pulling up to the sidewalk. It was the most beautiful bus I seen in my whole life. We tried not to run, but did anyway, storming up the bus steps.

Flower pattern shirts, cameras hanging from necks, all over forty, tourists filled the seats. Every eye was on the two men suddenly joining them. Two men in all black, carrying four duffel bags each, one with a bloody head. It was silent.

"Viva Las Vegas!" Howie yelled.

They hooted and hollered.

21

The Suburban was already at the spot when we showed up, Taunter and his homies leaning on the hood. I had a bout of queasiness at the sight and felt naked without the gun I'd dropped at the armored car. The amount of money we had with us anyone would consider killing for.

I got out and tried to sound confident. "You got my brother?"

"You actually did it." Taunter laughed.

"You thought we wouldn't?"

"I thought no one could, fool."

"You knew your information was wrong. There were three guards, not two. And one had an automatic. They didn't even stop at the spot you said."

"Whoops." He smiled and his minions laughed. "You still managed it though." I stared until he moved on. "Who's that fat guy they're after?"

. It was the only thing we hadn't planned and about the only thing that had worked in our favor. The rental car had been in dad's name. Within an hour of us getting away, a photo of dad was plastered on every news channel.

"Does it matter?"

"Guess not." He shrugged. "You bring the money?"

"You bring my brother?"

"Let me see the money first." I glared at him, thinking, then sighed at my hopeless position. I tapped the hood with my nub, and Howie brought out the bags. Four of them. He set them at my feet and opened them.

Taunter's eyes shone in the dusk.

"Now where's my brother?" He shook his head then coughed. Movement burst from everyone but me. Three guns pointed at us. Howie's pointed at them.

"Put the gun down." Taunter turned his sideways. "Now, fool."

Slow, I put my hand on Howie's gun. "We had a deal, you bastard," I said.

"A deal? Unless you can bring back the dead, you ain't got shit. Think I make deals with people who kill my own? You the bastard, a stupid bastard."

"I didn't kill anyone."

"Don't matter. I'm keeping the kid. For the money, I won't kill him. That's all you get. Now, I know there was two stops." I glared. He shot a round at my feet. "The other bags, fool!"

I made eye contact with Howie, the question in his eyes. I shook my head. We'd end up dead. I got the other four bags out and set them with the rest. "Taunter, please, let my —"

"You going to start begging?" He scoffed. "Let it go. Kid's mine now. You grew up to be a Chinese gangster, he'll grow up to be a homie." They all roared like it was the funniest thing ever said.

"I won't give up."

He surged over to me, pushing me over onto the hood, smashing the barrel into my cheek. I was sure Howie was going to shoot him. "That a threat?" He jammed the gun hard into my face. "Huh?"

I held my breath.

"What I thought." He stepped back. "If I see you two again, you're dead." The four doors to the Suburban opened, then they drove off. I hammered my fist onto the hood. Tears rushed out of me. I hit the hood again.

Howie put a hand on my shoulder. "You should've let me kill them."

I slammed my fist again. "The hell are we supposed to do?"

"We'll think of something, bro. We got to think of something."

The something we thought of stepped out of his car and moved toward a house at the far end of the block. He was dressed like the rest of the cholos we'd seen since coming to Vegas. Same shirt, pants, shoes. The house he disappeared into was the same as every other in the neighborhood. Two stories, mid-sized yard, knee-high metal fence out front, porch with a balcony overhang. Impoverished.

"That's the place?" I wondered to mom.

"And that's the guy. I know all Taunter's spots. Wanted the best one when we..."

"Robbed and murdered them?"

"Don't be all high and mighty," she said. "I ain't stupid. I got an idea what you two did."

That was hard to hear from her. The motives behind my actions might've been more righteous, but ask the people we'd killed if they cared about motives. Mom was an evil witch of a person, but she wasn't stupid. She saw the way of things.

"What do you think?" I asked Howie.

"With one gun? I think it's a bad idea."

"We know it's a bad idea. How are we going to do it?"

He looked at mom. "That's a trap house?"

"No. Just where they keep the shit."

"Who's going to be in there?"

"I don't know. His family and him I guess."

"His family? Why would he keep drugs in the spot he keeps his family?" Howie asked.

I laughed. "You're asking the wrong person that."

"Well, I know what to do." He sounded disappointed. "Look."

His finger pointed to the front yard we were watching. It was dark, but I could make out a trampoline, behind it some swings. I knew what he was thinking. "No," I said.

"It's the only idea I got."

I put my face in my hands. "How far will we go for this, Howie?"

"That decision is yours, but I'm with you no matter what, bro."

"Real high and mighty now, aren't you?"

"Will you shut the hell up?" Howie's hand clapped off mom's cheek. "I'm so sick of you."

"Try living with her your whole life," I mumbled. "Howie, if we do this, we got to make sure no one gets hurt. I can't take any more."

"I'm not taking the bullets out of the gun."

I followed Howie out the car and toward the house. We hopped the low fence, trekked through a sandbox, and crouched beneath a window on the side of the house. The neighbor's was close enough to touch, and someone would only have been able to see us from a small portion of the front and backyards.

I stood up then crouched back down. There was a living room, a couch beneath the window facing a TV across the room, and two bald heads on the couch. I shook my head and led Howie to the next window. A bedroom, empty. The next one held what we were looking for. I tried to open the window, but it was latched. Howie's hands interlocked at knee height, and I tightened the strings on my hood so that only my nose and eyes were out.

I whispered, "One, two —"

Howie threw me through the window. I landed, rolled, and turned. The kid wailed. I pulled Howie in then swooped the kid up as the door burst open and the light turned on. "Who's all in the house?" I asked to the homie's wide eyes. He stared at the beautiful baby girl in my arms. "Who's all here!"

"Just me and Sleepy."

"No women? Other children? Don't lie to me."

"Nah, man." His eyes moved to the gun Howie pointed at him. "Please, don't hurt her." The other homie appeared behind him.

"Tell him to stop moving. Don't you dare run off."

"Sleepy, chill!" The guy looked panicked. "Just chill."

I nodded. "Into the living room." As we went, I checked the rooms off the hallway. The house was empty. Howie directed them to the couch, gun on them the whole time. "Where can I find Taunter?"

Their eyes came together, then they shrugged at me. "You really going to be difficult?"

The anger in my voice made the baby cry. I bounced her, trying to soothe her, only barely thinking about how twisted that was given the situation. After a couple long shushes, I looked back to the gangbangers. "Tell me where Taunter is."

"Look, if we tell you, Taunter kills our whole family," said Sleepy. "We can't tell you shit."

I looked at them, looked at the baby. That had been the extent of my plan. "Give me the kid," Howie said. I almost asked him why, but caught myself. I passed her over. "Go find something to tie them up with."

I looked at the homies. "Don't try anything funny —"

"Just go, bro." There was a back porch. I found some twine that held rakes, brushes, and brooms together and took it back into the living room. Everyone was in the same spot. "Sleepy, you first," Howie said. "Hands behind your back."

I tied his wrists and cut the rope with Howie's pocket knife then did the same around the body. I did the other homie the same way. "That good?" I asked.

"Go bring the car out front." Again, I almost asked why. But if I couldn't trust Howie at this point, I'd never trust anyone ever. I jogged to the car.

"Back already?" mom said, smiling. I parked the car as close to the sidewalk as I could get. Howie was shepherding them out. He looked ridiculous with a baby on his hip and a pistol in his fist. I popped the trunk and got out of the car.

They went in without a fight. Their resistance amounted to Sleepy starting to beg as I slammed the lid down. My eyes roamed over all the nearby houses. The lot of them were dark and silent. Howie was bouncing the baby. She smiled at him, reaching for his face. "That's some evil shit," I said.

"What?" He laughed. "Look how cute she is."

"What do we do with her?" He quit bouncing, looked at me, and shrugged. Whatever his plans were, a baby shouldn't be there. I could take her to a neighbor's, but that might alert Taunter. Who knew how many people knew the man? He'd know exactly who'd done it; we'd gone straight from the meetup to here.

"Give her here," I said.

I took her back into the house and lay her down in her crib. She smiled up at me, waving a little arm. I pulled up her covers, more than was needed since we'd broken her window, and let her grip my pinkie finger. Then I whistled Perire's melody. Five minutes and she was asleep. On the way out, I locked all the doors.

"Her mother better live here too," I said, getting in the front next to Howie.

"I saw high heels," Howie said.

"What now?"

"We need a secure place." We turned onto a different street. "Somewhere quiet. Any ideas?"

I looked at mom in the rearview. "Only one."

If the last neighborhood we'd been in was poor, this was decrepit. Two houses, one on each side of the street, had plywood boarding up every window. All the yards were dirt, with no sign of upkeep. No flowers, grass, decoration. The parked cars were as run-down as the houses, paint chipped and metal rusted. I couldn't see one face anywhere though.

"Which one is it?" Howie asked, creeping down the block, headlights off. Mom pointed. "Go get the door open, Jim. We'll lead them all in at the same time."

A metal gate whined as I pushed it open, a roar in the black of morning. I pounded on the front door and turned away from the peephole.

"It's four in the damn —" The door opened. Coitus was as fat and hideous as ever. I shoved my foot in before it could slam. "Jimmy, I never meant — I moved away. I have nothing to do with anything. Please, you don't —"

"Shut up. I'm not here for you. I need to use your house."

"Why?"

I pushed past Coitus. The inside was worlds different. Immaculately clean, furniture in precise position, smelled like flowers. It surprised me.

Our trail of captives pushed into the house, crowding it. "What is this, Jimmy?" Coitus demanded. "Mom? Oh, no. No, no, no. Whatever you're up to, do it someplace else. I won't have it. This is my house. Mine!"

Howie lifted his gun. "We're using your house."

"Feel free." Coitus sat on her couch.

"Show us where the basement is," Howie said. "And we need some rope."

We filed down a narrow staircase. Coitus, me, mom, two homies, then Howie with his gun at the back of the last man. The basement was cramped. The dirt floor crunched beneath my feet, and the water heater took up most of the space. "You two —" Howie pointed to mom and Coitus. "Sit there and stay quiet. Jim, you watch them. You two —" He pointed at the homies. "Lay right here."

He pulled his pocket knife and sawed through the rope Coitus got him. A big wooden support beam was above his head, and he tossed one half of the rope over, then the other. "Tie one to him, bro. At his ankles."

We both got on the other end of a rope and hoisted Sleepy off his back onto his shoulders. We heaved again, and he was off the ground, swinging, his head scraping the ground. We secured the rope to the water heater then did the next guy. They were surprisingly quiet throughout the whole ordeal. That would change.

"Whatever you're going to do," Coitus said, "I don't want to be here —"

"Shut up," Howie demanded.

"Sure." Coitus crossed her fingers in her lap.

He crouched in front of the man's face and stopped him from spinning. "Are you going to be difficult?"

"Look man, we told you, we can't say shit, man, Taunter knows everybody, he'll kill my whole family, Sleepy's too, we can't say nothing man, please."

Howie sighed. Then he pulled the man's ear and slashed his knife through. It gave way, the whole top half. The man screeched. My stomach lurched.

"What about you?" Howie crouched in front of the other, Sleepy, showing him the ear. "You want to tell me where Taunter is?"

"We can't fool, listen to —"

Shuuuueet.

His scream was louder. "We can do this the rest of the night, into tomorrow," Howie said. "One of you will tell me what I want to know. Question is, how much of you two will be left when we're done?"

The answer was not much. Howie started with both ears. Next, shirts came off, nipples with them. He took fingernails, he sliced cheeks, he poked holes. Their willpower to stay quiet was impressive. Howie was about to start taking fingers when mom spoke up. "They're not going to snitch in front of each other."

Howie stared at her a long time then nodded. "You know what, you're right. We only need one." He cut Sleepy's rope without ceremony, sending his bloody face into the dirt. He groaned, then began to cry. "Coitus, you're going to help me. He dragged Sleepy to his feet. "You got a bathtub?"

We all listened as Howie forced the man up the stairs, Coitus following them. The hanging man's eyes were huge. "Make him stop," he said to me when it was but the three of us. "Please, you have to see, we can't say shit, we're dead if —"

A gunshot echoed through the house.

All went quiet. Howie's feet on the stairs were thunderous, Coitus's a tiny replica behind his. He came and crouched in front of the homie. His smile terrified me. "You ready to talk?"

He told us where Taunter was at what times and with whom. It spewed out of him in a continuous flow until Howie had to tell him to stop. Howie's huge palm patted the man's cheek, then he stomped back up the stairs.

A second later, Sleepy tumbled down the stairs. He had a strip of duct tape over his mouth and shivered uncontrollably. Howie started the process of hanging him back up. "Nice touch," I said as I helped him.

"Did you think I killed him?"

"Honestly?"

"No. Lie to me."

"Never thought it for a second."

The place was not what I expected at all. Taunter was a gangbanger, but I had to give it to him. His vision was big. I thought he'd have a simple house in a poor neighborhood with half a million worth of vehicles parked out front. That was about the furthest from the truth you could get. Taunter lived in a fortress in one of the nicest neighborhoods in Vegas. A ten feet high wall enclosed the entire place with but two ways in, a small gate for walking in and a large gate for driving. Both had two guys on it at all times.

The house itself peeked over the walls and looked just as daunting. From what I could see, it would be as difficult to get into the house as it would to get past the wall. The upper windows, the only windows visible from the street, were barred with thick steel grating. I had to assume the lower ones would be too. The house, hardly house-looking, was three stories and a perfect cube.

"No way," mom voiced my thoughts from the back seat. Coitus was next to her and had her very own set of bounds to match. Howie didn't trust her, so she couldn't stay at her house with the homies. I agreed.

"She'll probably try to screw them both," I'd told Howie.

"They've been through enough."

Mom was right though. How were we going to storm a place like that? I wished she'd decided to rob one of the other million Mexican gangbangers in Vegas, not the single competent one. I couldn't see one flaw, not one damn weakness, that would allow us entry.

Howie started driving away. "Where we going?" I demanded.

"There's no way we're getting in there, bro. Not with two of us and one gun."

That was obvious. "What're you thinking?"

"We need help."

"Arm them?" I pointed a thumb to the backseat.

"Fuck no!" He laughed. "We'd both be dead."

"You at least," mom mumbled.

"Who then?"

"There's only one person we can call."

"Who?"

He looked at me. "You know who."

I did? Oh. Of course, I did.

"Here it is!" I hollered needlessly to Howie. We were on the couch in Coitus's living room. "Finally. Look!"

"I see it."

"—robbery was by two masked men, neither being the man police had originally thought," Coitus's TV blared. "Suspects made off with nearly one million in cash and killed two people. Police say they have blood from one suspect and fingerprints on a gun, but need the community's help. If you have any information, please call the hotline. In other news —" I turned it off.

"A million?" Howie screamed at the same time I screamed, "Blood and fingerprints?"

"That's bad, bro."

"Really bad." I popped the knuckles of my finger on my knee.

"We got to get out of town, bro. Like yesterday."

The front door pounded, and my stomach dropped. I jumped and checked the peephole. I could only see the top of his head. I swung the door wide. "Mr. Long —" His arms were crossed and he glared at me. Howie had said that he'd sounded reluctant to come. I'd never been on the receiving end of his anger. "Mr. Long," I said and cleared my throat. "Thank you for coming."

"You disobeyed me." His voice was firm.

"I —" It hardly mattered at that point. "Yes, sir. I did. And I would again."

He stood there nodding, staring at me with those slanted eyes. "Your wife was very upset with me," he said eventually.

"We both were." I wanted to tell him how stupid he was. Stupid and hypocritical.

"Jessy enlightened me," Mr. Long said. "She has a beautiful way with words. 'False patriarch to a non-family,' I think she'd said."

He stopped talking. "Howie told you the situation?" I asked.

He nodded.

"Will you help us?"

He stepped aside, and I looked past him for the first time. Seven Audis parked in a row across the street, exhaust whispering out their tail ends. Mr. Long put a hand on my shoulder.

"Go get my grandson."

22

I tried not to think about the last time I was part of such a caravan, but the thought was there. We'd driven right into a trap, Howie'd been shot, then I rushed him across San Francisco. This time, we knew what was ahead of us. The knowledge wasn't comforting. My feet tapped the floorboard a thousand RPMs.

"What's your job?" Howie asked me.

"Find Pecu."

"Where do you do it from?"

"The back."

The closer we got to Taunter's, the faster my feet tapped. My pistol was already in my hand, had been since leaving Mr. Long and a few guys with my lovely family, and a clip weighed down both my pants pockets. I'd practiced unloading and loading a clip a few times at the house. It was awkward with my nub. I had to press the gun into my armpit, release the old clip, pull a new clip, then shove it in, all left-handed.

I realized something. All these men, most of them I'd only met in passing, were there for me. They were there to Save Pecu, but they were doing it for me. Any one of them could die. For me.

"This is what you do for family." Howie squeezed my shoulder. "It ain't always easy. Sometimes you have to make sacrifices, might even be you have to sacrifice yourself, but it's the only thing we got in this life."

And I had one. Finally. With Pecu, it'd be complete. My feet stopped tapping. Warmth flooded my stomach, killing the butterflies.

"Here it comes. Remember, bro, stay in the back."

We were three cars from the front and came around the corner onto Taunter's block as the first car rammed through the compound's steel gate. Gunfire erupted. On instinct, I ducked low. Howie stuck his arm out the window, and we screeched a turn through the gate. He fired three times. "Let's go!"

I jumped out the car and pulled the seat forward for the man in the back to get out. An explosion blasted behind me; I looked in time to see smoke fading from the front door. Five cholos lay about the yard, one of our black suits. Shots filled the air like fireworks.

"Last!" Howie yelled, running toward the house with his gun up. I ignored him, pressing in behind his massive back. We got to the front door. Something smelled burnt. The house opened up into a big front room, our men filling it. A hallway led away, doors on each side the whole way down. Two of ours moved to each side of a door, another kicked it in. Gunfire.

"Clear!" They came back out. Howie ran toward the hallway and got ready to rush the next room. Two shots. "Clear!"

"The back, Jim!" Howie shouted when he saw me close. "Look for Pecu."

The first room they'd cleared, I checked. Two dead Mexicans, white powder on a table, and a whimpering half-naked chick in the corner.

No Pecu. The next room was empty. One dead Mexican in the next. The rest were empty.

At the end of the hall, suits ran up a wide staircase in a line. Howie was pressed in with them. The quiet ended. Gunfire started in truth. Like war crashing through the building, shots fired from both sides. I crept to the bottom of the stairs. Our guys were crouched, firing over the top stair. One cried out, then Howie pulled him back and dragged him to the bottom.

He ran back to the top, gun high, fired a few rounds, grabbed another man, and pulled him down. The shots carried on. Eternity was in those moments, and eternity came for more than a few men. Gunfire stopped.

"Clear!"

I ran up. Stairs continued up, but there was a hallway. Bodies filled that hallway.

"Clear!"

Most our men gathered in the hall, pointing pistols at various doors, while a group of three cleared each room. The hallway went the length of the building. Taunter had bought an apartment building and made it a safe house. I started checking already cleared rooms. No Pecu.

I knew where he was. "He's on the third floor," I screamed, heading for the stairs.

Howie grabbed for me, but I pulled away. "Jim, wait!"

I brought my gun up and went up the stairs. The top floor was set up like the second. Long hallway, doors on each side. A door at the end was open.

And Pecu stood in the room beyond.

My feet carried me on their own accord. Howie yelled something, but I ignored it. *Pecu's right there!* I'd be the first person he saw. Pecu talked to someone I couldn't see. He looked scared, but he held back tears. Whatever the person said worked. Pecu smiled.

I saw the person he talked to before he saw me. Taunter. I brought my gun up. I stopped. All I'd been through, all the death behind me and around me, but I stopped.

I didn't shoot.

"Ah, ah, ah," Taunter said to me. "Stop there, fool." His hands came together in front of his face, then he tossed something to my feet. It was a little piece of bent metal. *A pin*, I realized. Taunter smiled at my realization. He wiggled the sphere in his hand. "Call your boys back or we all go."

I waved a hand behind me, forcing everyone to stop before Taunter could see them, and stepped forward an inch. "Don't do this, Taunter. Give me the boy, and we'll leave."

"You think I'm stupid?" Pecu tried to move toward me, but Taunter stopped him with the hand not holding the grenade.

"He doesn't even belong here. It makes no —"

"Belong?" Taunter yelled. "I don't give a fuck about that. He's mine to get back at his moms, nothing more."

"She's not going to get him back. I'm taking him with me."

"Oh, so give him to the guy who killed half my people. Turn around and leave. It's the only way we live through this, yo."

Howie appeared next to me. "Wait!" I shrieked, but he fired. A red cloud shot out the back of Taunter's head. "Run!" I screamed, running, yanking Pecu by his arm. I was halfway back to the stairs.

The grenade detonated.

Howie was behind me.

The world seemed to bubble, the floor expanding and tilting, then it popped. The explosion threw me down the hall, and I rotated so that Pecu landed on top of me. Another vibration in the floor and some of the building caved. One high-pitched tone tore through it all. I smelled fire.

When I could hear again, I looked back. Blue sky came through where the ceiling used to be and dust spiraled in the sunlight. The room where I'd first seen Pecu was gone. I stood, Pecu's hand in my own. Audis were visible below through crumbled walls. Parts of the walls that were still up swayed. Pieces crashed somewhere.

"*Gweilo!*" I looked back at a suit. "Place is coming down. We got to go."

Go? But Howie?

"Now!"

Pecu's hand pulling me shook the paralysis. I lifted him into my arms and went down the stairs two at a time. Something crashed, vibrating the building again, and it was followed by more screams to get out. We got to the bottom, and I saw the huge front room.

It'd been right below the grenade, and the entire building above it had fallen in. Thick metal wire tangled with huge cement pieces covered the place. Suits were crawling over the wreckage toward the hole, toward the Audis.

I started to climb, but stopped. Two legs protruded from beneath a cement slab.

"Wait for us outside!" I handed my brother off. I wedged my hand beneath the piece of wall crushing him. It hardly moved, but I heaved with everything in me. Something heavy fell into the rubble next to me and shifted the pile. The wall almost slipped from my fingers. "Slide out," I bawled through clenched teeth. I got the wall up then flipped it from him.

It was Howie. I knew by the size of his torso. Parts of the building fell as I stared, as my eyes began to swim, as I tried to make sense of something that couldn't make sense. His skull was misshapen, deflated like an old soccer ball. One eye hung from a slimy red string down to his mouth. Teeth were broken or missing. And his flesh, it was burned a black-brown.

"*Gweilo!*"

"What!" I cried, eyes on the carnage.

"The building. It hasn't settled."

Dazed, I wiped my face with my nub and started over the rubble. Crashing came from around me. I heard it. I felt it. But I didn't care. I was somewhere else, a place in my head, and I stayed there while I was directed to an Audi and until we were far from Taunter's compound. When I came back, I was in the back seat of an Audi with a squishy little hand in my own. Pecu must've seen my return from wherever I'd been.

"I missed you, Jimjim." He said it with such big, understanding eyes. I cried. Pulled him to my chest and cried.

"You too, buddy. You too."

"You lied." He was crying into my shoulder. "Mama's not dead."

"I —" I wanted to lie again. "I know. I'm sorry." He patted my back. We rode in silence for a long time. The mission had been successful. I had my brother back. He was unharmed. We'd won.

Howie was dead.

"Why?" Pecu asked. He pushed the tears off my cheek with his palm. "Why'd you say mama's dead?"

I almost lied again, but I couldn't make myself.

"Because I wish she was."

23

Mr. Long sat across from me in Coitus's living room. Everyone else had already left town. The attack was all over the news, and the Audis were impossible to hide. They were all probably in San Fran already.

The attack wasn't the only thing on the news; my face, along with Howie's, was too. They'd found security footage of us when we were running on foot. It hardly affected me. In fact, I was having a hard time giving two shits.

"This isn't good, Jim," Mr. Long said. We sat on Coitus's couch as we watched the news coverage blast a reward for information about us. I focused on bouncing Pecu on my knee. Mr. Long was as calm and sure as ever, but I could see the loss in his eyes. He'd loved Howie too. "We will have to put you in hiding for a while. I don't know how much they have on you, but I'll find out. It won't —"

"Mr. Long, I need you to do something for me."

He looked at me. "Another favor?" His tone was fierce. "Is it as severe?"

Only to me. "No." He lifted his chin and looked down his nose at me. "I need you to take Pecu to Jessy."

"Take him... Can I ask why you can't take him to her?"

I thought about that. "No," I decided.

"Can I ask where you'll be going?"

"No."

"Is this going to upset Jessy?"

I held his eye. "No."

He sighed then tossed me keys to an Audi. "Howie told me how much you love those things. Don't get pulled over in it."

It wasn't funny, but I laughed anyway. I owed him that. "Thanks," I said.

He stood. "Let's go, Paul. Come take a ride with grandpa."

I set Pecu on his feet. "Will you give us a second? I'll bring him out in a moment."

After he left, I took Pecu's hands. "You know I love you, right?" He nodded. "Good. No matter what happens, remember that. Everything that happened, everything I've done, I did it for you. Okay?"

He stared into my eyes. "Okay." His smile was sincere. I hugged him as hard as I could and held him. Mr. Long honked his horn outside, and I released Pecu. Tears flowed off my chin. I let them fall and smiled at my baby brother.

"You be good," I said, buckling him into the backseat. Mr. Long was next to him, a driver up front. "Listen to Jessy, all right?"

I went to close the door. "Jimjim!"

"What, buddy?"

"When will you be coming?"

I shook my head and smiled the hardest smile of my life. "Soon."

The world is such a cruel place, I thought as I went back inside. Even the people I loved, Pecu, Jessy, Howie, they hurt me then. They hurt me because I hurt them. *A God-awful place, this world.*

The light clicked on in the basement. Everyone was right where I'd left them.

"Did you get him?" mom demanded.

"I did."

"Is he safe?"

"He is." I crouched down in front of Coitus. "Are you going to act stupid when I untie you?"

She shook her head.

"Mom," I grabbed her arm. "Up the stairs."

"Do I get to see him?"

"No."

"I'll find him," mom said. "I'll never stop until he's mine again."

"I know that, mom."

She had no response. I untied Coitus and helped her to her feet. Mom was still staring at me when I walked toward her. Her frown I'd never seen before. She wasn't sure. "Let's go," I said and pushed her up the stairs.

"Where're we going?"

"For a drive."

Two steps up the stairs, Coitus yelled, "Jimmy!" I looked back. "What about these two?"

Both homies stared at me with the same question in their eyes.

"Keep 'em," I said.

24

Some things in life are worth everything. That standard we live by, the one that tells us right from wrong, used to be one of those things for me. Used to be I believed if I did my best to adhere to it, I'd be a good person and good things would come back to me. *Stupid and naive.* That standard left a pile of dead at my back. That standard left me with nothing but bitter memories. That standard ain't worth shit.

How noble I was, willing to die for what's right. Been that way since I was a kid, and it was never easy growing up with the adult figures I had. I was always better than them though, because I was willing to sacrifice myself for what was right.

Dying is easy though.

I drove mom east from Las Vegas. The lotus flower was in my lap.

"Surprised you still have that thing," mom said after hours of silence. "When I was packing your shit after Wyoming, I found it hidden in your drawer and put it in your pocket. Didn't take you for the sentimental type."

I focused on the road ahead of me.

"You found it in the gift shop of a truck stop when you were a bit younger than Pecu," she continued. "You'd run off, and I'd spent half an hour looking for you. When I found you, you were staring at it with those big, beautiful eyes you had. You'd been so cute back then. So nice, so ... loveable. When you turned those eyes on me and asked 'mama, please,' I had to get it for you."

Something tore inside me. The lotus had been the only beautiful thing in my life for so long, the only calm under my family's terror. It'd been my secret refuge. It'd been something only I had, something that separated me from the Torqueres.

But *she'd* given it to me.

I spent the next hours going over all that happened, all the things I could've done differently, all the people I could've saved. But everything came back to the words my mother had just uttered.

I had to get it for you.

We rolled into the Casper around dinnertime, looking as out-of-place in the Audi as Satan at the Last Supper. People stared and I was happy for the tinted windows.

"Why are we here?" mom asked.

"You know why."

"Jimmy, if people see —"

"Where's she at?"

"We can't —"

"Just show me so we can get out of here."

Mom pointed the way. Paved road turned to dirt, and I stifled a sob. It was the same road that Amanda and I had first made love. Mom told me to stop.

"Whatever you're planning, it's stupid, Jimmy."

"Where?"

She coughed, and her eyes studied the dash. "See that shrub?" I pointed out her window. "No, the overgrown one next to it. She's behind it. We dug deep though, Jimmy."

"Don't get out of the car."

The only sign of Amanda's burial was uneven ground. It rose in a lump. I crouched and settled a hand on the dirt. I stayed there like that for a long time, thinking about where Amanda would be right now if she'd never met me. I smiled. *Stripping her way through college, just as she wanted.*

"I don't know why I came," I whispered to her. "I could probably talk to you as easy from anywhere."

A low cry, the wind, was the only response.

"Maybe I had to be sure. I always felt it in my heart, knew my family couldn't have let you live, but there was always that hope. I came back as soon as I could. I —"

Droplets sprinkled into the dust, fat tears from my eyes.

"I'm sorry, Amanda. I could've saved you, but didn't. I guess that's why I came. To tell you. I'm sorry."

I kissed my fingers and pressed them into the dirt, knowing how wasteful the trip was.

Sorry does less for the dead than the living.

Four hours of driving, north and west, and the phone Mr. Long had given me rang the whole time. Jessy wanted to know why Pecu had shown up without his big brother. At first she left messages, begging that I answer. Then they turned angry. She had something important to tell me, apparently something she had to tell me in person. I had better get home if I knew what was good for me. I left the phone in a ditch next to the interstate.

"That's not how you treat someone you love," mom had said when I'd done it.

I slapped her.

I stopped in some no-name town for some food and as I turned onto the interstate to leave, red and blue lights spiraled behind us. "Great." I pulled the steering wheel right and slowed down. "Just great."

"We're screwed," mom said. "Both of us. Thanks a lot, Jimmy. I'm sure I have warrants all over this damn county."

"Shut up and put this shirt over your wrists. Don't say a word."

A deputy with a comb-over blowing in the wind tapped on the window. "Evening, sir." He leaned so he could see in. "License and registration please."

I popped the glove box, pulled out the registration and my Jim Thompson ID, and handed it to the cop. "Is there a problem?" I asked.

"Not yet. I pulled you over for not using your blinker." I looked down. It was still blinking. "Everything all right with her?"

Mom's eyes were sunken into her skull and surrounded by black. Her cheeks were sharp, pale skin stretched tight over them. Two teeth stubs stuck out of her closed mouth. She looked the same as always.

"She's sick," I said.

"Hmm." He stood straight and put both hands on his belt, one on his pistol. "What you guys doing all the way from California."

"Visiting."

"Visiting who?"

"Old friends."

"Stay here."

He walked to his squad car. Through my rear-view, I watched him talk into his walkie-talkie as he held up my ID. This was bad. It'd been days since leaving Vegas, and I had been too in my head to try to listen to the news. They'd had my face when I left. *Do they have my name yet?*

"We're screwed," mom reiterated. "We're so screwed."

He was in his vehicle too long. He quit talking into the radio on his shoulder and stared at the back of my car. "He's waiting for something," I whispered. Then the other car appeared behind him, speeding toward us with lights blaring.

"Nope." I threw the car into drive. "Not today."

I floored the accelerator and kept it there. The speedometer climbed, and I zipped by vehicles like they were still. The cops faded behind me, their cars too slow to attempt a chase, and I took the first possible exit once they were no longer in sight. We ended up on a highway heading east.

"Only a matter of time, Jimmy."

"I know."

25

I took too many turns trying to avoid busy roads and got lost. Too many highways veined through that part of the country, and I took whichever felt right at the time. I realized where we were at the same moment mom did.

She wiped sleep from her eyes with her bound hands. "Jimmy, this looks like —" We drove past the spot where she and Stupro had made Pecu. "What're you doing?" She was awake now. "Why are we here?"

I focused on the highway.

"It's too soon," she continued. "Anyone who sees my face will know I had the house where..."

"Where Stupro murdered my father, your husband?"

"Oh my god." She paled. "You're turning me in. You're going to —"

"No one's turning you in. Sit still and shut up."

I took us to the exact same hotel I'd stayed at the last time I was in Whitehall and rented the exact same room. Mom was right, it was too soon to be here. The cashier gave me a funny look when I slid him the cash for the room, but kept his mouth shut.

"You're stupid to bring us here," mom said as I set her down in the room. "We'll both be in jail before the night's up."

"Go take a shower." I untied her wrists then her ankles. "Don't do anything stupid. I'll order a pizza."

She glared, but decided to bite down whatever she'd been about to say. As the water turned on, I used the hotel phone to order pizza then leaned my head back on the bed.

I woke to knocking. The shower wasn't running anymore. Mom stepped out. "Get the pizza," I told her and threw my wallet.

She laid the pizza on the bed and started eating. She stared at me.

"Eat."

After we ate, I tied her back up. She went into the bathtub. I sat down at the table and lifted a pen.

Dear Jessy,
Thank you for showing me what a family is.
There's a floorboard loose in your old room beneath
the pink rug. Use the money to raise Pecu. I love you.
Your husband.

I had more to say. I wanted to tell her everything. It would've helped neither of us though. I slowly walked to the mailbox by the front desk, kissed my letter, and tossed it in.

"Goodbye, Jessy."

Inside the hotel room, I picked up the phone and dialed three digits. "Yes, I've heard gunshots. I'm at the Jefferson Inn, room twelve." I hung up the phone and went into the bathroom. Mom was in the bathtub, with no water. Her eyes were as wide as they could go. She stared at the gun in my hand.

I set the lotus flower on the tub next to her. It pained me to see it so wilted. I knew that it had died the day someone forced it into that globe, but now it truly was dead.

"Why did you kill your father?" I asked.

Her eyes wouldn't meet mine. She swallowed.

"Just answer the question."

"He put a needle in my arm when I was eleven years old. By the time I grew tits, he had me fucking junkies for dope. One night, he wanted a turn."

I nodded, staring at the lotus, tears filling my eyes. "The lotus is a miracle," I whispered. I imagined Jessy sitting at the edge of my bed, admiring the lotus when it still held its glory. "It grows in the filthiest of waters but remains unstained. It rises above the filth, untouched and perfect." I paused and felt a tear roll down my face. I steeled myself.

Sirens wailed. Blue and red lights flowed in past the curtains.

I set the barrel on mom's forehead.

"But not everything can rise – can it? Some waters are too deep, too dark to escape. Some things must be swallowed by the filth."

26

Clang, clang, clang!

"Thompson, Gallagher, wake your asses up," came from the steel door. "Pack your shit."

The cell was ten by eight, with a toilet, a desk, and two bunks, one atop the other. Jim Thompson hopped down from the top and shook Tree. "Wake up," Jim said. "We're going to mainline."

"The fuck you so excited for?" the big white boy demanded. He had 19 tattooed under one eye and 88 under the other. "Wake me up when breakfast comes."

Jim paced until two trays slid through the trap, ate, then continued pacing. Tree sat up in his bed now, watching him. "You going to pack that up?" He pointed a spork at the manuscript on the desk.

"Nah." Jim didn't look up from his pacing. "There's no point."

"No point? Kid, you been working on that for weeks."

Jim didn't respond.

The prison staff came, handcuffed Jim and Tree, and brought them across the prison grounds. When they entered their new unit, Jim was surprised at the volume. Cards snapped on tables, feet battered on doors, inmates hollered over it all. Jim glanced at every face.

"The top tier already got out," the guard told them as he walked them up the stairs. "You'll get out in the morning." He jammed a key into a door.

"Bottom!" Tree yelled as the door slammed behind them. He threw his bundle of clothes, sheets, and blankets onto the bottom bunk. "I won't be here long, so you'll get it when I leave."

"You'll be here longer than me," Jim mumbled.

"What's that supposed to mean? You got a life sentence. Or do the feds really got something on you, kid?"

"No. I'll be fine." Jim tossed his own bundle on the top bunk. "So everyone in the state with a life sentence is in this unit?"

"Don't be scared, kid. Not all of them. Some have leveled down."

"You going to help me with this?" Jim pulled a little metal binder clip from between his butt cheeks. "I have until tomorrow."

Tree's eyebrows came together. "Tomorrow? Don't make it worse for yourself. Chill for a little —"

"You going to help me or not?"

Tree sighed. "I'll show you the best spot to cut from."

Jim started sawing the steel bunk with the clip frantically. It took all night of sawing in shifts, but come morning Jim had a shank as long as his hand. It had no edge, just came to a single point like a pencil. He cut a strip off his sheet and wrapped it around for a handle. The sun would be up in an hour. Jim paced.

"I've seen that look before, kid." Tree stared at Jim from his bunk. "What you thinking about doing?"

"Something I should've done a long time ago." The door popped, and Jim looked at Tree. "Stay in here a while, yeah?"

Jim shoved the shank into his waist and stepped out the door. His cell was second on the range; no one had come out the first. The guard popped open the rest and went down the stairs. A fat man with grey, slicked-back hair came out the cell next to Jim's.

"How you doing?" he said. "Name's —"

"I'm looking for someone."

"Looking for someone?" He looked into Jim's eyes and backed off a step. "I ain't him."

"Big guy. Long, dark hair. Creepy."

"Walks with a limp?" The guy cleared the walkway so Jim could get by.

"Where is he?"

The man pointed to a cell.

Jim stuck his face in the window. One person lay in the darkness. Light from the window shone on a form two sizes too big for the mat. Long, slow breaths were the only movement.

Jim grasped the door handle. His heart pounded. He felt sick. He wanted to run away.

But he'd already made this choice.

Jim charged into the cell and brought down the shank in a hammer swing. It buried to his hand, and Stupro groaned beneath it. He lifted and crashed it down again. It sank deep. Stupro rolled and made eye contact. The wonder in his eyes was like a drug. Jim breathed it in.

Again, the shank came down, but Stupro caught it. His fist pounded into Jim's ribs, then smashed into his nose. Everything spun, but Jim yanked back, breaking free. He watched the bastard climb to his feet. Jim wiped blood from his nose with his arm.

"How'd you get here?" Stupro demanded.

"Killed mom."

Jim leaped toward him and brought the knife up like he was going for the neck. When Stupro reacted, Jim stopped and kicked as hard as he could. His foot connected between the legs. Stupro bent at the waist; the knife came down and pierced midway down his back. A wheeze squeezed from Stupro. He fell back onto the bunk. His hands came up like a prayer.

Jim smiled.

He stepped forward. "Stop!" Stupro tried to breathe. It was gurgled. Jim stepped again. The knife came down. Jim didn't care where it landed. Stupro bled from two wounds in his chest that had his white shirt stained from neck to groin.

Stupro leaped off the bed and swung a meaty fist, but he was too slow. Jim ducked and stabbed, tearing into soft belly. Stupro dropped to his knees.

"Stop." He pressed his hands to his stomach, trying to keep his insides in. "Please, stop."

Jim crouched so that he was eye level with Stupro. "I bet Amanda said those very words. I know Jesse did."

Stupro's mouth opened then closed.

The shank went into Stupro's neck and back out before he could understand what had happened. The same place dad had been stabbed. Blood poured from the hole. Stupro slumped. A puddle grew at Jim's feet.

He took a deep breath.

Blood covered his clothes. Blood coated his arms. Blood leaked from his face. He didn't care. He turned, flushed the shank down the toilet, and walked out onto the tier. Every face stared at the door as he stepped out of Stupro's cell.

He went to his cell, climbed into his bunk, and asked Tree, "How long I got until the guards come back?"

Tree's eyes were huge. "A couple hours. Maybe three."

"Perfect."

Jim rested his head on the mat and slept better than he had in months.

A week after the incident, the feds came back. His door popped, and they came right into his cell.

"You bastard," Mustache greeted.

"What happened?" Jim stretched his back without sitting up. The special housing unit had given him plenty of time to rest.

"Stupro Torquere. The only reason you're here, isn't it? You son of a bitch, his death is on me."

"Don't let it bother you," Jim said.

"Mr. Torquere, you deserve it. And you'll die too, without us. Now you hold up your end of the deal. Who is he?"

"Who's who?"

He ripped a photo from his back pocket. Howie on the Las Vegas strip with cash-filled duffel bags in his hands. "Tell us where to find him," the man growled.

"Never seen him in my life."

"What!" He showed another picture. Jim running next to Howie.

"That's not me."

"Mr. Torquere, you had better think hard on this. You're facing the death penalty in Nevada. You promised that if we gave you two more weeks in this damn prison you'd tell us everything. Don't you get it? If you don't give this man up, you're a dead man."

Jim put his hand behind his head and smiled.

"I'm ready."

Dear Jim,

I like to imagine that you read every letter I send and will read this last too even if you never respond. You left me a hard life to live. Pecu remembers too much. Your son asks him questions. Little Howie looks just like you, Jim. He wishes he could've met his father. I thought for a long time about going to your execution. I won't be behind the glass. I can't do it. I hope you don't blame me for that. I love you, Jim, always and forever. And I forgive you. I think I do, anyway. Goodbye, Jim.

Love,

Jessy

Acknowledgements

This book was written in a dark place: prison. Words were written with pencil onto 90-cent notebooks and then typed out for a nickel a minute through Corrlinks, all with the ever-looming possibility that correctional officers could come in and take the stack of notebooks at any time for being over the lawful amount allowed. Looking back, it was a ridiculous task. But it would have been impossible alone.

Thank you to all the people who helped me within those walls and without. Aj, Brandon, Andrew, Travis, Scourge, Byers, Hayden, Thibodeaux, Tumbleweed, Grinch, Elz, Wyatt, and all the homies with names ranging from Penguin to Clavo to Junior. This book would have never been finished without your support, whether you knew you were supporting me or not.

Thank you to my family. Without you, I would not have been released as early as I was. You never gave up on me, and that has instilled a drive that can only result in success.

Thank you to my soon to be wife. Christina you've provided another reason to actually do something with all these books I wrote in prison. Without you, this book would still be a pile of printed paper with a Corrlinks header at the top of each page.

And thank you, reader, for giving this book a chance.

ABOUT THE AUTHOR

Dacota was sentenced to over 18 years in federal prison for a drug crime when he was 20 years old. This tragic mistake of his was made into one of his greatest blessings. Before prison, he'd never been interested in reading, but with that being the only form of escape left to him he developed a love for fiction. One day it dawned on him that maybe he could write stories too.

He began small, writing short stories that developed into longer works, but he soon realized that he didn't want to be a short story writer; he wanted to be a novel writer, so he began writing in longer form. While incarcerated, Dacota wrote four novels, a few novellas, and dozens of short stories. Due to good behavior and changes in laws stemming from the First Step Act, Dacota was granted compassionate release, and now he is out of prison and ready to share his stories with whoever will read them.

Printed in Dunstable, United Kingdom